MW01592621

All best to Ed
& Susan Werner
— who rescued
the undersigned from
a car wreck!

James P. Merrill

TOUCH A LONELY STAR

[BY]

GEORGE P. MORRILL

TRAFFORD PUBLISHING™

This book is a work of fiction.
Names, characters, places and incidents are either products of the author's
imagination or are used fictitiously. Any resemblance to actual events,
locales, or persons living or dead is entirely coincidental.

© Copyright 2006 George P. Morrill.
All rights reserved. No part of this publication may be reproduced, stored in a retrieval system,
or transmitted, in any form or by any means, electronic, mechanical, photocopying, recording,
or otherwise, without the written prior permission of the author.

Note for Librarians: A cataloguing record for this book is available from Library and Archives
Canada at www.collectionscanada.ca/amicus/index-e.html
ISBN 1-4251-6739-x
First Edition

TRAFFORD
PUBLISHING™
Offices in Canada, USA, Ireland and UK

This book was published *on-demand* in cooperation with Trafford Publishing. On-demand
publishing is a unique process and service of making a book available for retail sale to the
public taking advantage of on-demand manufacturing and Internet marketing. On-demand
publishing includes promotions, retail sales, manufacturing, order fulfilment, accounting and
collecting royalties on behalf of the author.

Book sales for North America and international:
Trafford Publishing, 6E–2333 Government St.,
Victoria, BC V8T 4P4 CANADA
phone 250 383 6864 (toll-free 1 888 232 4444)
fax 250 383 6804; email to orders@trafford.com
Book sales in Europe:
Trafford Publishing (UK) Limited, 9 Park End Street, 2nd Floor
Oxford, UK OX1 1HH UNITED KINGDOM
phone 44 (0)1865 722 113 (local rate 0845 230 9601)
facsimile 44 (0)1865 722 868; info.uk@trafford.com
Order online at:
trafford.com/05-2331

10 9 8

For *Phyllis Mae — A Girl of the New England Coast*

ABOUT THE AUTHOR

George P. Morrill

George P. Morrill grew up in a small New England town bordering the Long Island Sound. Author of many stories and articles in major magazines, as well as the distinguished novel *Dark Sea Running,* he has had his work hailed by eminent writers as diverse as William Manchester and Gladys Taber.

In *Touch a Lonely Star* he writes vividly of the Great Depression and World War II, having experienced them both. He and his wife Phyllis have four sons and four grandchildren. He lives in Higganum, Connecticut, and Saxtons River, Vermont.

Warm Praise for Books by GEORGE P. MORRILL

Dark Sea Running

"Morrill knows the life he is writing about ...
Dark Sea Running is both convincing and absorbing."

— *SUNDAY TIMES OF LONDON*

"... abounds in grotesquely humorous and ribald
phrases making for life and reality. Brilliantly (done)."

— *NEW YORK TIMES*

"Tough sea narrative ... first rate."   — *CHICAGO TRIBUNE*

"Alternately appals, touches, raises hair, and lumps
throats with its almost agonizing directness."

— *WASHINGTON TIMES & POST*

Snow, Stars, and Wild Honey

"A charming, poignant memoir by a gifted writer.
I recommend it unreservedly." — *WILLIAM MANCHESTER*

"In a text as consistently poetic as the lovely
title, Morrill holds the reader enthralled."

— *PUBLISHERS WEEKLY*

"... vividly recalls hardship and beauty ... Morrill
made it in the wild world and in the often wilder
world of words."   — *ST. LOUIS POST DISPATCH*

The Blake Streak

"An original story with splendidly crafted
characterizations and a compelling plot that simply
will not let the reader go."   — *MIDWEST BOOK REVIEW*

"A great, great book. What intrigues, outside the
wonderful intricacies of the plot, is the author's
knowledge of the United States Navy."

— *GEORGE RICHARDSON*

— Worthington, Krantz Fiction —

TOUCH A LONELY STAR

[BY]

GEORGE P. MORRILL

PART ONE

> *Drake Ranch*
> *Calif. 99085*
> *Oct. 6, 1955*

Dear Jack,
    My Michael is coming to West Stod-
dard next week—Thursday, Oct 12, I think
it's time to tell him the whole truth.
    Gently, please. He's my only son.

> *Love,*
> *Eva Drake*

The words hit Jack McGreggor like cold surf.

He leaned against Village Garage's rusty mailbox, the pink envelope crushed in his fist. A full half-minute passed. Then he hollered to the Millay kid servicing Roy Kingsland's old Essex sedan at the Texaco pump.

"I'm going up to the cemetery awhile, Ted. Oil Van Taunton's Caddy next."

He drove up Horse Hill road. Radio news was crackling. Blacks were boycotting buses in Montgomery, Alabama...President Eisenhower's heart attack was under control....

He punched the off button. His yellow jeep bounced through Blackthorn Cemetery's granite gateposts. White gravestones slid by on fragrant, new-cut grass.

So it all comes out, Miss Drake. Didn't we know it would—sooner or later?

The marble markers turned to brownstone. And here was the Griffin family tomb, the only structure in the place, loom-

3

ing like a monstrous bathtub upside down. He got out. He set his back against the tomb's bronze door, staring at Long Island Sound five miles away. A sort of primal calm seeped into him—the mystic warmth of Blackthorn that never failed to steady his thinking.

This was West Stoddard, Connecticut, founded in 1663. Its young men had marched from these home acres to Washington's army in Boston. In 1861 they had boarded shoreline trains to meet Lincoln's appeal for troops. They had answered every national call since the birth of the Republic. Then they had come home to marry, grow old, and die in their paint-peeling Colonial houses.

This burying ground—with its single, slope-roofed tomb—was their final rendezvous. And Jack, fingering the balled-up envelope in a sinewy hand, wasn't the only villager who came here to grapple with private quandaries.

My God, Miss Drake, how is Michael going to take this?

He smoked two cigarettes, cradling the butts in his palm from long-ago habit as a World War II Marine. Then he drove back. Ted had the Cadillac hood up, dumping in oil.

"I put my time on your blotter, Mr. McGreggor. Four hours since Sunday."

"Good. See you tomorrow."

He watched the boy's bony shoulders cross Route 1. They reminded him of himself 18 years ago when he had cranked gas for Old Man Chapman at the garage. On a warm morning in August 1936 he had walked out to Miss Drake's car, wiping his hands on a grease rag.

The tan convertible with the bright California plates was streaked with road dust. Its top was down. An athletic-looking woman bent over the wheel listening to the radio. She had wide shoulders in an open corduroy jacket. And a nice full chest. She looked up. Blond curls slid on her loose gray collar.

"Franco has just bombed Madrid," she said.

Jack unscrewed her gas cap. "That Spanish guy?"

She got out and walked to the edge of Route 1. Her back was to Jack. As she looked at the passing cars he saw her touch her temples—very lightly. Then she came back and paid him out of a sleek alligator purse, the costly kind that rich women carried.

She smiled and her eyes were different from any Jack had seen. Green-gold. When she flashed them it was honey melting.

"What's your name, fella?"

"Jack McGreggor."

"You go to West Stoddard High?"

"Yes mam."

"Well Jack, I'm Eva Drake, your new History and English teacher. So this is New England?"

Then she was gone. Heading for Mrs. Kelsey's Shore Rooms on Sand Block Road. Old Man Chapman came out scratching his leg and looked at the dust the Packard had kicked up.

"Those West Coast drivers," he said. Then, "Say, I think that young woman was crying. Did you see her eyes?"

At 6:30 Jack locked the garage and drove home. Had Miss Drake really been crying back then? He hadn't noticed anything. But Old Man Chapman seldom missed clues. And as it turned out, she'd had plenty to grieve about.

He swung into his yard remembering the cruel appraisal Joe Tutynski had made of her the first day of school. Joe, slouched in the next seat, twisted his deformed moose-jaw and cracked, "We gotta take a semester of shit from this chrome-plated California bag?"

Holly came out the kitchen door and kissed him. "The twins are eating at Sherwood's. We dine alone—hooray."

"Steel yourself," he said, "Michael Drake is coming to town."

She stopped wiping her hands on a red-checked dishcloth. Her pretty eyes widened. "Michael Drake? Here?"

"She wants me to tell him the whole story."

"Everything? Wow."

5

Supper was uncharacteristically subdued. It wasn't just that the kids weren't there. It was that they were both thinking back to the old Depression days at West Stoddard High...back to the sudden change that had blown in from the Pacific altering everything.

"I don't know how you're going to handle it, honey," she said, "But keep in mind that Miss Drake saw things differently. She'd want a merciful judgment of Joe Tutynski—not bitterness. Not now."

"I know that," he said.

———•◆•———

Joseph Tutynski, momentarily alone in his expansive Washington DC office, lighted a cigar. He closed the mahogany door to his secretary's chamber and sank into his recliner. From a teakwood drawer he lifted a leather-backed notebook marked Private. He uncapped a gold fountain pen.

Columbus Day, 1955. Autumn again, he wrote, *Why do I always think back to West Stoddard when it's leaf-falling time? And to Eva Drake? I can't say I miss the old coastal town—the scene of my suffering and humiliation. But there's a curious pull...the lure of the Sound with its fresh salt scent and restless waves...*

As he scribbled, the day's upcoming agenda of official meetings and interviews fell away. His mind clamped onto memories. From the start in 1936 he had sensed something phony about Eva Drake. He was 15, very precocious. And the physical infirmities (which the world now knew about and ignored) had inclined him to be an intriguer—a 10-cent Inspector Poirot.

He had liked to sharpen his brain on the little mysteries of the place. West Stoddard of 1936 was bogged down in the Depression. But in the 20's it had been a bootleg stop on the Sound, an exciting stretch. It had spawned legends of souped-up fishing boats trading gunfire with the Coast-Guard... New York gangsters prowling West Beach at night

First, he'd discovered that her full name was Eva von Etherington Drake. A mouthful like that would stand out anywhere.

He spotted it in the office file at school. He'd jumped to the conclusion that the German *von* hardly went with *Etherington*, an English surname.

Then he'd checked her car, a classic 1932 convertible slightly pocked with rust. And discovered that Packard had never made an assembly-line model like that. It was a special-built supercharged job.

Everything about Miss Drake—her husky voice, her musical laughter, her luminous beauty touched with abstraction—said she was not a teacher. He decided she was an heiress who had been bruised in the stock market. Or a Hollywood actress down on her luck. Her age seemed about 26-28.

How he had scorned her! He'd given everybody a hard time in those days. He'd discovered the power of his intellect and liked to throw it around.

"But you wouldn't scorn an innocent person—not you," said his loyal, dumpy Miss Fox when he'd inadvisably confided in her, "This Drake woman must have asked for it."

"My only excuse is it was a long time ago."

"You're censuring yourself over a very old memory, Mr. Tutynski."

Well...yes. At the moment he judged himself a restructured, balanced human. His professional record included calming down nuclear scientists and counseling corporation presidents.

But he'd been wrong about Miss Drake. The fact chewed on him still. Wrong about her motives, wrong about her character. He wished he could pick up life like a deck of cards. He'd shuffle through the kids he had known—and plagued—at West Stoddard High. He'd look at faces and try to figure out how such an ordinary gang of wet-eared teens could attract so extraordinary a person as Eva Drake.

She had *purposely* sought out their small poverty-wracked coastal town—apart from any other. Why?

His phone started to ring. As he picked it up, he puzzled for the hundredth time over why she had taken such tender care to lift him after the unnatural way he had behaved. And why—when he owed her so much—she had vanished from West Stoddard 18 years ago without saying goodby to anybody.

"Listen," said a strange male voice, "I'm coming to see you in 45 minutes. Please be there, Mr. Celebrated Attorney."

Click went the receiver.

o○○○o

PART TWO
1936 – 1937

A Novel By George P. Morrill

Geraldine Prue

I was vacuuming Apartment 5 at Mrs. Kelsey's when this leggy woman with wide shoulders came in and tossed a doeskin suitcase on the bed. I yanked out the plug of the clattering old Hoover.

I said, "Mrs. Kelsey will kill me for not finishing this earlier."

She took a silver comb from the richest-looking purse I ever saw and began stroking wind-tangles out of her yellow hair. She smiled.

"No grief, honey. The place looks fine."

I wound up the vacuum-cleaner wire. She started humming The Lady is a Tramp and peeled off her shirt—just as if I wasn't there. Her full brassiere jiggled. I'm flat-chested. I tried not to look.

She went in the bathroom. Then, without even closing the door, she put on a tight blue bathing suit with a white dolphin on the hip. I got a glimpse of naked thigh and back.

"You're Geraldine?"

"Yes mam."

"Mrs. Kelsey told me you're in West Stoddard High"

"I'm a Junior."

She tapped me on the shoulder in a friendly way. "Good. I'm Eva Drake, your new teacher. We'll have a time. But at the moment —"

She grabbed a towel and swung out the door "— I'm going swimming."

11

Through the upstairs window, I watched her tall, curvy body run down the sand. Her bright hair was streaming back from her shoulders. She hit the still water and started a smooth crawl outwards—just like Olympic swimmers in Pathe News at the movies.

I carried the vacuum cleaner to the utility closet. I thought: *something different has zinged into this busted old town at last. O Yes.*

Holly Millay

I saw the new teacher up on Stannard Hill her first night in town. She was standing beside the old granite horse trough that's been abandoned for years near Holbrook Lane. She had hands in her jacket pockets, watching car lights wink on Route 1.

She was very pretty—squarish jaw not harshly lined, mop of golden hair balanced lightly on strong shoulders. Even not moving, she gave the impression of a long-legged ballet dancer about to sail into the stars.

Looking down on her I didn't make a sound. I was up on the circular walk of the big water tower, which is only 60 yards away from our home, a restored Colonial with wide lawn and flowers. I often climb the steel ladder to watch West Stoddard sink into the sunset.

I do it out of love for our broken town. Up here I can see the shabby roofs of the North Road...the falling-down dock for fishermen's boats...the unlighted hulk of Griffin Leather Belt Company, closed for good. I can feel the scary silence of people moving around, keeping lights off to save money. I can *feel* them sewing old clothes...sitting down to bread and potatoes at supper.

Sometimes I stay here until total darkness. I stare at the Sound, our one beautiful thing—all wriggles and starlight. Then I carefully pick my way down the rusty ladder. I go home to rich food and warm bed, feeling bad. I say to myself: *If you love this town so much why don't you do something for its pain?* It's a question that makes me feel useless.

The only way I can shake this feeling is to switch my mind to Jack McGreggor. He works at the garage. He reads history and kids around and seems to make sense of the way things are. It doesn't bother him that his family is poor.

He's also handsome. I'm in love with him, but I don't think he really knows it.

Suddenly the new teacher looked up. I ducked back from the railing. Then she saw the ladder and started to climb it. Oops. I slipped around the circular deck out of sight. What was going on?

A few minutes later, I edged back around the big tank. She was up here leaning over the rail, looking down on the whole scene. Minutes went by. I had just about decided to walk up to her and say hi when I saw her shoulders quiver. She lowered her head on the rail.

Silently she began to cry.

Jack McGreggor

The day before school started I accidentally dropped an un-opened can of 10-30 oil on the hood of a new Ford at the ga-rage — ker-clunk.

"Hey!"

A red-headed kid in a rich brown sweater jumped out, dou-bling his fists.

I wiped the hood. "Sorry. No dents."

Suddenly he swung. I ducked and knocked him down. He got up holding a hand over one eye. He climbed back in the car."

"You're gonna get yours, *peasant*!" he shouted.

I expected to get fired. But later I heard Old Man Chapman's voice at the desk phone, clipped and hard. "No Mr. Fiske, I can't accept that. Your son attacked. My man defended himself. Well,

I value your patronage, sir. I hope you'll reconsider. Goodby."

Then he came out and stuck his big, calloused hand in mine. "We small town peasants got to stick together these days."

West Stoddard was hurting. Up in Doane's woods an old man in a tent had died from hunger. A lot of families had put their Model A's on blocks and walked for groceries. The roads were potholed everywhere. And Griffin Leather Belt — our lone factory that had paid a decent 55 cents an hour — was four years gone.

The beaches were doing okay, what with summer folk down from Hartford throwing nickels and dimes around. They frolicked in our gorgeous blue water. But the rest of the town, mostly out of work, tended to hang together and live poor.

My one-punch fight got blown up big. Hymie Volenski made me out a hero dripping blood as I defended West Stoddard honor. The word spread. The afternoon I checked into Miss Drake's history course she read my name on a card and whistled softly.

She said, "Is this Jack McGreggor the Lion Heart? He who waded through crimson gore to hold our escutcheon high?"

So you could kid with the new teacher? I shuffled my feet. "That wasn't gore, Miss Drake. It was ketchup. I was eating a hamburger."

She looked me over — like she was seeing a guy she could connect with. "It figures, General McGreggor. An army travels on its stomach."

Then she started upstairs to History room carrying some papers, holding a yellow pencil in her teeth. Suddenly she turned and cupped a hand behind her ear.

"Who said that, Jack?"

"Napoleon," I said.

She jabbed a thumbs-up at me and left. I went to the dictionary and found that *escutcheon* meant ornamental shield.

Right from the beginning I liked Miss Drake. She tunneled into how we lived and what we thought. She shoveled History and English into our brains like they were the most important things in our lives. Some of the kids were practically in rags. But she ignored that.

"Let's zero in on what matters," she said, "Who said what in the Continental Congress? How ignorant does it sound if you use a double negative? Pack it all in —" she tapped the eraser end of a pencil against her temple "— up here."

Eva Casserino

When I heard the new teacher's name was Eva—like mine—I told Elaine Bordan, "Maybe this jerk town is waking up, no? Eva means 'life.' Look it up in the dictionary."

Elaine shrugged. "If she's such a five-star special, what's she doing here?"

We filed into homeroom. Miss Drake was bent over some books on the chipped oak desk that had been there since Year One. She was wearing a white cardigan sweater with a fresh sprig of goldenrod on the shoulder. She had on brown, tortoise-shell glasses and lipstick bright red. She was quite tall and very, very pretty.

"Hi, new generation. I'm Eva Drake."

Nobody spoke. Hymie Volenski, our runt clown, closed his eyes and stuck his tongue sideways in his cheek. Miss Drake picked up a small, gray paperback.

"Can anyone tell me who Oliver Wendell Holmes was?"

Nobody spoke. Hymie raised his hand. "I think he was Sherlock Holmes's little brother. Yah."

Miss Drake lifted an eyebrow. "You may be confused with Low Cost Vacation Homes from *Better Homes and Gardens*, fella. But nice try."

We relaxed. Miss Drake explained that Oliver Wendell Holmes was a great jurist who was also a philosopher, son of a famous 19th century poet.

"He died just three years ago. Here's what he said. 'If you want to hit a bird on the wing, you must have all your will in a focus. You must not be thinking about yourself. And equally you must not be thinking about your neighbor. You must be living in your eye on that bird. Every achievement is a bird on the wing.'"

A few feet shuffled on the splintery floorboards.

"I think he meant *Do something on this earth*." she said, "Project yourself outward so you have a wide choice. Then set your sights on a bird."

She got up. In the seat behind me Fred Millay exhaled like he always did when a female moved near him. Miss Drake had on a creamy tan jumper, white socks, and saddle shoes. She looked a little like Dorothy Lamour in *Swing High, Swing Low*.

"Think about that, new generation. Now sit still."

She walked down the aisles. At each desk she paused and looked in our faces without saying a word. Her glasses dangled in her hand. And when she found one of us staring at our lap she touched the glasses to our chin and made us look up.

It got embarrassing. I started thinking what a crummy little bunch we must seem to this fancy skirt from the Golden West, no? There was Jack McGreggor, our auto nut with the half-moons of grease on his fingernails. Elaine Bordan with the slinky shape under her hand-me-down blouses. The spoiled Millay twins, Fred and Holly, lawyer's kids — the only two who wore sweaters with no patches. Shy Tom Kingsland. Giggly Geraldine Prue. Sibyl Noyes, our angry village moll.

For non-Yankees we had me and Tony Tragonni from poor Wop families that drove gravel trucks. Hymie Volenski, the Jewboy from East Side New York, living with his mean uncle the storekeeper. Not to mention the two colored brothers, Gene and Vince Bigelow, always sitting together, always dressed in faded khaki pants.

And of course Joe Tutynski the Brain, so badly deformed you wondered how he could walk.

Adding in the other half-dozen kids, our class numbered only 19. We should have been sent to Kenbrook High in New London, which had a chem. lab and tile bathrooms. But town meeting had voted no to save transportation and tuition costs.

Miss Drake sat down at her desk and pushed back an ink bottle. She looked out the window at sunlight glinting on the Sound. She said, "In life's journey some pilgrims don't leave enough tracks to trip an ant. But I think this class is going to leave elephant tracks."

She wrote on the board with squeaky chalk: LET'S FIND THAT BIRD ON THE WING. Then she added the word DESTINY and told us to bring in a one-paragraph explanation of it tomorrow.

We trooped out, lifting eyebrows at each other. Hymie said, "What's with this Hollywood chick—she got ants?"

Hymie Volenski

I looked up DESTINY like the new teacher ordered. The dictionary said: *Something to which a person or thing is destined. See fate.* So I copied a poem out of a book titled Echoes of the Great War and read it in class.

"Destiny," I said, "is what troops in France worried about when one of them wrote this verse in a Paris hospital:

We'll all come home to the USA,

And get drunk on soda pop.

Cause the slackers have voted the country dry

While the doughboys went over the top.

Destiny to these guys turned out to be bootleggers, gangsters, gunfights, and rot gut hooch."

The kids laughed. Fred Millay put his fist to his mouth like he was gurgling whiskey.

Miss Drake said, "Mmm, the destiny of this class is in a different direction, fella. Okay Fred Millay, explain the Prohibition Amendment."

We caught on pretty quick that she was serious about putting something in our heads. She mixed History and English—and everything else—together. In the Current Events period if somebody griped about a national event (like how the Navy was bungling the search for Amelia Earhart) she'd assign a committee to get the facts and report back. She was fussy about spelling. She pinned a word over the door to homeroom every Monday morning. And expected each of us to score 100 when tested on them. Yah.

"This week's word is RELEGATE," she said, "Look it up."

Joe Tutynski gave a loud groan. He rocked his head back and forth, holding a finger to his forehead like a pistol. That spurred Jack McGreggor, the one guy who never held back because Joe was a cripple, to sound off.

"Give us a break, Tutynski baby."

"Screw you," said Joe out loud.

"Hold it," said Miss Drake."

She quieted them both. But we cheered in silence. We liked it when Jack tangled with Joe's mean, stuck-up ways. Jack was my hero. He could fix a Model T Ford. Laugh. Fight with his fists.

Two days later he didn't hold back against Fred Millay either—who was his buddy. He saw Fred making dirty signs with his hands when Miss Drake's back was turned.

He said, "What's with the finger-wiggle, Fred?"

"How'd you like to do push-ups with a chassis like that, McGreggor?"

Jack didn't even smile. "Give her a chance, guy."

Sibyl Noyes

Miss Drake's heart must have stopped when she first saw West Stoddard High. The floors slanted up and down. The blackboards were cracked. The storeroom leaked, so everything was piled in the hall—dog-eared reams of paper, pencil cartons, erasers.

But the first week I saw her smiling and talking to the other teachers. Trying to tie in.

A Novel By George P. Morrill

Our faculty numbered five. Miss Wainwright taught Biology—but never mentioned how babies were made. Miss Pope taught Chemistry—but allowed few experiments because of the bad smells. Miss Baker taught Industrial Arts—which meant that each of us nailed together a flowerpot stand for Christmas and a flag-holder for Memorial Day.

Mr. August Plimpton taught Citizenship—while doubling as principal. The girls called him Fat Augie. The boys a dirty name. He liked cigars. He'd usually light up the minute he stepped out the school door, blowing stinky smoke.

The second week in October we had a fire. Fat Augie's roll-top desk blazed up. The Volunteer Fire Department arrived and squirted water over everything. The building was saved. But the whole west side was charred.

Instead of rebuilding the office the town boarded it up. Miss Baker had her carpentry unit partition off the south end of the hall for Fat Augie's new office. For weeks the big issue around town was whether Fat Augie had been smoking and started the fire. He denied it. First he said his phone had short-circuited. But when somebody pointed out that phones don't carry enough juice to start a fire, he said he meant his desk lamp.

"Maybe a spark slid out of his brain, down his nose, and blew up," I said to Elaine.

"A spark in Fat Augie's brain?" she said.

We were in an angry mood. The whole class was sore because we shouldn't have been going to this school at all. Up until 1936 West Stoddard had sent students out of town for Junior and Senior years. Now the school board had decided to keep us home and save money. But this year's Seniors were allowed to finish up in New London.

As Hymie Volenski put it, "We love the tomcat stink of this building. It helps our poverty image. Yah."

We were isolated from the outside. There was a wall of ignorance between us and America. A lot of one-horse burgs in New England were like this these days. Everyone was scared. There was no money to do anything. So Selectmen hugged the purse strings.

But things seeped in. We had radio and the movies. We had the *New Haven Register* and the *New London Day*. Gradually it dawned on us that Franklin D. Roosevelt was going to stay President no matter if West Stoddard had gone against him 963 to 227—and we needed the few bucks his WPA was bringing in. We learned that bullets were tearing apart kids our age in Spain...that the Japanese had bombed a U.S. gunboat on a Chinese river. A few of us actually caught the idea that the King of England's dumping of his throne for Wally Simpson—the top news—wasn't the most important thing on earth.

The first time I talked to Miss Drake, I was snotty. I said, "In this dumb school you can't do anything you really want."

She tapped a rubber-ended pencil on her blotter. "Mmm. What do you want to do?"

I expected her to snap back at me the way Big Ass Pope did when I sassed her in Chemistry. I grew flustered. What did I want to do?

"Why can't I be a doctor some day?"

"Why can't you indeed?"

My face heated up. I hadn't thought the thing through yet. "I-I mean, Miss Pope doesn't want anybody to go for anything different. She's against..."

Miss Drake waved me silent. She said her great aunt had been a surgeon in San Francisco. And that she'd started as a girl dissecting a dead chipmunk on her father's ranch. I told her that I'd fixed a crow's broken leg with toothpicks and scotch tape.

An hour went by. The sun dropped behind her desk, making pink light on the ceiling.

"Now here's an idea," she said, putting on her coat, "I have an acquaintance in New York who sells formaldehyde to laboratories. He'll send a free sample. Want to dissect a frog with me?"

I blinked. "Yes...*yes*."

"Good. We'll have to find someplace. Maybe Mrs. Kelsey will let us have a room down cellar."

Walking out, I started making cracks about other teachers again. It didn't seem right not to let Miss Drake know she was starting off better.

"In Chemistry, the test tubes are growing barnacles. Miss Pope won't—"

We stopped by her car. For a second all you could hear was the *bhaaahhh* of a big ship passing up the Sound. She put her fingers to my lips.

"Hush, Sibyl."

"But if you could see..." I went on stubbornly.

"Hush." She leaned over and drew some letters in dust on her Packard's hood. "You want to be a doctor. Here's something all doctors must have."

The letters spelled COMPASSION. She told me it came from the French meaning to bear or suffer. She gave a crooked little smile. Then she kissed me on the forehead and got in her car.

"I'll write for the formaldehyde tonight," she said.

Jack McGreggor

We had raunchy names for our teachers. *Big Ass Pope...No Balls Plimpton*—like that. But we never hung one on Miss Drake. She had a swinging way all right. But she also had a kind of dignity that ruled out wiseguy labels.

She'd walk up from Kelsey's, her yellow hair blowing...her dimpled knees bumping her skirt. She'd wave to everybody. But she carried a bulging briefcase, so her smile—a flash of white teeth—was quickly over. You knew she was thinking school and wouldn't be distracted.

Even when she stepped close, sometimes giving a guy horny thoughts with her stacked figure, she was *Miss Drake*, period. Our new kind of teacher.

One noon she found me alone at my desk, eating lunch out of a paper bag. She slid into the adjoining seat. "Jack, were you the fella I spotted up at Blackthorn Cemetery last Sunday sitting against that old tomb?"

"Yes mam."

"Mmm. You go there often?"

"Yes mam."

Her forehead creased into little lines. "Really? What in the world for?"

"The people who built our town are there."

"Ah, the history bug...."

"Yes mam. I like leaning against that Griffin tomb and looking at the Sound. The grass smells good. The air is fresh."

She smiled at me, resting her chin in her hand. "Mmm. Haven't you ever thought maybe the outsize tomb is a bit much for this Colonial village?"

"No mam."

"Well, it does stick out. All the other graves are ground level."

I told her that the Griffin family was the only big-time name in town. If they wanted to blow their horn in a public boneyard it was okay with me. Old Jonathan Griffin, the first immigrant, had been a hero in the French and Indian War. His three sons had been officers in the Revolution. His great-great-great grandson Ethan had founded the leather belt factory. He had generated the only important money West Stoddard had ever seen.

I added, "Griffin Belt went broke in '31. Too bad. The family's all gone now."

"All?"

"The last one, Clay Griffin, joined the French Foreign Legion four years ago."

Miss Drake had stopped listening. She wheeled around and picked up an eraser that had fallen from the blackboard. She gave a little backward wave and walked out of the room.

Joe Tutynski

I decided to always call her Teach. No "Miss Drake" for me. That respect stuff was for the sheep who sat in our crumbling classroom, pretending to absorb knowledge.

I raised my hand. "Teach," I said, "What are we going to read this semester—Rebecca of Sunnybrook Farm?"

She took off her glasses and looked at me. "Mmm. I didn't have that in mind, fella. But if you're passionate about it, go ahead."

"I don't want to read anything that might be beyond your plans."

She tapped her pencil against her cheek. "Well, I was thinking more in terms of Peter Rabbit or Mother Goose."

The class laughed. I felt my cheeks grow hot. She had taken a crack at me. That's the way it has always been—people putting me down. Insulting me. Turning *my* cracks into *their* cracks.

"Nice pitch," said Jack McGreggor, leering at me.

"Screw you," I said.

"Gentlemen..." said Teach.

I snorted at her. She gave that phony smile—supposed to be tender and understanding but edged with a kind of toughness. She had started using this rich-bitch approach to lure us into crazy projects outside school. Projects that often had nothing to do with History or English. Some way to be a teacher.

"Okay," I said, "Peter Rabbit or Mother Goose."

Geraldine Prue

The second week of school we found new copies of Webster's Collegiate Dictionary on all our desks—19 of them.

Miss Drake said, "It's your private possession. Put your name on it. I hope to see it tattered from thumbing by next semester."

Each book cost $4.95. She had paid for them herself. That really made us blink. These days 25 cents looked big.

"A stinking rich Teach," snorted Joe Tutynski, "Ain't we lucky."

But most of us felt warm toward her. I smoothed the crisp red cover of my copy. I decided my first thing would be to look up words describing her.

Lithesome: *pliant, bendable.* That was Miss Drake as she stooped at the blackboard to write, her limber wrist moving, her golden hair bouncing.

Beautiful: *comely, pulchritudinous* (wow) She stood, holding a yellow pencil against her cheek, her red lips pursed. Then suddenly she'd smile, showing bright, even teeth—and you'd think of one of those Greek goddesses.

Brainy: *astute, perspicacious* (wow again) When she cocked her head, her brow crinkled in thought, you knew some bright word—maybe a funny crack—would pop out to make you think.

Benevolent: *tender-hearted, humane.* The morning after Elaine Bordan's father was arrested for stealing food at the A&P, Miss Drake stayed close to her in class. Her hand touched Elaine's desk as she taught. She was protective without really showing it. After class I saw her call Elaine into her car and drive off.

Humorous: *facetious, jocose.* Miss Drake could grin while she was saying "Mmm" to a joke. Or she could bend over laughing from her stomach. And she could take a witty poke at herself. One afternoon she ran down from History to home room, tripped and fell. An armful of themes flew in all directions. We ran to help her. She sat up on the stairs and said, "Tommy Kingsland's short story exploded in my hands. Now, that's creative impact."

I kept scribbling out words from my private dictionary, having a real time—o yes. I found a section that had rhymes that would help me with poetry. I laughed when I ran across the word "doohickey." It was how Miss Drake described the little drawings she put at the end of each corrected theme—along with her signature: *Drake.*

A Novel By George P. Morrill

Excellent  Good So-So Terrible

Jack McGreggor

As soon as Miss Drake discovered I was from an old West Stoddard family—and that I read history a lot—she cornered me for information. It was Saturday morning.

She said, "Jack, drive around with me. Let's have the real scoop on this place."

I told her I was just a saltwater Yankee who liked living on the New England coast same way that Thoreau liked hanging out at Walden Pond.

"You'd get a better run-down from one of the Selectmen, Miss Drake."

She swung out the Packard's heavy door. "Get in here, Henry David."

First I took her up over a bumpy dirt road to McGreggor Pond. We got out and waded through high sweet-smelling grass. The water was clear. Frogs honked. When we reached the bank they went silent.

I said, "That big busted-up barn is the old McGreggor ice house. My great grandfather built it. When the ice got a foot thick my old man and other guys would saw up chunks and float them to the barn. Load them with a hoist powered by a Model T engine. Pack them in sawdust. Come summer, my cousins and me would peddle ice to the beach houses."

Miss Drake squinted at the water. "Mmm, I can almost see it."

I took her to Nathan Swamp and told her iron ore had once been fired here to make Revolutionary cannon balls. She picked up one of the rusty lumps inside the crumbling stone works. She carried it to the car.

"I know it's only slag. But still...."

I took her to the abandoned railroad Station where P.T

25

Barnum once parked a dying elephant. I showed her the Congregational minister's house where Lafayette stopped for lunch on his 1824 tour of America. We drove around all morning. Miss Drake saw tired old men working on our WPA bridge project over Pequot Brook. She took off her shoes at Wright's Pond and waded across the sunken dam.

When we got to the beach I pointed to a bootlegger's dock, now sagging with rotten timbers. "A lot of hooch came ashore here in the 20's."

"Heavens—right out in the open?"

"Yeah. My Uncle Terry owned that wharf. In 1927 he got four years in the Federal penitentiary."

"Oh dear."

We ate lunch on the splintery benches at Shoreline Dog House. Briny air blew from the Sound, making the marsh grass bend with a *swish-swish*. I said this stretch of salt-scented water was the best thing about West Stoddard.

"I think it purifies the air. It keeps the whole town healthy."

I was due at the garage by two o'clock. But we made one more stop—Leatherman's cave. The cave was tucked in a towering ledge outcrop back from Clinton road. She crawled in the low entrance behind me. Sunlight glinted through narrow slits in the ceiling.

"Golly," she said, running her hand along the rough stone wall, "Somebody actually slept here?"

I told her how in the last century a Frenchman—destitute, disappointed in love—had dressed himself entirely in leather, and begged around the county. Everyone called him the Leatherman.

"He had caves in a lot of towns. Slept in different ones, summer and winter."

"Lordy, didn't he freeze?"

"He kept sewing layers of old leather on his clothes. He would burrow down in leaves to keep warm. He died up here—after eating some bad stuff he'd found at the town dump."

She stepped around, her sneakers crunching the dry leaves.

She said nothing. But her eyes glimmered with a kind of gentleness — as if they were looking at a broken-down hovel full of hurt memories.

Driving back to the garage, she was quiet. "Well, I never heard such a strange, sad story."

Joe Tutynski

When it dawned on me that my old man was an ignorant fool, I started hanging around at Leatherman's cave. I'd bring a book from the library — any book, fiction, science, politics — and go through it in 20 minutes or so.

I'd read some passages aloud to Luke the Leatherman who seemed alive in the solid stone walls — and understood me like nobody else in West Stoddard.

Then I'd sleep in the leaves. When I woke up I'd pile dry sticks in the rock firepit outside the entrance. I'd put a match to it. The smoke would curl up through the tall maples and drift off toward the Sound — just the way life drifts.

If the book was stupid I'd toss it in the flames.

Almost every sundown I clawed my way to the ledge-top above the cave. I'd sit on an old stump and watch the colors change on the Sound. The beaches and sailboats were four miles away. But they gave a feeling being close. Sometimes the blueness of the water, checkered with white, looked like a huge, soft bed blanket — like the one I saw when I peeked in the window of Mr. Kelsey's boarding house one day after school.

Elvira Wainwright, Biology I

I told the other teachers — Virginia Polk and Susan Baker — that we must welcome the new faculty member, even though we knew nothing about her credentials.

"Mr. Plimpton says the Board hired her at a bargain price after she passed California examination. She seems bright.

Hopefully she'll develop our way of pedagogy."

From the start, however, Eva Drake showed alarming familiarity with her students. She had a classic vocabulary and used it in English class. But launched into inappropriate slang whenever she wanted. She wrote insightful examinations. But allowed the most immature student questions to dominate class discussions.

Once I stopped outside her room to listen. A student, that ghastly crippled boy, was half-shouting, "So what if the Japanese shoot up Manchuria. Too many Chinese in the world anyhow."

She said, "You're around the bend, Joseph Tutynski. Uncle Sam stands against that kind of flippancy."

Then that little snappish girl, Sibyl Noyes, blurted, "You'd send our troops to get killed out there, Miss Drake?"

"Well, that's for FDR and Congress to hash over. Right now we're neutral. But if tyrannical powers start zapping us, who knows?"

"War is great, hey Teach?"

"Come off it, Joe. War is hell—as Sherman said. But sometimes the most peaceful people get shoe-horned into it. Okay, class, hit page...mmm...page 64. *Origin of the Versailles Treaty.*"

That sort of language is hardly appropriate for a high school faculty member. And she didn't seem to understand that teachers have to keep voices down so Board visitors won't think we can't control West Stoddard's young.

Also, her after-school life was...well...unusual. She swam at Mrs. Kelsey's beach in a bathing suit that showed her physical qualities in...shall we say...*bold outline.*

Fred Millay

I never wanted to work the way Miss Drake wanted us to work. She divided us in groups of three to research pre-Revolutionary America. She made us prepare five-minute speeches. She tightened the easy-float of school so that each morning you came through the door a little on edge.

How will she sock us today?

Our school building was an old farmhouse, partly unpainted. Built in 1766, it featured eight rooms, four of them upstairs. It had six stone fireplaces plugged with brick. You started in homeroom and walked creaky floorboards to Chemistry, Mathematics, Industrial Arts, History and English, each in its separate torture cell. You passed the office where No Balls Plimpton sat farting and shuffling papers. He headed up our faculty of five. Yeah.

Up to now I hadn't minded the poorhouse feel of the place. I just wanted to loaf and look at Elaine Bordan.

Elaine burned me up. If she knew I existed she never showed it. Here I was, the only guy in West Stoddard with money to spend on a girl—and she looked through me like I was a dirty hunk of cellophane. It didn't help that she came from the down-at-the-heels Bordans and I was from the top-line Millays.

I hate that snooty bitch, I'd tell myself.

Then she'd come by, swinging those soft-grooved legs and flouncing that hazel boy-cut hair. She'd be humming Red Sails in the Sunset. My stomach would flip over.

Miss Drake made me study. She gave me an assignment on King Philip's War to write in one night. "Just a sketch for class tomorrow. Couple of pages," she said.

I couldn't believe it. "It'll take till midnight to do this."

Her green-gold eyes took me in—all my phony indignation, my laziness. "So hitch up your pajamas and give, fella."

I tried my sass-back approach. "Lose a night's sleep for a lousy Indian fight? Nah. That's bad for your health."

Her voice had a new brassy ring, "It'll be worse for your health if you don't get it in."

I wrote it—because right off the bat she was getting a reputation for tough grades, and my father was a gorilla about report cards. But I was sore. All next day I wouldn't turn my face to her.

29

After lunch she told the class to follow her up Stannard Hill, a ledge outcrop which jutted behind the school. We trudged up there, glad to be trying something different. The town stretched out below, crumbly-shingled roofs following a line of giant elms. The New Haven Railroad tracks looked like long strands of chromium holding the beaches in place.

"Now stand in a circle and clasp hands," she said.

What was this? We followed orders. Something about this teacher didn't encourage non-cooperation. The high sun glinted on the Sound. Everything smelled good — the cow grass...the September leaves...the girls' fresh dresses.

"Close your eyes," Miss Drake said.

Giggles. Mutters. I took my sister Holly's hand on one side and Jack's rough fist on the other. I shut my eyes and tried to forget everything except the pleasant heat on my face.

"Now think outward, everybody. Consider yourself a strong electric current generating power."

Crazy, I thought. But I let myself float.

"Keep thinking outward," said Miss Drake, "You're drawing strength from each other. You're sending signals far, far away."

A bunch of gypsies playing with magic? But suddenly I *did* feel a kind of power, yeah. I sensed a strange unity with the guys...the girls. A feeling that we were together against something. Startled, I opened my eyes. And there was Elaine Bordan across the circle, her China-blue gaze fixed on my face.

The next day I asked my father if I could do something at his office on Saturdays. "Carry papers, sweep floors. I just want to see how things work."

He gulped and tried not to look surprised. "By all means."

I began reading. My mind began to function — a little. The day came when I described to the class how laws were written in Congress, and I wasn't self-conscious a bit. Somehow out on Stannard Hill, Miss Drake had touched a button and started my motor sputtering.

Then I got into poetry. Miss Drake had a habit of breaking into History class with bits of Donne or Wordsworth. And her

A Novel By George P. Morrill

English class was alive with verse.

"Poetry is music," she said, "Wouldn't it be terrible to go through a single day without music."

She set aside 20 minutes each day for us to read poems aloud. Most of the kids intoned stuff like Trees or The Cremation of Sam McGee. But one day I recited a lyric from an obscure magazine called the Cardinal:

Come sit beside me on this sand, and let
Me take your head between my hands and kiss
Your cheeks, and ask of those soul-searching eyes
If there be truth, and faith that we can share;
If love there be which knows no bonds of time.
Eternity were then a briefer life
Than this, the transient wand'ring of two souls.
If I, forever bound in your embrace
Could press your head against my breast and say,
"No sorrow can destroy our shrine of faith."
Then surely God and Man were one against
The hurts and melancholies that deny
The joy of perfect unity in which
We two could reach those golden shores beyond the stars.

I looked up. Hymie Volenski and Eva Casserino were drawing pictures. Joe Tutynski was carving something with a jackknife, muttering to himself. Gene Bigelow was staring out the window. Nobody was listening except Miss Drake and Elaine Bordan. Elaine raised her hand.

"Who wrote that?"

I looked at the magazine. "Somebody named Penelerim."

Miss Drake said, "I want a copy of that, Fred."

As I was tying my shoe in the hall, Elaine came up hugging her books. "I liked your poem," she said.

I walked her home. We started going together. One night my father let me take our Roadmaster Buick to Guilford to see Flying Down to Rio with Fred Astaire and Ginger Rogers.

Afterwards she and I drove to West Beach and got out.

The sea breeze was freaky-warm for autumn—quite sweet when you breathed it in. We sat in the sand watching the moon make silver squiggles on the water.

"The new teacher is making us different, you know?" she said. Then, "Whew, I'm taking off my sweater."

I helped her with a sleeve—and her perfect breast bumped against my arm. It was like a signal. All of a sudden she was naked to the waist, her hard nipples pushing into my palms. We couldn't stop kissing.

"Freddy...Freddy..." she said.

The breeze was freaky-warm, yeah. The moon dropped those silver squiggles on the water. Neither of us knew how to do much. But all at once I was on top of her, looking down on closed lashes. I felt a warmness...a wetness...an incredible giving way.

"Are you there?" she whispered.

Elaine Bordan

I always needed rhythm in my life. My family was dirt poor. The only birthday present I remember is a harmonica my father tossed to me on my 10th when he was drunk. By the time I got to high school I could play every popular song on it from *Tea for Two* to the *Dipsy-Doodle*.

When Miss Drake introduced us to poetry it was like a fire going on. I used to walk home from school reciting *Annabel Lee*. Then Fred Millay read a love poem that throbbed with sweetness—and I melted like a Popsicle.

I'd always considered him out of reach. But he started rushing me. We began to touch and kiss. I found it breathtaking.

When we came together at West Beach, it was an explosion. I remember squirming under his hard stomach and saying to myself: *This is better than anything in the universe.*

We became like rabbits—everywhere. On the back seat of the Buick...in the forsythia behind the town hall. We were pretty careful in public. We figured we were fooling everybody. But one day Miss Drake called me to her desk after class.

"You trouble me, Elaine."

"Me, Miss Drake?"

She started to say something, then looked at her fingers. Her beautiful brow was puckered into little thought-creases above the nose.

"You're all melody, all lyricism, dear—"

She turned her face on me. It was so full of softness and sympathy that I felt tears pushing up behind my eyeballs.

"But that's good, isn't it?" she added quickly, "Of course it is."

"Without music I'd die, Miss Drake."

She smiled. "Well, do you know that new Tin Pan Alley song. *Butterfly, Be Careful of your Wings?*"

"Yes."

She handed me some sheet music with a girl wearing gold wings on the cover. "Look over the words tonight."

I walked home. I already knew the words by heart.

Butterfly, be careful of your wings,
Careful of the care tomorrow brings...

She was trying to warn me. But it was too late. Her teaching had opened up life for me like a flower. I was going to bloom and blossom from now on.

Fred Millay was special to me now. But I knew there'd be others. In school I found myself musing over the sinewy, licorice-black arms of Vince Bigelow. I watched him open a book... scratch his dark, perfectly shaped ear.

Sometimes I looked at Joe Tutynski—and shuddered. He was a wreck except for his one left arm, which looked like something from a Roman statue—rippling with muscle. I made secret glances at that powerful-looking hand—and wondered how it would feel if he touched me.

When you erase barriers between kids and fill them with strange, wonderful ideas, how can you know which way it's going to push them?

Sorry, Miss Drake.

Eva Casserino

Miss Drake put me with Jack to do a paper on Algonquin influence in pre-Revolutionary West Stoddard. He dug into the research like a crazy man. He read histories from Hartford Library. He wrote to the Indian Institute in Washington.

I was no help at all. I just sat in the library and watched him probe through encyclopedias. And scribble in his notebook.

I said, "You're part of this place, Jack. Yes? You go down in Yankee ground like an old tree. But my roots are back in Italy."

I thought he might be sore. But he looked up and smiled.

"You're our Roman connection, Eva. Wait till Miss Drake gets us to the immigration wave of the 1890's."

Holly Millay

Miss Drake didn't stop at having us read poetry. She got us writing it.

"Let's give it a shot," she said, "Maybe we should concentrate on a single subject at first so we can compare. Mmm. How about Autumn? Or the Sea?"

The sessions didn't go over with everybody. Hymie laughed at them. Eva Casserino polished her nails instead of listening. And of course Joe Tutynski just snorted.

The class voted to use Christmas as a subject. Everybody had to produce something. Hymie came up with:

> *We three kings of Orient Ar*
> *Tried to smoke a White Owl cigar*
> *It was loaded*
> *We exploded.*
> *Silent Night.*

A Novel By George P. Morrill

And Joe wrote:
> *The day of*
> *Christ's birth*
> *marked the beginning of*
> *Duplicity*
> *Fanaticism*
> *Inquisition*
> *Christmas Trees burning down houses*
> *Poor people burning up money*
> *Ministers burning out their guts in hollow pulpits*

> *Otherwise,*
> *it was just another*
> *offhand child-dropping*
> *amidst the*
> *camel dung.*

But the rest of us leaned toward the ordinary holiday feeling. We tried hard to write a few words that had rhythm and sentiment. Most came out like 5 & 10 Christmas cards. But Miss Drake encouraged us. She read aloud my poem, *December Thought*, and pronounced it good:

> *The sweetest of things,*
> *As everyone knows,*
> *Is a kitten asleep*
> *in a basket of clothes.*

> *But the dearest of sights*
> *(I hope you'll agree)*
> *Is the Christ-child awake*
> *And smiling at me.*

"It has traditional melody and feeling," she said.

Nothing got by Miss Drake, however. She knew she couldn't keep the class awake with just rhymes. Her technique was to find what each person was interested in and push that guy into doing something about it.

She pushed different people at different speeds. When she saw I knew quite a bit about plant life, she lined up a botany project for me — studying West Stoddard flora and building an exhibit to enter at the National Botanists Convention in Atlantic City. A big job.

But with Elaine Bordan, who also liked flowers, she was less demanding. She helped her paint some water colors of goldenrod and roses. And she began steering Elaine into acting out skits in class, which to everyone's surprise, Elaine did better than anybody else.

It didn't matter if what you liked was a million miles away from History or English, Miss Drake backed you up. She hovered around, friendly, interested, her sweet-smelling hair swinging on her shoulders.

Joe Tutynski

At the end of that poetry crap session I waited until Teach and I were alone in the room. Then I said, "Doesn't the U.S. Constitution say that church and state are separate?"

"Why yes, it does."

"How come this Christmas stuff in class then?"

She blinked, then smiled. "By golly..."

"Hymie Volenski's a Jew. Why should he write Christmas stuff?"

She sat down at her desk. "Mmm, He seemed to enjoy doing it, Joe. His poem was funny."

"Well, I didn't enjoy writing my poem."

She stared. "Really?"

"No. I'm an atheist."

For a long time we just looked at each other. Then she got up and smoothed her sweater down, making her big tits bulge. I put on the blue leather cap I always wear, summer or winter.

"Well, I never expected this," she said, "Your poem was dark. But highly original. Too bad it didn't give you a kick."

"Atheists don't want religion in school."

She cocked her head. Her yellow curls fell onto one shoulder. "Mmm. How about doing a paper on the Supreme Court, fella?"

Jack McGreggor

As weeks passed Miss Drake and I grew closer. I wasn't one of those talents she spotted and started building into something—Fred Millay, the lawyer-to-be...Elaine Bordan, the actress. But I was the kid she could talk to. I was taking in the real jazz about life outside. Truck drivers from New York and Boston...jitterbuggers from Rhode Island roadhouses...hungry guys in jalopies hunting for jobs—they all stopped at the garage.

She saw early on that I was going to stick in West Stoddard. Maybe buy the garage someday. Soak up all the books in our two-bit Carnegie library. And eventually be planted with my ancestors up in Blackthorn Cemetery.

"Mmm. You're destined to be Mr. West Stoddard, fella," she said, poking her finger on my chest, "The vital Socrates every town's got to have."

I said, "Fame is a food that dead men eat. I have no stomach for such meat." (I'd picked it up from a book of old English poets.)

She blinked, then laughed. "Well, I never!"

Less than a month later she motioned me to her desk after the bell. She flipped back her yellow curls and tapped her pencil on the red blotter. "Jack, when I need to know something, you're the connection? Right?"

"Maybe."

"Okay. I've got to know Joe Tutynski better."

I looked at her. "Nobody in Middlesex County knows him, Miss Drake."

Silence.

"Mmm. You mean he has no ties with you-all?"

I nodded.

She got up frowning. She leaned against the blackboard, tossing a hunk of chalk in her hand.

Joe Tutynski

I was five years old when the creature I was finally seeped into my consciousness—and I tried to kill myself.

My parents had gone back to Poland to sell a peasant property they inherited. They left me with my Aunt Anna in Bridgeport.

The kids in the tenement came to stare at me. My aunt worked from 7 to 5 in a shoe factory and couldn't keep them away. I kept the door locked like she said. But the kids would peer in from the fire escape.

"Jesus, look at him."

"Lookit his arm—dingle-dangle."

"That hump...them legs. He don't walk, he crawls."

I was used to people staring at me. But these kids wouldn't let up. Then they started talking friendly. One of them handed me an all-day sucker through a hole in the screen.

"Hey kid," he said, "You wanna be in our circus?"

They put me in an old piano crate behind the garage. I didn't mind at first because they kept giving me candy. But then three of them told me to take off my clothes. I cried and fought, but they tore off every stitch.

"Jesus Christ."

"I never seen nothing like —"

"Lookit his lumpy dong."

All afternoon they charged kids a penny to look at me. I tried to double up in a corner, but they poked me with sticks to make me move around.

When my aunt came home, they ran off. She carried me naked to my bed. She was sobbing. She said, "You little Satan from Hell, I ought to *zmucic* you. Don't I tell you to stay inside?

38

Now neighbors see—oh my God."

At supper she wouldn't give me any dessert. As soon as she went to bed, I crawled to the bathroom and drank a small bottle of iodine. I screamed all the way to the hospital in the police ambulance.

After that, my voice always sounded like stones rattling. And I couldn't taste salt.

The creature I was (and am) isn't easy to describe. Just say I was born from a diseased sperm and a lop-sided egg. I came out with no right shoulder and a right arm as thin as a snake. My left arm was overlong. Oddly, it would grow thick with powerful muscle. My right leg was six inches shorter than my left. There was a hump on my back, which mushroomed as I got older.

My head was misshapen. And because of my practically non-existent shoulder, it tilted to one side.

Enough? Well, there's more—the ultimate mockery. My forehead, eyes, and nose were handsome, Greek classic. But my jaw sloped outward like an ape's. When I talked I looked like a prehistoric monster chewing.

By the time I was four I had taken to standing in my mother's bedroom staring at myself. I'd move sideways so my withered arm and leg wouldn't show. I'd hold my left hand over my jaw. That way I actually looked handsome.

When I started reading fairy tales, I'd dream that the Good Fairy came down and touched me with her wand and made me like everybody else. But in the morning there I was.....

I learned this: Don't trust anybody...anywhere...anytime.

But there was, as the humanists say, a noble compensation. My mind. Early in the game I discovered I could read faster, think quicker, and absorb more than any kid I knew. My father, a laborer on the New Haven Railroad, brought home books from the company library. He couldn't read them. But when his drinking buddies were in the tenement, he'd open one in front of me and order, "Read."

I'd read the page in seconds. Silently.

He'd shut the book and grin. "Wha it say?"

I'd recite the page verbatim. He'd roar with laughter. "By Jesu, des keed mak me million dollar someday."

Before I entered Shoreline Grammar School, I had read the complete *Railroad Journals of America* from 1878 to 1928—and could recite them all from memory. I memorized a set of Funk and Wagnalls encyclopedia up to Volume 6 (as far as we had them). I had devoured junk novels as far back as Elinor Glynn. I had raced through quite a bit of science and religion.

At school they didn't know what to do with me. A state lady gave some intelligence tests—and my scores ran off the board. Finally they put me at a desk by myself and let me read grown-up books—while other kids were laboring through *Dick and Jane*.

For me the only activity close to athletic was the cultivation of my left arm. I'd lie on my back and lift anything heavy—sledge hammer, grain bag, scrap iron—until the muscles went dead. As a result the arm developed to massive size, keeping me somewhat off-balance.

So that's the freakish mutation I was, a voracious intellect in a crab's body, when Eva Drake came to town. I had developed in crazy directions. Nobody had put the engine of my mind on a single, straight track. After I collided with her over Christmas poetry in public school, Teach found out I had read everything in our two-bit Carnegie library. She started bringing me books from Hartford.

"Let's get something coherent going," she said, "How about a study of New England Indians—their roots and their displacement by a militant white culture."

I was looking at the smooth furrow of flesh along her collarbone. Every time she turned, I followed the curve of her right breast (which was big enough to fill a small salad bowl).

"If you say so, Teach."

She put on her coat. As she poked her arm into the sleeve, she leaned back slightly—and her muscled legs pressed against her skirt like tree boles. For a second her mound of Venus bulged out. And her yellow hair bounced against her white collar.

I took that vision of her to the Leatherman's cave. I lay down and hugged the fresh leaves I always kept in a mound along the back wall.

Elvira Wainwright

When Miss Eva Drake began taking her classes on nature walks, I said that's about enough. I've taught Biology here since 1927. I don't appreciate anyone poking into my territory.

I asked Virginia Pope how she'd like it if an unqualified teacher began chemistry experiments? I warned Susan Baker that Miss California might start doing projects in Industrial Arts.

Of course, we stayed polite to the new teacher. But when we met privately we agreed something had to be done. We aired our view to Mr. Plimpton—who had been elevated to full-time principal.

He said, "I couldn't agree more. We've got to re-establish a little restraint around here. I'll handle it."

Jack McGreggor

Miss Drake liked to explore West Stoddard. After school we'd see her big Packard with the roof down poking into dead end roads. She always let her yellow hair flow loosely. She nibbled an ice cream cone and hummed old jazz tunes.

At first some people seemed sore when her supercharged boat popped up where houses were unpainted and grass was ragged. But, as she leaned over the door smiling and asking questions about the town, they softened. They showed her the old stagnant quarry pond off Little Italy. They took her to remote Kill Horse Cliff where in 1865 a returned Union Army veteran had driven a neighbor's four-horse team over the edge after finding adultery in his home.

"They showed me the horse bones under the cliff," she said, "Golly, what a terrible rage must have driven that soldier."

Any resentment over her fancy car died after what happened at Jake Doane's farm. She was poking into the wood lot trail that led back from Chalker Beach. She came upon Jake grinding the starter of his 1930 Reo truck.

"The damned thing won't kick. And me with a cord to cut for town office before nightfall. There go eight bucks."

"Mmm," said Miss Drake, getting out, "Let's see...."

In the end, she and Jake hooked a manila line from her car to the Reo. She towed it out of the way, then backed the Packard over the homemade treadmill he had built to use wheel-power for sawing wood. She revved up her wheels. The circular blade whined. She sat on a fence and watched while Jake cut the cord.

"I surely thank you, Miss Drake."

After that, the whole town just smiled when she showed up in off places at odd hours, sometimes scribbling notes in a little rawhide-covered book. And when she parked at the beach after supper to watch starlight turn the Sound to jewelry, they said approvingly, "That teacher likes beauty."

Elaine Bordan

"Sometimes I don't see the point to anything." I told Miss Drake.

We were sitting alone on two desktops. School was half-an-hour over. A State Police officer was coming to pick me up. My father was in Haddam jail again, drunk after beating up my mother. The police were keeping my baby sister at the barracks until I got there—because my mother was drunk too.

"Sometimes life is anguish," said Miss Drake, "but we have to ride it out anyhow. So we might as well lean to the sunlight."

I said, "I don't see any sunlight. Look at the kids in this

42

room. We're all alike. We live in a poor town. We're all going to grow up, marry, work, and die."

"Mmm, but..."

"Look at poor Joe Tutynski. All knotted up and turned mean inside."

When the cop arrived, Miss Drake kissed me. She tucked a two-dollar bill in my hand.

"Chin up, now," she said.

I walked to the patrol car, looking at my feet. I didn't look back or wave or anything.

I was out of school two days. After mother dried out, things were okay—or would be till the next time—so I spent 35 cents of the two dollars on a glass ruby for my hair. I'd never had a barrette before.

"Today," Miss Drake said, standing in the bright sun by her window, "We will seal our dusty books. We'll seek the solace of the bosk on Stannard Hill."

Somebody asked her what *bosk* meant.

"Look it up," she ordered, sitting down, "Right this very minute."

No other teacher did things like this. We crossed Route 1, laughing and talking. Miss Drake led the way uphill, her skirt flashing against those solid calves. She pointed to a squirrel high in a maple tree. Now and then she stopped to say something about a bush or a flower.

"These lilacs...see? They tell that people once lived here. Yes, there's the cellar hole. Now look at that barn foundation. Each generation has left its mark on our town."

I only half-listened. So people had grubbed along ahead of me. Whoopee.

At the top of the ledge Miss Drake climbed up on a big white stone. Her hair was blowing. You could see the outline of her graceful, muscular body under her clothes.

"This rock," she said, stamping her foot on it, "was brought by the glacier from thousands of miles away. And look out there at our beautiful Sound—so blue, so sculptured. The geology of this area is worth studying, worth writing about. Now who wants to do it?"

She was trying to hook us into projects again. Well, there wasn't anything in West Stoddard that interested me one iota.

Holly Millay and Eva Casserino agreed to do a paper on town geology. Miss Drake pointed to a tanker steaming up the Sound, and Vince Bigelow agreed to write on local maritime history. She waved her hand at the New Haven tracks. And Jack signed up for a railroad story.

This is the craziest classroom ever. Teacher standing on a rock. Kids sprawling around chewing stems of grass.

"Now here's an assignment for everyone," she said, climbing down, "On the way back, pick up one object—just one. A leaf, a pebble. Anything."

We were getting used to her weird ways. Vince peeled off a hunk of bark from a black birch. Sibyl Noyes found an old, peach-colored brick. Jack dug a rusty bolt from the tar shoulder of Route 1.

I broke off a sprig from a weeping willow.

Back in homeroom Miss Drake swept her hand over the pile of stuff on her desk. "Look at this. Flowers. A brick. Even a Baby Ruth candy wrapper. Now what do they tell me? They tell me you're all different."

We quieted down.

"Nobody came up with the same object. Oh, I know some of you were looking for silly things. But even that says *individuality*. We have humorists in the crowd, and that's good."

She leaned against the window, her glasses winking in the sunlight. "If you forget everything else we discover this year, remember this. You're a private person, unique and filled with a special destiny. Maybe you don't know yet what talents you have—but they're there."

A bee zoomed through the window and out the door. Miss Drake tilted her elegant jaw away from it. "Your job is to find those talents and put them to work."

Nobody said anything. It was as if Miss Drake had hung

some kind of an arrow on each of us saying: *go this way.* My arrow said: *be an actress.*

I think Miss Drake came from a star in outer space—I truly do. One night Hymie and I were walking up by the Green. We saw her step out of the library.

The sky was shiny with milk-white stars. She paused, looked up, and lifted her arm in a prayer-like way. It was like she was adding something to the dark—like a magician tossing a ball into nothingness.

"Did you see that?" I whispered to Hymie. He nodded. But he said that Miss Drake was only batting a night moth.

I don't think so.

Now they talk about celestial people coming down to visit us—Buck Rogers types and all. God-like creatures from distant worlds who have watched our development for millions of years. We're only laboratory animals to them up there.

Maybe Miss Drake was one of them. She loved us and felt sorry for us. So she broke away from her star and came down, trailing silver mist....

Jack McGreggor

West Stoddard had a nine-hole golf course. Before I got into garage work with Old Man Chapman I did a lot of caddying. I could earn 35 cents a round.

It was an okay job. Hot sun on your back. Grass smelling good. I liked it—even if I was lugging the bag for some stinker who yelled at me for not finding a ball he'd sliced into the rough.

We caddies played, too—around dark. We'd get in some shots from the Eighth and Ninth tees before Truscott McShane, the pro, drove up in his motorized golf cart. We'd run. He'd cuss. He'd shout that not a god-damned one of us could ever work for Pequot Country Club again.

But next day we'd be back. The club needed caddies.

By the time I was 13, I could whack a ball over 200 yards. When the Colonial Driving Range started up on Route 1, I tried it out only once, spending 25 cents on my 16th birthday. I slammed a ball 211 yards. Watching, a couple of beach girls clapped and said. "Say-y —!" Then a Trinity College golfer named Peter Hollinger — whose family lived year round at swanky Indian Beach — walked over to the tee.

He said. "You that guy who pumps gas at the garage?"

He looked me up and down. I was wearing oily dungarees and a torn shirt. I said, "You the guy who drives that Pontiac with the piston slap?"

We faced each other. He started practice-swinging a shiny Bobby Jones driver. He was older than me. I knew he didn't like the idea of a rag-tag guy playing on his turf.

"Watch this." He teed up a new white Top-Flite. He belted it past the 200 marker.

It was a challenge. I teed off with my wooden-shafted driver. But the best I could do was 197 yards.

He laughed. "Your swing is weak, guy."

My face heated up. "Yeah? Lemme try your Bobby Jones."

He stepped back, hugging the club. "Not on your life."

We traded insults. I got sore. Finally I blurted, "Wiseguy, you're looking at a hoss who has hit 300 more than once."

"*Three hundred!*"

"That's right."

"I got 25 bucks that says you're lying."

He grinned. I was trapped. I had shot off my mouth. And he wouldn't let me off. He maneuvered me into betting 25 dollars that I could hit a ball 300 yards. The only condition I hurriedly added was that I could pick the place and time to do it.

All summer long Hollinger kept bugging me. He'd pull in for gas and say, "I don't see any rush to pop those 300 yards."

I snorted. "Just keep those 25 clams handy."

But I was mighty nervous. And everybody in town seemed to know the bind I was in.

School started. Autumn rolled in, bright and sun spanked.

A Novel By George P. Morrill

The first cold snap came in December. Gene Bigelow and I visited my traps at Wright's Pond. We stood on the dam shivering from wind blowing across the ice. All of a sudden I clicked my fingers.

"Gene," I said, "Tell the guys to take all the bets they can get from Hollinger. I'm gonna fix his ass next Saturday."

The guys and girls had their doubts. But they bet nickles and dimes out of loyalty. Hollinger, sitting in his Pontiac, wrote the bets in a notebook.

On Saturday morning he announced, "Come one, come all. See the dog-faced boy bang the little ball 300 yards."

Even Miss Drake got interested. She gave Elaine 50 cents in an envelope with a note saying, "Put this down on our Superman."

"Okay, Hollinger." I said, "Head up to Wrights Pond."

The whole town knows the rest. I teed up a golf ball on the dam. Whacked a low drive across the ice. It picked up a following wind and rolled on...on...on. We lost sight of it heading down the half-mile-long slab of blue ice.

Sibyl Noyes

After Miss Drake helped dissect the frog I caught in McGreggor's Pond, I realized she was my friend. She bent over the table, a faint perfume floating from her rolled-up sleeves and bare, strong hands.

"That looks like a heart ventricle—there," she said, "Slip your knife under that sinew, Sibyl. Mmm...see?"

She worked with me two hours in Mrs. Kelsey's basement. Then she drove me home. I was embarrassed for her to see our little, unpainted Cape Cod that my father had bought with a $800 mortgage before Griffin Leather folded.

"Pretty place," she said.

"Aw, it's all right."

I didn't ask her in. I didn't want her to see my father's overalls hung on a nail in our unpapered living room...the rug made from grain sacks sewed with red-and-blue twine that was supposed to look colonial. I was ashamed of our kitchen with its old fashioned icebox instead of a refrigerator.

She waved goodby. My father appeared in the door. He was unshaven, chewing something.

"Who's that?"

"My teacher, Miss Drake."

"What's she driving that big car for?"

"She came from California."

"One of them rich ones, ain't she? What business has she got taking the taxpayers money outa town? By God, West Stoddard is going to hell, hiring teachers we don't need from them movie-star places."

My father wasn't always like that. Before mother died he'd had steady work at the factory. He'd brought home food. And even picked up our secondhand Essex on installments. Some Sundays we would drive to New Haven for a show. And eat sandwiches on the way home, talking about Joan Crawford, Gene Autry, Humphrey Bogart, and the rest. Sometimes my father would laugh.

But everything changed. He had been a top leather-stitcher at Griffin's, starting in 1923. Since the factory folded, he'd scrounged for jobs parking cars, digging ditches, mowing lawns, shoveling traprock, unloading freight at the railroad depot. His last job was with the WPA, pushing wheelbarrow loads of cement at Pequot Brook.

"I don't fancy shoving that cussed concrete around," he told mother, "I'm a sit-down worker, not a damn gorilla."

Those nights in bed I'd hear mother rubbing his back in their room. Talking low as he groaned. Then in the late dark I'd hear him stumbling down the back step to the outhouse, lighting matches to see his way. It was scary—with a freight train rumbling for Boston... unfriendly stars glaring through the cracked glass of my window.

Then mother died. We sold the Essex to buy a coffin.

A Novel By George P. Morrill

One day, long after Miss Drake and I had finished with the frog, I walked all alone through tall weeds to the deserted Griffin factory. I climbed up on the loading platform. I rubbed dust from the side door. I gave the door a little push. To my surprise it opened. Somebody had broken the lock and left pieces on the floor.

I explored the whole building. It smelled musty. It had long lines of benches. Oily stitching-machines. And heavy leather-cutters, powered by overhead belts. In the front office an antique Underwood typewriter sat on a roll-top desk. I punched a key and it stuck against the dry ribbon.

In the storage room I stumbled over chunks of tanned hide. I picked up samples of stinky pieces I had learned when my father had taken me through here—chamois, suede, pigskin, horsehide, doeskin. Even bits of alligator, sharkskin, and buffalo.

Well, I felt like crying. Here was everything that had made West Stoddard almost prosperous when I was in grammar school. Now it was dead and gone. Through some horrible magic the workers who had talked and laughed while these machines whirred were now out in a sour countryside scratching for work. Their nights were like the nights at my house—fathers squirming in beds, talking in their sleep, seeing dollar signs dancing.

Like me I'll bet the kids got that cold, angry, frightened feeling that made your throat go dry when you opened the icebox and saw only a half-eaten apple inside.

On the way out I noticed that one of the benches was missing its rusty old stitching-machine. There were marks on the floor where it had been dragged out. Who would steal a dumb, useless thing like that?

I walked home. Up North Road I waved to Jack McGreggor who was turning his jalopy into the cemetery. I said to myself: *Sibyl Noyes, you're going to be a doctor. Nothing is going to stop you, hear?*

Then in my father's room I found a big stitching-machine

behind his bed, hidden under an old khaki jacket. It was oiled and polished like new.

Hymie Volenski

I liked West Stoddard the way it was before Miss Drake came. I could make guys laugh. Yah. It gave me rank. If I was running dry I'd grab some practical joke stuff from my uncle's store—itch powder, fake dog turds, toy chocolates that blew up. But I preferred to spout original wisecracks.

One day I was sitting in the boys' toilet. I finished—and there was no toilet paper.

I hollered to the next stall, "Got any toilet paper over there?"

Fred Millay's voice came back. "No."

"Any newspaper—an old magazine?'

"No."

"Got five ones for a five?"

Fred made a choking noise. Fast comebacks like that always got a good laugh. I was forever racking my brain to have the smart-ass reply ready when I needed it.

Miss Drake tried to crowbar me into thinking different. "Let's face it, Hymie," she said, "You haven't been reading and writing enough. The language is your prized possession. Take hold of it."

She meant business. She made us write a theme a week. She went over every paper like a hawk. Her remarks, in bold purple ink, always ended with her scrawled signature and a goofy little drawing:

Wanders all over the lot —*Drake*

Get in one tense and stay there —*Drake*

Will you kindly learn to spell "Coming"? —*Drake*

Once she had us write definitions of words we knew but that

were difficult to explain. She read a definition of mine and liked it: "A circle is a line that meets its other end without ending." *Pretty clever. But the rest of your paper is atrocious. Write and hand in a correct sentence using the word "which."* —*Drake*

I wrote, *which is a word with five letters in it.*

She wrote back, *Flunk is another.* —*Drake*

I griped to Fred. "Why is this babe laying into us?"

He was no comfort. "She's hot to cram culture into brains—even a gooey mushroom like yours, Hymie."

"She's trying to intimidate. That's unconstitutional," I said.

I battled back. When she wrote that my paper titled Ways to Get By Without Sweat seemed a little money-mad, I said, "That's right. I've never had any money and it makes me mad." "When she had us explain what top jobs we aspired to, I wrote, *The biggest: washing elephants in a zoo.*

She didn't get sore. She just said, "You're quite the oil merchant, Hymie. Now let's get some of this wit down on paper."

By mid-semester my act was running low. The cracks I was picking out of 10-cent joke magazines weren't busting up kids the way they used to. The reason was everybody was growing interested in Miss Drake's approach.

She was supposed to be teaching only English and History, but she dug into any subject that came our way. When she found out Tutynski was a science nut, she wangled him a $50 grant from the American Society of Civil Engineers to experiment with stresses on wood. (Joe snorted—but took the check.) She kept in motion all the time—going with Geraldine Prue to copy Revolutionary epitaphs in Blackthorn Cemetery...helping Tony Tragonni build a model of a moon ship from *Amazing Stories* magazine.

After she discovered Elaine Bordan could sing the words of every popular song published since 1928, she brought in some old cylindrical records to show the development of American music.

"Music knits generations together," she said, while Elaine

nodded happily, "Civil War troops sang to each other across the lines, you know."

She started a special art class for Sybil Noyes and Holly Millay.

How could I compete with that? I was losing center stage to something we had always scoffed at—a teacher. Miss Drake spoke to some kind of pride in each of us that we didn't even know we had. Yah.

She said, "Look on yourself as a storehouse—a small castle of brain, sinew, and memory in a vast Universe. The songs and sadness of all the ages have come down through generations to you. Be a good custodian."

I started falling under her spell. She was so gorgeous, sitting at her desk with those shapely legs sticking out the side, touching her eyebrow absently with a yellow pencil. But I was sore that it was happening.

One Sunday I saw her coming out of the Congregational Church. (She went to different churches—Catholic, Protestant, Jewish. The town wondered about this.)

She fell in step with me, swinging a white, broad-brimmed hat. "What goes, Hymie?"

I felt the need to disappoint her somehow. "Not church—that's for sure."

"No?"

I blurted that I never went to synagogue. I didn't believe in religion. Rabbis and priests got a free ride. And guys like me paid their way.

She looked at me, lifting a brow, "Oh? How much is it costing you?"

My cheeks heated up. "I mean my uncle pays. I'll be expected to when I'm older. But I'm not going to."

"Why not?"

I said all ministers were greedy. And the money they got went for clothes and cars. I kept expanding my case. I said the churches were merely businesses that gnawed on the economy and produced nothing. I implied that anybody who went to church was a jerk. Why, the money would do more good if it went into building roads. Laws should be created to make churches leave people alone...not trap kids to learn crazy traditions.

She started grinning at me. "Mmm," she said.

Suddenly I realized I was talking idiot stuff. And it was getting wilder and wilder. I felt my face redden, my stomach flip over. She turned off to where her car was parked.

"By golly, I'll have to think about all that," she said.

Elvira Wainwright

Virginia and Susan asked me—as the oldest faculty member—to inform Mr. Plimpton that we continue to be disturbed at Miss Drake taking students out of the building during school hours.

I said, "Mr. Plimpton, our new colleague should understand that English and History are her areas—not Science, Recreation, Nature Study or some other sprawling interest."

He nodded. "I'm concerned, Miss Wainwright."

"I understand she's encouraging projects far afield from her specialty."

"I'll address the problem in good time."

Geraldine Prue

Miss Drake swam at all our beaches. She went alone. But if you happened to be there she'd sit in the sand and talk. O yes.

One Saturday she dropped down beside me and said, "Gery, I've heard there are two legends attached to the Sound hereabouts. You know them?"

I told her about mean Mr. Hughbottom, a down-on-his-luck fisherman who had stuffed a mother cat and her five kittens in a bag and dumped them four miles offshore.

"Good heavens!"

"Another fisherman, Ezekiel Stevens, found them alive. Floating on driftwood. He brought them back. Then he went up to the Hughbottom shack with an empty fertilizer sack—and said he was going to stuff old Hugh inside and plant him off Kelsey Point. They got in a terrible fist fight."

She exhaled slowly. "Mmm. I hope the good guy won."

I went on to the famous incident back in the 20's when Ralph T. Harlow had a shouting match with his wife over money. She ran to the beach, sobbing. Back at their house, he suddenly realized she was gone and sprinted after her. People found them standing waist-deep in the water, hugging without saying a word.

"Mr. Harlow became a Representative in Congress," I said, "The voters kept re-electing him, saying he was the most even-tempered man in Washington."

"My! Well, I never...."

Later, when Tony and I were heading into the Saturday night dance at the West Beach Rink, he pointed at the water.

"Hey, is that Miss Drake out there?"

She was standing far out on the low-tide flats. Little waves, tinted red with sunset, were sliding in at her feet. We watched her turn toward Long Island. She lifted her arms in what seemed like a caress—a prayerful embrace of sky and water.

"What the dickens is she doing?" he said.

I knew. Miss Drake was saluting the liquid magic of our Sound, which glued West Stoddard to the earth...which healed lovers like Ralph T. Harlow and his wife.

Fred Millay

In History Miss Drake got me thinking about times past...about things that happened right here in West Stoddard. I worked cleaning the American Legion House for the 1936 Armistice Day dinner. I found old newspapers advertising *Over There* and other Great War sheet music. I blew dust off a yellowing snapshot of three young guys in uniform. Their rugged calves seemed about to burst through their puttees. They were standing in front of a ruined French cathedral...holding up those round, old-fashioned helmets on sticks. They were grinning.

Holy cats, was that, Mr. Jacobs, our fat butcher? Were those other two guys Mr. Leland, our skinny town treasurer, and Second Selectman John Grannis who walked with a cane?

I stared at them. What had happened to them? These guys were now unmistakably—even pitifully—*old*. Their vivid selves were gone. They now seemed strangers on a fast sprint to extinction. It gave me a weird lump in the stomach.

That night, waiting on table, I watched husbands and wives singing *There's a Long, Long Trail* and *K-K-Katy*. Later I stepped outside to dump some leftovers.

A warm November moon was glinting through the elms. Beyond, the Sound gleamed. Mrs. Jacobs the butcher's wife, and John Grannis, Second Selectman, were leaning against the clapboards, kissing. His blue Legion overseas cap was pressing her head back...back...

"Oh John...John dear," she whispered.

I was sort of stunned. I dropped the garbage can cover. *Clatter-bang.* They separated as if touched by electric wires.

The next day, while having my theme conference with Miss Drake, I was still puzzling over the way Time robs everyone. She had on some new perfume that smelt faintly of roses. Her clean pretty hands shuffled my papers.

"Let's see, Fred. Mmm. You handled the Continental Assembly very well. But you blew the summary. Look at this sentence..."

My hand was on the desk beside hers. Our fingers looked good beside each other. They seemed to have a kinship. I thought: *the accident of Time has clothed her bone in flesh a few years ahead of mine, that's all.*

Suddenly it was as if she were not my teacher but my girl.

"And for the love of Moses, Fred, don't repeat *observed* four times in one paragraph. Sprinkle in a *he saw* or *the record shows."*

Miss Drake had once been as young as Elaine. Elaine was mine only part-time. And it hurt. Miss Drake's strong tan fingers attaching a paperclip to my theme would be different. They would cling to the single hand they chose.

I couldn't take my eyes from those blunt, clean fingernails.

"Generally speaking, this is very good work." She wrote a B+

on the paper and drew a little ☺ beside my name, my first.

A sort of warm gush went through my chest. "Thanks, Miss Drake."

That afternoon I tried to describe my experience to Jack, disguising it by pretending I'd read it in a *Saturday Evening Post* serial. He listened as he tinkered with a broken fuel pump at the garage. He glanced up, grinning.

"In a way, we're all lovers," he said.

Joe Tutynski

Two days before our European history exam, Germany signed an anti-Comintern pact with Japan. Teach used that fact as a springboard into Toynbee's "challenge and response" theory—and I noticed that her voice was a little huskier than usual.

She's edgy about this, I thought. *Can I pry out her secret thinking?"*

"What does this alignment mean?" she was saying, "We don't know. Both the Soviet and Germany are police states. But Hitler's pact with Japan is clearly a slap at the Russians. Thus do totalitarians quarrel."

She pointed a yardstick at the world map hanging on the blackboard. I saw a little spot of white come out on each cheek.

"It seems clear also that this is a slap at the Western democracies," she went on, "An historian named Arnold Toynbee has developed a thesis—". She said that the German-Japanese pact was a definite challenge to free nations. She applied Toynbee's reasoning to the thing. I had already read the ten volumes of Toynbee's *Study of History*. I agreed with her that Western civilization must respond to the surge of modern barbarism or go down. But as a cynical pragmatist I didn't care either way. I was just curious about Teach's hint of passion in the matter.

I raised my hand. "Isn't this merely the case of two have-not nations banding together against the have nations?"

Did she color slightly? The rest of the class was half asleep. Vince Bigelow dropped a book with a bang and picked it up.

She said, "You mean a simple case of those innocent lambs—Germany and Japan—protecting themselves from wolves?"

I nodded. "Germany is choked economically by Britain and France. Japan, by the U.S. They have a right to be afraid of us."

"And this pact is merely their defensive response?"

"That's right. I think they did it to insure peace among the major powers."

We faced each other. I knew as well as she did (maybe better) that all historic indicators pointed toward world explosion. But long ago I had decided to enjoy the spectacle. Let the dumb mobs of the world fall on each other. I'd just ride the bloody waves and stay afloat to see the outcome.

"Well, I never," she said.

I had gotten to her. She walked to the window and looked out. A sparrow flashed by our whitewashed flagpole, dipping below the limp Stars and Stripes.

"Will the brutes of the world force us to out-brute them, if we're not to be destroyed? Peace is hard won and easily lost," she said, her voice trembling slightly, "We're inclined to forget that fact—with our comforts and all. But right now, over in Spain, people are battling tyranny. Why, I know a man, an American, who—"

She paused. A few kids looked up. I didn't change my expression, my moose jaw clamped shut. But every nerve of me strained forward, listening.

The bell rang.

As I limped out, I glanced sideways at her. Her head was down, and she was thumbing hurriedly through some papers. She was holding her lips in a tight purse, as if to keep them from quavering.

Almost caught you that time, Teach.

Jack McGreggor

Joe Tutynski corked me off big-time. But I was the first one to realize that he had a sense of humor. Bitter, sardonic, and buried. But it was there, see?

Miss Drake often used jokes to get through to us, but she never had any luck with Joe. He'd sit in his back seat, a scowl on his ruined, deformed face. Sometimes when she said something funny, he'd snort out loud.

One day somebody wrote on the board:

WE'LL CONQUER THE WORLD.

—Class of 1938 —

Later, looking through an outside window, I saw Joe limp into the empty room, peer around, and hurriedly scrawl words underneath:

THE WORLD IS FLAT

— Class of 1491 —

An evangelist came to town and thumbtacked a placard on the town bulletin board: JESUS DIED FOR YOUR SINS. The next day I recognized Joe's handwriting alongside: BUT DON'T WORRY—THE VIRGIN MARY IS PREGNANT AGAIN.

He was a back wall Shakespeare. He couldn't resist adding his bit to posters and notices, no matter where he found them. If there was nothing written in a public place, he'd scribble down an original comment with a thick black pencil. BRING BACK PAGANISM he wrote in the Methodist Church entryway.

It got so all us guys looked for Tutynski cracks and passed

them around. When we went on field trips we tried not to go into a rest room until after Joe had used it. Usually we were rewarded.

In the Peabody Museum men's room in New Haven underneath a sign saying SAVE TISSUE, PLEASE he wrote: USE BOTH SIDES. At the Mohegan Hotel in New London he answered the management's: DON'T THROW TOOTHPICKS IN THE URINALS with THE CRABS HERE CAN POLE VAULT.

He didn't take sides. He pasted everything. Some Trinity students draped a banner on a Hartford fence saying: WHY SHOULD WE GIVE OUR BLOOD FOR CAPITALISTS? Next to it Joe wrote: WHY NOT? —COUNT DRACULA.

Under a Bridgeport sign saying SUPPORT OUR POLICE FORCE he scratched BRIBE A COP TODAY.

It's a wonder he didn't get caught because he left his mark in some sensitive places. The Bible in the library turned up with his words on the flyleaf: JUDAS NEEDED THE MONEY FOR HIS SICK GRANDMOTHER. And Mr. Jacobs, our butcher, was outraged to find a message finger-written in grease on his store window: ONLY TOP GRADE HORSEMEAT SOLD HERE—A BILLION FLIES CAN'T BE WRONG.

Miss Drake first noticed Joe's talent when she was washing her hands at the utility sink in the basement. I saw her glance at the sign the janitor had nailed up there. She blinked—then laughed. Underneath CONSERVE WATER Joe had written: BATHE WITH A GIRL FRIEND.

"I spy a budding Rabelais in our midst," she said.

After I told her who it was, she was careful not to let Joe know. She didn't want to destroy his spontaneity, she said. But she got me to feed her some of his stuff. I gave her only Joe's clean comments from walls or posters—things like:

MACHINES CAN NEVER REPLACE HUMAN STUPIDITY. Or: IMAGINE HOW YOU LOOK TO A NEAR-SIGHTED TAPEWORM.

Our secret about Joe made our relationship special. Miss Drake trusted me. Sometimes she'd talk about her teaching problems. She took care, however, not to put down a single kid. Or spill too much.

One afternoon as I was helping her load some books in her car, she said, "I still haven't reached Joe Tutynski."

I shrugged, "He's all by himself out there, Miss Drake. He wants it that way."

"I'm not so sure. This graffiti may be a cry of loneliness."

"He *loves* loneliness."

The next day she called me into the cellar storeroom. It was a junk bin, piled high with old desks and books. In one corner a cracked mirror hung sideways. She pointed to a chair drawn up in front of the mirror, then at a blue leather cap that had fallen underneath. It was Joe's.

"I think he sits here and looks at himself in the mirror."

She lifted the hinged arm of the chair. She touched her finger to some black-crayon letters written on the bottom of it.

"We've got to try harder with Joe," she said.

He had scrawled: IS THIS THE END-RESULT OF EIGHTY THOUSAND YEARS OF EVOLUTION—BROKEN ME?

Geraldine Prue

Sometimes I noticed Miss Drake seemed hurt in class. She tried to laugh and smile like always. But that stinker Joe Tutynski was always giving her a tough time. In History he scoffed at her idea that historically America offered the best chance to the down-and-out.

He said, "Tell it to the guys in the breadlines."

"Well Joe, we're having troubles all right. But we seem to be electing leaders who know it. They're experimenting with ways to recover."

"They're all dead from the neck up."

"I suspect that's what George the Third thought of Franklin, Jefferson, and Adams."

"So? Maybe he was right. Perhaps we'd have done better to

stay in the British Empire."

In English, Joe was savage when she called on him to judge the playlets we were writing and acting out:

"Miss Millay's skit is a dog. Who did the make-up? Does her complexion have to be seasick green? I don't like the dialogue either. To cackle, 'I wish better things could happen in this life' is not Shakespearean eloquence. It's banality enthroned."

"Now Joe..." said Miss Drake, as Holly turned red.

One afternoon a big A&P van blew two tires down on Route 1. It lurched sideways. Its steel rear door clanged open. Crates of baked goods... cartons of canned food tumbled out on the cement.

She told us, "Mmm. Take a look. Then back to your jobs."

The spill was spread wide. A lot of cans rolled into a ditch 50 feet down the highway. We looked, then returned to our desks."

Miss Drake stayed by the window gazing out, tapping her yellow pencil on the sill. I watched her pretty lips make a frown, then soften. Then she bit her lip gently. I said to myself, *Why, that's how she must have looked as a little girl about to cry.*

I got up from my desk and walked to the Britannica shelf. I sneaked a second good look at the accident. Cars had stopped. Grown-ups and kids were scrambling to pick up food. One State cop was trying to stop them, blowing a whistle, moving back and forth.

But more people kept appearing. Grabbing bread, cans, cartons—and running away. O yes.

Elaine Bordan

Miss Drake got me doing things I never believed I could do: recite poetry in front of the class...act out little skits. Before then I'd thought I would faint if I stepped onto a live stage.

My first part before a grown-up audience (as Hester Prynne in *The Scarlet Letter*) found me scared stiff. The town hall was full. I told Miss Drake I couldn't walk into those bright lights.

"Nonsense," she said, "Pick out the most hostile-looking face in the seats. Play to that face. Throw every line at it. Now get out there, sweetie, and *perform*."

I saw a scary old man in back with a beard and squinty eyes, and I acted just for him. Next day everybody said I was the star of the show.

By mid-semester Miss Drake had talked the New London Players into giving me a bit part in Clifford Odets' *Golden Boy*. Then the New Haven Group put me in the chorus of Rodgers and Hart's *Babe in Arms*.

All of a sudden I was something at West Stoddard High. I kidded and laughed with everybody like I never had before. For my semester 15-minute speech I talked about a little book of poetry I had bought for 10 cents in an old bookstore in New London. I talked straight at Joe Tutynski because he was a guy who sneered at everything. He had once called me a two-caret lunkhead.

"See this little torn book?" I said, holding it out toward Joe, "It was published in 1833 by a poet so poor his friends had to buy his shirts. But he had music in his heart."

I described McDonald Clarke, known as The Mad Poet of New York, who had married the actress Mary Brundage. But penniless, the couple had had to separate. Later he had gone insane.

"I found beauty and song in these pages. You won't find this forgotten poet in anthologies but listen to this sample of his verse..."

I held the book straight out at Joe. His lumpy jaw was twisted sideways. He gave me a look of pure disgust, but I kept on "The Mad Poet wrote: *Now twilight lets her curtain down, and pins it with a star.*" Isn't that something!"

The class was silent. Miss Drake asked for comments.

"I call it transcendental garbage," said Joe.

Sibyl Noyes

We didn't have a radio. On the nights when President Roosevelt made his fireside chats my father would walk to Hammock Fish Market to listen. I stayed home with my baby brother.

When he got back I knew he'd give one of two set opinions: "That rich man don't know nothing about how folks gotta live."

Or: "By God, FDR is right about them damn big business crooks."

I would sit in our weedy yard and look at the stars. One night Miss Drake rode by and stopped.

She said, "A star-watcher! Anything new and shiny up there, Sibyl?"

I stood by her car. "Oh, Miss Drake, I love the sky at night. It seems so soft...so friendly."

It sounded stupid the minute I said it. But she didn't laugh. Instead she opened her door and sat sideways, looking up.

"Out West when I was a girl my father and I would ride to the north pasture and watch the sunset. He always watched Venus, the evening star. It came out bright and all alone over the Pacific."

I said, "I see it sometimes."

"Well, I used to turn my horse and look to the east. After awhile a dull little star began to wink along the horizon. It wasn't flashy like Venus. I didn't know its name. But I'd watch it while the sky filled up. Pretty soon it was lost in the crowd of brighter stars.

She broke open a Hershey bar and gave me half.

"One time, my father said, 'Venus looks close enough to touch tonight, Eva. Give it a pat.' But I said, 'I'm waiting to touch my lonely star in the east.'"

Joe Tutynski

Once a week I went to the North Road overpass to meet the 6:15 A.M. Yankee Express coming down from Boston.

It was tough hitching myself down the brownstone blocks to the small gravel plot just six feet from the tracks. But I did it. The New Haven rails glimmered, only a step away. No one could see me except the engineer and the fireman as the locomotive thundered by.

I'd get there early. I'd peel the shirt off my big left arm. I'd clench and un-clench my over-size fist so the heavy muscles on my shoulder and forearm would stand out. I'd tense my biceps until the purple veins bulged.

When the Express whistle wailed, I'd see the train's steel nose coming down fast from Saybrook. I'd get set. I'd hunch down by the tracks concealing my withered legs. I'd hide my skinny right arm under my shirt. I'd lift my rugged left elbow up so it covered my lower face.

I'd hold myself like a statue. The roar would grow. The monster drive-wheels would churn past — so close their wind would blow cinders on my forehead. In the cab the engineer flashed in and out of view. He'd shake his fist at me. Or maybe the fireman would lift his shovel and shout something I couldn't hear.

I knew what they were thinking: *What's that damn fool doing on railroad property, crowding in close like that?*

I knew and I didn't care. They were seeing a rugged fella with a mighty arm and a rock-like fist. They were two guys in the world who saw Joseph Tutynski as a force. That's all I had to show them.

After the train was gone I'd hitch out onto the tracks. I'd sit down on the stack of creosoted ties under the overpass. I'd inhale the fumy stink left in the train's wake. I'd imagine what those guys would be saying at the railroad hotel in New York tonight:

Say, there's this cuss who keeps showing up on the West Stoddard stretch. Powerfully built fellow. Holds up this big, tough-looking arm with a clenched fist. Doesn't move an inch. Anybody know who he is?

A few minutes later I'd haul myself up the brownstone blocks. I'd limp to school, chawing an apple for breakfast.

Geraldine Prue

I never thought of myself as a snob. But before Miss Drake came, I stuck pretty close to my family—which was fourth generation Swedish. The Prues rated high in West Stoddard because, even with the Depression, we kept our barn painted. O yes.

I took the job cleaning rooms at Mrs. Kelsey's to save money for college.

Miss Drake got all of us looking at things we'd never noticed before. She told us the Sound was West Stoddard's unique claim to undiluted beauty. She explored the old piano factory crumbling by the Pachaug River and found some yellow ivory chips. She called them Exhibit A in an Historical Museum she set up in the back of home room. Pretty soon we were filling up the table with arrowheads, old photographs, and Civil War letters.

She examined the Roller Skating Rink at West Beach, where summer dances were held, and pronounced it an original Victorian "promenade house," rare because it was made of English brick.

Her easy-going way loosened me up. I got friendly with Elaine Bordan, a drunkard's daughter, and Eva Casserino, who wanted to be a jazz band singer. Their ways of life—so different from mine—showed me that West Stoddard was a world in miniature, a bubbling hodgepodge of different creatures.

I started wandering around offbeat places. I walked the New Haven tracks and discovered a camp where out-of-work families and tramps parked. I saw sedate Mr. Brooks at the drug store taking horse bets. One day after school I came across some legs in dungarees sticking out from under Miss Drake's convertible at Mrs. Kelsey's.

"Is that you, Miss Drake?"

Her face slid into view. She rubbed her cheek with a small wrench and left a tiny grease mark.

"What do you know about leaky radiators, Geraldine?" she said

I helped her clamp a hose on her water pump. She started the motor and we poured some sealer into the radiator.

"Jack sold me this stuff," she said, "Mmm. If it doesn't work he says we'll have to weld."

It wouldn't have surprised me if she meant she'd do the job herself, borrowing an acetylene tank and goggles somewhere. O yes.

I'd reached the point where Miss Drake was a kind of goddess with flashing sword. Capable of anything. When she played tennis at Madison Courts, she beat college students from Yale. When she talked politics at the Post Office, she dropped facts like rain.

On the other hand, when she called at our houses, she was reserved and gentle. She put our parents at ease. She said something good about everybody in the Class of 1938.

That's why I got mad when I overheard Fat Augie Plimpton complaining to her one late afternoon. I had come back to school to pick up a sweater. His voice floated out his office cubicle.

"...hardly conducive to calm education, Miss Drake. Young people are unsettled enough at this age without churning up their minds."

"Young minds should be churned up, Mr. Plimpton. That's what teachers are for."

"*Not* at this school. We're here to help ordinary, down-to-earth citizens-to-be acquire the tools to hold good ordinary jobs..."

"There's not an ordinary person in my class."

"Well, I'm glad you think that way, Miss Drake, but—"

He went on. Arguing, reproving, trying to pour Miss Drake back into the same mold that I'll bet had shaped every West

66

Stoddard teacher since the Spanish-American War. He accused her of offending town opinion by taking her classes out on hikes, giving them a hundred separate projects.

"The town wants solid, nuts-and-bolts education," he said, "Not fancy, progressive frip-frap."

"I'd be happy to have my students compete with other Connecticut 11th graders — on any level of analysis," said Miss Drake.

"You miss the point. What I'm saying is West Stoddard High School will not tolerate a teacher who uses bizarre methods. You can't hold free-for-all gossip sessions with students and keep their respect. You can't appear at student parties. Play baseball. Dress in...aaa...trousers when you're off duty. A teacher must be a lady 24 hours a day."

Miss Drake's voice stayed soft. But she wouldn't give an inch. She said she was making progress with her methods.

"My students are finding new horizons," she said, "I mustn't stifle self-discovery."

Fat Augie's words hardened. "I have to inform you, Miss Drake, you are risking dismissal."

Silence. Then the steel edge we'd experienced came into her voice.

"I have to inform *you*, Mr. Plimpton that I have a two-year contract. You can bring charges against me only on the basis of incompetence or moral turpitude. That will require a hearing before the schoolboard. I'll welcome a confrontation there."

A chair scraped. I slipped away. But before I got out of earshot, Fat Augie spoke again — in a voice with a sort of nervous hiss.

"Incompetence is not an issue, Miss Drake. As for...aaa...moral turpitude, well it's my duty to keep a continual check on all school employees."

Joe Tutynski

As weeks went on the class got crazier. Talk sprouted up about anything, anything at all. Elaine Bordan mooned about acting. Geraldine Prue simpered about flowers. No-Brains Volenski tried to explain the radio humor of Eddie Cantor and the A&P Gypsies. In between, we wrote essays and took true-false tests in American history.

Big Tits Drake was no teacher. She jumped on any subject that interested the jerks here. She got Jack McGreggor to bring in an old one-lung engine he'd rebuilt and start it up. The noise brought No Balls out of his office on the scramble, shouting, "Just a minute...now, now..."

He demanded what was a mechanical contraption doing in a history classroom? Teach said we were covering the Industrial Revolution in rural USA.

"Jack returned to life this butter churn used in the 1880's," she said, "Isn't it wonderful?"

I cruised along with her idiot ideas because they amused me. I wrote the assignments and took the tests. But now and then I'd toss in a shocker. When she assigned poetry in Creative Writing I wrote:

> *As the drunken squirrel*
> *goes up the tree,*
> *His asshole looks smaller*
> *and smaller to me.*

I expected her to blow up. But she just pursed her lips. "Don't you think this is a bit tasteless, Joe?"

When she asked us to write on a needed legal reform, I wrote:

NO PAINLESS EXECUTIONS FOR CRIMINALS
The case for slow strangulation

"Well, you don't lack for ideas, Joe," she said at our private conference.

"I keep an open mind."

She made a silly smile. "Someone said if you're too open-minded your brains fall out."

"What does that mean?"

She sighed. "Just an expression. I've been troubled by...well, by your penchant toward the violent and painful. Your last theme was titled: Ten Reasons for Legalized Torture."

"Historically a valid position."

"Mmm. Joe, you think society today would tolerate—?"

"Society? Society's a fraud. By the time young people find that out, it's to their advantage to continue the fraud. So it goes on forever. That's why a bunch of old folks—like you—are cheaters. You know the game is rigged, but you go on with it."

She stood up. I hoped I was getting her sore. But she laughed. "I didn't know my gray hair was showing, fella. How about writing up your remedies for our stinking society next time—mmm?"

But the next time was that hot Indian Summer day she brought apples to class—and gave us a special writing assignment that was totally nuts...

Jack McGreggor

After lunch Miss Drake set a bag of apples on her desk. She took one out, tossed it up, caught it behind her back.

"Come and get it," she said, taking a bite, "Food for the brain, fairly earned."

As we filed up to stick our hands in the bag, she added that this was a reward for a good bunch of papers she'd corrected last night.

"You Yankee scholars are really coming on. I think it's time we forged into new territory."

We all sat there chewing apples, wondering what next? She finished her apple, then sent the bag around for cores.

"All right—here's the pitch. Try writing something only for

yourself. Secrets, if you want. Thoughts that you keep to your-self for whatever reason—fear, embarrassment, anything. For a week think about it, read it, evaluate it. Then destroy it."

Everybody perked up. Elaine Bordan blushed. The Bigelow brothers exchanged glances.

"I firmly believe that each of us has some ironclad private matter that shouldn't go beyond our own conscience. But it definitely should be a *part* of our conscience.

What the hell...? I looked at Fred. He shrugged. Hymie stuck his tongue in his cheek and blinked like a zombie. This caper seemed far out. But what wasn't in this class?

I raised my hand. "Suppose one of these crums steals my copy?"

"Guard it with your life, Jack. Hide it in an old crankcase at the garage. Stuff it in a used tire."

"Jack's an open book anyhow," said Holly, "We know all about him."

That's what *she* thinks. I took one of the blue-cover compo-sition books from the pile on Miss Drake's desk. And sharp-ened my pencil with my jackknife.

She said, "You-all have an hour. When you get done, fold the book and stick it in your pocket. Don't forget. It's *yours*, nobody else's. I'll never read it. But I jolly well expect you to stay in one tense. And double-check your spelling."

She paused at the door. "When you're finished, you may go. Me? I'm going swimming."

We heard the Packard start. Then everybody settled down. I wrote:

I'd like to hang my best left hook on Joe Tutynski. He's crippled. So I shouldn't think that way. But he's an arrogant, growly son-of-a-bitch who never even tries to smile. He's got a brain that can knock you down. But he uses it to hurt. I could have busted his nose the day he lowered the boom on Holly Millay. And I don't go for the way he pours the shit on Miss Drake either...

A Novel By George P. Morrill

Joe Tutynski

I hated to admit that our California whoopee-lady did anything right, but the assignment to write a paper not to be seen by anybody appealed to me. I wrote, PRIVATE on the inside cover of my bluebook, then I put a title underneath:

The Suicide Plan of Joseph Tutynski.

I wrote I would end my life on Thanksgiving Day 1937, exactly 377 days from now. I picked Thanksgiving—so that Teach could see that all her sanctimonious optimism hadn't deluded at least one of her students.

After considering poison, drowning, throat-cutting, suffocation, and Oriental means such as harikiri, I chose vein-opening by jackknife. This would be relatively painless. I would slowly pass out—like that old Roman who bled to death in his warm bath.

I wrote that this final act will be at Leatherman's cave. The only witness will be Luke. He'll come out of his stone wall, grinning. I'm sure he'll get a kick out of a fellow outcast joining him.

What's the reason for this dramatic exit? It's designed to make West Stoddard get a scary look at a decaying human wreck lying in blood-soaked leaves. It serves them right.

I finished writing. I jammed the bluebook in my desk.

Elvira Wainwright

There was no sound from Miss Drake's English class when I passed her door. But I noticed she wasn't at her desk. Later I found out that the students were alone, writing an assignment and their teacher had *gone swimming!*

I was stunned. At any moment ungoverned students might erupt—and then where would we be? I told Mr. Plimpton this was the limit.

Jack McGreggor

After school I was pumping gas at the garage when this ratty 1929 Hudson chugged in. Kids hanging out the windows.

I figured: *No sale. WPA customer. (Water, piss and air.)*

Two girls and a boy, dressed almost in rags, ran for the rest room. A skinny unshaven man got out and stooped at his front right tire. Then a woman with a tired face came up holding a cellophane cup.

"May I get a little water, please?"

I nodded. "Cold drinking fountain inside."

The man walked over to our used tire rack. Then I noticed that the Hudson's front right was practically flat.

"These here tires for sale, I reckon."

"That's right," I said.

"This here 20DK Goodyear—you take 75 cents for it?"

I went on wiping the globe of our Texaco pump. We were getting a lot of these families. Hungry folks from New York looking for work in Boston. Hungry folks from Boston looking for work in New York. For the last four years, grown-up family people had been sinking. It didn't feel right for me to see it.

Old Man Chapman was home to lunch. I wanted to give this guy a break. But *75 cents!*

I said, "I can go to three bucks."

He shook his head slowly. "I know that's a good price. But..."

Just then Miss Drake's Packard pulled in. She got out and tapped the hood. "Full—when you get to it, Jack."

She took off her sunglasses. She nodded to the family—three barefoot kids...a sick-faced woman, carrying water to a rusty old car. She walked over and began talking to the kids.

I heard her start, "You folks from New York...?"

"Listen, my boss isn't here," I was saying, "But he might okay $2.50. So I'll go to that."

The guy rubbed his bristly jaw. He gave a long sigh, then looked around the lot. "Your air hose here? I'll just blow up the old tread for now."

I filled Miss Drake's tank while the guy fussed with the air hose. She came over and bent down to the guy, holding something in her hand.

"How do, mister," she said, "Your children showed me this medallion. I collect these things. Mmm. Would you part with this for ten dollars?"

The next day I saw a busted little Hudson emblem sitting on her desk. It looked mighty lonely in the midst of pencil stubs, erasers, hairpins and other junk.

Holly Millay

"This is a new feature—the Speak Up Session." said Miss Drake, "Anything goes."

She said that we had an hour and a half to say whatever we wanted. She pointed her pencil at me."

"Holly Millay will give us a few words. Holly?"

Oops. I froze. I couldn't talk in front of people without notes.

"N-No...no..."

"Right this very now," she ordered, beckoning me to her desk.

I stood there, twisting my fingers behind my back. The faces of kids I knew looked like white watermelons.

"I...I...." I said.

It was torture. But Miss Drake asked me questions. What did I like about school? Hate about school? Who was going to find Amelia Earhart?

Gradually the sound of my own voice calmed me. Out in front the watermelons turned to faces again. Kids started talking. We got onto Hollywood. Who was better looking—Robert Taylor or Clark Gable?

"I vote for Andy Gump," said Hymie.

The laughter was like warm water over my body. Suddenly I

felt wonderful.

"Now," I said, "I'd like to talk about flowers, which you all know I'm interested in. West Stoddard is full of beautiful wild things growing."

"Like Jack McGreggor," put in Hymie.

"He's the *ugly* thing growing," said my brother.

Jack, in the back row, stretched lazily. "Our one-cylinder pettifogger spills his brains.

"All right now," said Miss Drake.

After she'd gotten Tony Tragonni to thumb his dictionary and report that pettifogger meant disreputable lawyer, she nodded to me.

I talked about bloodroot, orange plume, and yellow adder's tongue. I told them that red chokeberry and jewelweed grew beyond the tracks. It was incredible how the words flowed out.

Before long the whole class was joining in. Now and then Miss Drake got others to take over. Standing by her desk, they lost their scared feelings. She kept putting in a word whenever she felt like it—just as if she was one of us.

Tommy Kingsland said that you do your best studying after midnight, and she added, "On the other hand, keep in mind the quatrain:

Late to bed
Early to rise
Makes a kid baggy
Under the eyes."

Eva Casserino said it was a shame the way old people grew grouchy in West Stoddard, and Miss Drake said it was no different here than anywhere else.

"We're all born to be young—but we can't help growing ancient," she said, "I've met many an old timer here happy as a dog in a meathouse. Look closer."

Finally we got around to complaining about the U.S. government. How come this lousy Depression? Why couldn't Franklin D. Roosevelt do more about dividing up the wealth?

"That would be communism," said Fred.

"What's so horrible about communism?" said Joe Tutynski.

The talk became hot. Miss Drake sat back and listened. Her legs were crossed, and one saddle shoe—with a thumbtack stuck in the sole—bobbed gently in front of my desk. At last Joe talked down everybody but Jack. He showed that communism was the perfect system. Everything fair. Everybody equal.

He said, "The Soviet set-up makes ours look like a broken-down streetcar."

"Baloney," said Jack.

Somebody asked Miss Drake how she liked communism.

"Looks good—on paper," she said.

How was it working over there?

"It doesn't," she said, "They've got no freedom of speech, no freedom of movement. They don't enjoy a quarter of our consumer goods."

Joe scoffed. He defied her to find a better constitution than the Soviet's. What could be fairer than the communist creed: *From each according to his ability. To each according to his need.*

"It's a beautiful thought," Miss Drake admitted, "In long range terms the world may be moving in that direction."

But, she added, the Soviet way of forcing reforms was creating more tyranny than it was erasing. Anyone out of step with the government was in danger of going to jail. Or being executed.

She said, "What good is a system that works fine for angels but not for people? People are the clay we have to work with. Now the Founding Fathers—Adams, Monroe, Jefferson, and so on—understood this. They knew that men and women sometimes lie, cheat, steal, and betray. So they set up a government that would operate with these imperfect creatures. I think they did very well."

Jack McGreggor

When Joe blew off about how sweet the communist creed was—and Miss Drake answered, "It's a beautiful thought. In long range terms the world may be moving in that direction."—I said oh-oh to myself. Her whole talk had been against the crazy Soviet system. But those words wouldn't look good if dragged up by themselves.

I told Fred, "If you hear Joe spreading the dumb quote of hers around, let me know. I think No Balls is looking for ammunition to shoot her down."

Sibyl Noyes

Uncle Breck told me if I'd help him on his boat he'd give me a big fish for Easter dinner.

"Might be a jellyfish, might be a killer shark—I dunno," he said, "Ain't no way you can tell what's coming up in the Sound these damn days."

Like Jack's uncle—who had served jail time for rum running—my uncle could never get over the big money he'd made during Prohibition. He figured the waters off West Stoddard were not worth working now. They couldn't produce the kind of living he'd had in the 20's.

"Roosevelt ruined everything with his goddam repeal."

I rode out with him past Cornfield Point. The pum-pum of his high-powered engine...the swish of salt air...the twinkle of morning sun on turquoise wavelets—seeped into me. I stretched out on the splintery foredeck. I tried to forget I'd had only a pear and an apple for breakfast.

"There's that rotten bait to throw overside, Sibyl. And you kin wash out the catch bins. Git that done, you kin lug them hook-boxes back on the fantail. And sea-mop the cabin."

By noon I was dirty and covered with sweat. Uncle Breck produced four cucumber sandwiches and two bottles of hard cider. I wolfed the stuff down.

"Hey—my brother ain't feeding you so good, eh? Well, we fishermen got it tough too. Try gassing up a power motor like this—and then pulling in enough catch to pay for it. We used to laugh at the Coast Guard. Now they're watching us go broke."

By three o'clock we had pulled in a small pile of fish, silvery and flopping. We headed back. A mile off Cornfield the massive engine began to sputter.

"Goddammit!"

We were running out of gas. Uncle Breck idled down the throttle and headed for the beach. I lay down on the deck. Every bone in my body ached.

"I'll ground her on Indian Cove sandbar, Sibyl. We'll have to wade in. I'll go git gas."

The boat bumped the bar and tilted sideways. I splashed overside into water two feet deep. Then I lugged a burlap bag full of fish up onto Indian Beach. I sat in the sand, panting. The sun blistered down.

"Here's your fish, niece."

A slippery 30-inch, silver flounder slapped down on my legs. I wrapped it in a hunk of burlap from the bag. For the next half-hour I guarded the bag against beach kids attracted by our stranded boat. I dozed, my head resting on fish that were starting to smell through the fabric.

"What have we here?"

I opened my eyes. Miss Drake, in her frost-blue bathing suit, stood over me, her pretty eyes questioning.

I said, "My uncle took me for a nice ride."

"Mmm."

"We had a lot of fun, Miss Drake. Yes, we did...we did. You should feel the wind when it blows out there. Sweet. Cool. You can see the gulls scooping up silvery fish. The waves are so beautiful—deep blue. And they smell so good. You should...."

I don't remember all I said. Miss Drake listened, smiling. After my uncle came back with a can of gas, she drove me home. I held the fish in my lap. It smelled a little, but she didn't seem to notice.

Joe Tutynski

Teach got me to help correct a bunch of 9th and 10th grade themes that the state had sent down.

"They're every sort," she said, "Essays, book reports—even some short stories. Hartford wants a cross-section evaluation of writing in the system."

There was 40-cents an hour in it for me. And if I didn't take it, Fred Millay—the only other advanced English student—would. So I started reading the stuff.

It was devoid of thought. Could kids between 14 and 17 be this stupid?

I was just supposed to check grammatical errors. My blue pencil raced over the pages, jabbing here, jabbing there. For the first time I saw the bitter drudgery of teaching. Teach was luckier. She would re-read this crap for content.

Content? There wasn't any content. Here was a guy writing about his grandmother's cat...a girl trying to describe a mountain. Then my eye caught a sentence that woke me up: *The Climate of Death Valley is such that the inhabitants have to live elsewhere.*

Hah.

I started looking for bloopers like that. It made a quest out of a lost afternoon. I found a sentence that read: *After 1870 most Plains Indians were put in reservoirs.* Another saying: *Following the American Revolution crowned heads trembled in their boots.*

I made a check mark beside each of the howlers so she wouldn't miss them. Before the end of the afternoon I had found six more:

Nearly at the bottom of Lake Michigan is Chicago.

Never break your bread or roll in your soup.

In Pittsburgh they manufacture iron and steal.

The canoe went gently across the pond exactly like a cannonball wouldn't.

A burning glance froze him on the spot.

And best of all, in a pompous essay on European history,

flawlessly typed and bound in cardboard: *Dante stood with one foot firmly planted in the Middle Ages, and with the other he saluted the dawn of a New Era.*

I handed the batch over to Teach. She gave me a voucher for four hours work—$1.60. The next day after lunch she called me up to her desk.

"What do you think of Connecticut's budding penmen, Joe?"

Her eyes searched me. I stared at my feet. "Shakespeare is safe."

"Here's one you missed: *In the Amazon rain forests, the hand of man has never set foot.*"

I said nothing.

She smiled. My eye was on the movement of her breasts. "These are hilarious, Joe. You have the start of a humor article here."

I just looked.

She crinkled her green eyes. "Didn't you get a chuckle? Just a little one?"

Stay away from me, Teach.

She lifted a finger, still smiling. "Now, here's a word by Rabelais: *One inch of joy surmounts of grief a span. Because to laugh is proper to the man.* Think about that Joe."

Hah.

Eva Casserino

Miss Drake was standing on the schools so-called playing field when Jack McGreggor knocked a softball across Route 1.

Vince Bigelow ran after it—and a passing truck had to slam on its breaks. Pssssssft-schreeeeech. The driver stuck out his head.

"Hey nigger boy," he shouted, "You wanna be chocolate pudding?"

Vince said nothing. Cursing, the driver shifted gears and

roared off. I noticed a few kids exchange looks. Vince kept his eyes on his feet as he walked back.

After lunch Miss Drake pushed aside her history book and tucked the yellow pencil behind her ear. "Let's talk about names. Mmm?"

She went to the board and wrote *kike*. She pointed the chalk at Hymie and said, "What does it mean?"

Hymie turned pink. "It's a dirty word for Jew."

"So it is."

She said that America was loaded with expressions like that. They were the natural result of the greatest experiment in history: the mixing together of peoples.

"These words are little wedges driven between us. So let's look them over. Sibyl Noyes, you're Irish-American. What names have you been called?"

Sibyl examined her chubby hands. "Well...*harp*."

"Right, said Miss Drake, "How about *mick, shanty, and pig-sty?*"

Sibyl nodded.

Miss Drake went around the room getting us to say these words out loud. Sometimes we laughed. But the laughs were kind of strained.

Tony Tragonni said, "Italians get it worst — *wop, dago, guinea, ginzo, zool.*"

"Yeah?" said Vince, "How'd you like to have somebody call you *nigger, spade, moke, shine?*"

Miss Drake wrote them all on the board. Pretty soon we had a list stretching to three columns. We had *polack, bohunk, spic, dinge, jigaboo, yid, sheeny, hebe*—and a lot more. Hymie, who was half German, came up with *kraut, Hun,* and *Boche.* Vince's brother Gene got in an argument with Tony over *greaseball*—which Tony claimed was Italian.

"I've heard it for Spaniards, Greeks, and Mexicans." said Gene.

Miss Drake stood there, juggling the chalk in her hand, listening with a half smile. Everything came out. Joe Tutynski deigned to contribute something from his reading—*gook* for Filipino-American and *mockie* for a Jew who spoke with a thick accent.

"Well, we've got quite an alphabet stew here," said Miss Drake, "What's missing? I guess *chink... squarehead...*"

"Teach, what are you?" growled Joe.

She considered the list. "Mmm. I'm part French, part German, mostly English."

Vince rocked forward on his desk and gave a chuckle. A good feeling had drifted over the class—like we were a family.

"That makes you a *frog, kraut, limey,* Miss Drake."

Everybody guffawed. The class ended. Walking out, I heard Sibyl talking with Vince about the chances Tommy Dorsey's *Harbor Lights* had of making number one on the Hit Parade this Saturday.

Holly Millay

I never gave a thought as to why Miss Drake came to our town—until my brother Fred raised the question.

He said, "Why would a brainy, good-looking babe from California choose West Stoddard, for crying out loud?"

"She wanted to teach, of course," I said.

"In a busted-down burg on a Yankee coast?"

I began to wonder. That's the reason I did what I did when Miss Drake made her routine social call on our parents.

Our big restored Colonial on Stannard Hill had a green-velvet lawn, arched over with elms. Miss Drake arrived just as Fred and I were finishing the supper dishes. She stayed for coffee. She was radiant in an apricot corduroy jumper with a ruffly white blouse.

"Such stars tonight," she said, "Absolute fire-diamonds."

She charmed our mother and father. About 8:30 they walked her out to her car and watched it disappear down our curving, cut-stone drive.

"A brilliant and lovely lady," said my father, "The board was lucky to find her."

After they had gone in the kitchen, I crossed the lawn past the tennis court. I climbed up on the roof of our summer gaze-bo—thinking to watch her car go down Route 1.

Her car was stopped by our beach lane. And she was getting out.

Huh? I jumped down and ran past the garden shed. I slipped over the wall that ran beside the lane. I followed Miss Drake's shadowy head vanishing down the hill.

It was a sweet night, very warm for October. Vines that over-tangled the stone wall gave off a heavy smell. Miss Drake's ath-letic strides took her through our bottom gate and out onto the sand. She sat on a driftwood log. She peeled off her shoes and socks.

I sneaked up behind our beach hedge. Miss Drake was softly singing something:

"Roll out the barrel-l, We'll have a barrel of fun-n."

She sang it in a quiet way—as if it were part of a memory. There was a wavery strangeness to her voice. What was our teacher doing here, anyhow?

The tide was out. Sand flats gleamed all the way to Salt Is-land. Silvery. Giving off a wet, salt breath. The island loomed, its profile low in the sky.

She walked to the island, kicking puddles. I waited until her silhouette climbed over the island's lone hillock, then took off my sandals and followed.

Salt Island and I were old friends. I knew every dip in the grassy five acres, every sea cave formed by the boulders. I crept through the dwarf cedars on the western end. There, on a gran-ite outcrop we call The Knob stood Miss Drake.

She was holding her arms over the ocean with her palms up. She could have been testing for rain. Or just, stretching. Then she began walking around. Looking here, looking there. Exam-ining the shape of the big, tilting stones.

I watched her kneel by a lumpy boulder shaped like a dog's head (named Nero's jaw) and begin to dig with her hands. She dug slowly. Now and then she'd stop and stare at the sea.

"Oh!"

Her voice startled me. She lifted a small, dark object from the hole. She stared at it. She bent down, her curls tumbling over her clutching hands. She looked like she was praying. Or trying not to weep.

I sneaked away, splashing through the tidal pools, I felt like crying myself. Something awful had happened to Miss Drake... some cruel hurt. Nothing was as secure as I thought it was. Nothing was *right*. I felt as bad as the day Joe Tutynski had made a fool of me in front of the whole class.

I climbed back on the gazebo roof. I watched Miss Drake's taillights grow small down Route 1 and turn toward Mrs. Kelsey's.

Fred Millay

I ran into Jack at the garage fixing a door handle on old lady Wainwright's gray Studebaker. I told him about my sister seeing Miss Drake dig up something on Salt Island last night.

"After dark?" Jack said.

"Yeah. And she thinks the thing—whatever it was—made her sad."

Jack just arched his eyebrows and said nothing. He was closer to Miss Drake than the rest of us. She liked the way he talked—straight out. And how he knew everything that had happened in West Stoddard.

Finally he said, "Well, what did she dig up?"

I told him my sister couldn't see. But Miss Drake had hugged the thing to her chest as she walked back to the car. I said, "I wonder what could make a hit like that on our classy ranch queen?"

Jack shrugged. And went on working with a screwdriver and wrench.

Jack McGreggor

Fred's news got me thinking. I had grown used to seeing Miss Drake take her Saturday walks in Blackthorn Cemetery. Her saddle shoes flashing under the big maples...her arms swinging. Whenever a car job took me up North Road I'd glance over. Quite often she'd be sitting on the granite bench by the tomb. Taking in the best view in town—the blue Sound, white beach, and fluttery sailboats.

Nothing unusual about that. Everybody who walked at Blackthorn ended up on that bench.

But now I remembered once seeing her walk around the tomb, stop in front, and prop herself with both arms against the bronze door. I had slowed the wrecker, intending to drive in and talk with her a minute. Then I saw her head was down. Her brow was resting against the corroded metal—like she was thinking something private. I drove on.

In school I cornered Geraldine and asked if she'd noticed anything new in Miss Drake's apartment.

"New?"

"Well, different. New to you."

"I clean only once a week, Jack."

She walked away, then looked back. "There's a little toy boat on her bureau. Cast iron...rusty. It wasn't there a week ago. She must have found it in an old stone wall or someplace."

Eva Casserino

One Saturday Geraldine was sick. I was happy to take over her cleaning job at Mrs. Kelsey's—and get a good look at Miss Drake's apartment.

Everything in her four rooms told something about her special ways.

There was a little bird feeder at her window she'd built with sticks and glue. A half-tame crow she'd named Edgar Allen Crow flew to it daily. There was a quartz arrowhead on her night table. She'd found it near the grave site of an Iroquois chief buried standing up in the Indian Beach meadow. Her outdoors equipment hung everywhere. Bathing suit...corduroy jacket...sun glasses...knee-high boots...hunting knife.

I vacuumed the rug, scrubbed the bathtub. Straightened out the books and papers on her desk. Bending over the bureau I spotted a little toy boat that had slipped down behind.

It was a chunk of rust—shaped like those German-made wind-up boats that rich boys played with in the 20's. Attached to it was a card:

Found! Exactly where you said you hid it from your brother at age 8 — you little devil!

Joe Tutynski

Teach stayed away from religion in class after I registered my gripe about it. But on a later outing to Stannard Hill, Holly Millay got back into it.

She was giving her 15-minute speech on wildflowers, after laying them out on the ledge. We sat in the wire grass around her.

"Okay on questions," said Teach, sitting down on a big glacial rock, "But courtesy to the speaker at all times, please."

I didn't listen. The girl's chatter about stems and petals invited coma. But suddenly I heard her mumbling something about "...Nature's divine scheme of things." I propped myself up with my good arm.

She knelt there with the wildflowers, one hand clasped over her Indian-bead belt. Her small, Yankee-patrician nose was tilted up. Her voice was so soft you could hardly hear it.

"I think it's part of some Plan that the bluest iris and the yellowist goldenrod grow along the railroad tracks. God helps cover up ugly things, I guess."

I didn't intend to wreck her whole infantile philosophy—just kick it a bit. I raised my hand. "You figure that freight trains dropping fertilizer, coal dust, and other trace elements have anything to do with this divinely-inspired plant growth?"

She blushed. "Well, maybe, but—"

"So God has time to fiddle around with West Stoddard flora while he juggles stars and planets."

She fingered her belt nervously. But her head went up and she looked straight at me. "People have different ideas about what God can do. I have this...*feeling* that He is behind all good things, and these flowers are so beautiful that He *must* help them get that way."

"God is all-good, eh?"

Teach took off her glasses. She touched them to her chin, studying me. I sensed the class stiffen slightly.

"Yes, He is all-good," said Holly.

"And He's all powerful too? Yeah, He must be—if He worries about our town landscape while He keeps the universe banging along in high gear."

She looked down at her wildflowers. She looked at Teach. Jack McGreggor turned and put a cold stare on me.

"Yes, He is all-powerful."

She was trapped. I watched the red creep up her neck and deepen her blush. A voice in my head said: *Stick the dagger deeper.*

"Let's see," I said, "If He's all good how come He lets wars happen? How come crime? Famine? Automobile accidents?"

"Those are man's things. God can't help it if—-"

"Then He's not all-powerful?"

"He is *all-powerful*. But God isn't going to interfere with every single thing people do."

"Then he can't be all-good. If He won't use his power to stop boys from shooting each other in Spain, He's a pretty mean fellow, wouldn't you say?"

We trooped back to school silent as death. Holly carried some wildflowers. Teach thumbed through a big, red-backed *A Century of English Poetry* on her desk.

She said, "Now here's a verse to wind up the period. It's by John Tabb;"

Out of the dusk, a shadow
Then, a spark;
Out of a cloud, a silence,
Then, a lark.
Out of the heart, a rapture,
Then, a pain;
Out of the dead, cold ashes,
Life again.

The bell sounded. As I shuffled out in my crab-like step, Teach handed me a note. Before I passed the window between the room and the hall, I saw her helping Holly and Sibyl arrange the wildflowers in a vase. Holly's face was paste-white. Teach slipped an arm around her.

The note read:

Cleave ever to the sunnier side of doubt,
And cling to the Faith beyond the forms of Faith,

—Tennyson

I crumpled it and flipped it in the trash barrel outside the Industrial Arts room.

Sibyl Noyes

Miss Drake dug up some brochures on nursing schools. She said there was a good one in Middletown. "If you're bound and determined to go into medicine this can be a start."

"I'll work for it," I said.

She got me a job sorting out books in the stock room down cellar. The state would pay 40 cents an hour.

"Stick with it awhile, Sibyl, and I'll half-Nelson the Commissioner into coming up with something better."

I was on my knees in the piles of paper and old volumes when I heard the scrape-scrape of Joe Tutynski coming into the back room where he often sat by himself under an old busted mirror.

Then I heard another step. And a tense voice saying. "Dammit, I'm warning you, Joe...."

I recognized Jack McGreggor's tough tone. Joe's rattle-voice shot back.

"About what, McGreggor?"

"Lay off Holly Millay."

"What? So you can lay *on her?*"

Silence.

"Man, you're begging for a fat lip."

"Hah. I already got one, grease monkey. See?"

I got up and peeked around the door. The two boys were facing each other, not looking at me. Joe was holding his ugly, deformed jaw up at Jack. Jack was clenching and unclenching his fists.

Joe said, "I gave that wimpy broad the lumping her stupidity deserved..."

"Oh, man...." Jack's forearm muscles bulged. He knotted his fist and drew back.

"Hey, you guys," I said, stepping into the room.

Jack turned and walked out, breathing hard.

Joe looked me up and down. "Whadda want?"

That night I told myself, maybe I'd stopped a murder. Or at least a dirty fight that would have made Miss Drake feel awful.

Geraldine Prue

Miss Drake had a book with a rawhide cover and leather thongs which rested on her night table. It was titled *Eva von Etherington Drake* in gold letters. I figured it was private. I warned myself not to open it.

But I was curious. So when I was dusting and the book fell open on the rug, I couldn't resist running my eye over a page.

Well! The page was in Miss Drake's ink penmanship all right. But it said nothing. It was squiggles and dashes...tiny circles and dots...wavy lines of varying lengths. And here and there a "word" such as *bght* and *dfkijerh*. The whole thing was crazy. O yes.

But looking closer I saw that these weird inkings were set up like ordinary sentences and paragraphs. The page looked like a story written in a wild language that didn't exist.

The very next Saturday Miss Drake came in from swimming and hurried to her desk in her wet bathing suit.

"Quick, Geraldine," she said "I got an idea."

She opened the rawhide book and wrote in it for five minutes. Then she turned and smiled.

"Done." She held up the book. "I should have warned you, Geraldine. This is my journal. It's full of my thoughts and hopes. I write in it every day."

I nodded, trying not to look guilty.

She laughed. "It's in my private shorthand—which I invented years ago." She held the book out to me. "Nobody but me can read it. See?"

Fred Millay

The Depression choked town baseball. My father bought caps for the West Stoddard Minutemen. But we had no uniforms. (I played third base.) We had to chip in to buy baseballs and bats. Some of the guys wore striped shirts left over from the days when Griffin Leather financed the team.

Yeah, we were shabby. But pretty good. Before Miss Drake arrived we were leading the Old Saybrook Wreckers in the 11th inning of the Shoreline League finals when Jack McGreggor broke our only Louisville slugger. We couldn't hit beans with the junky Woolworth bats that were left. We lost 7-6.

In September Miss Drake used to watch us practice. Sometimes she picked up Jack at the garage and brought him to workouts. Jack was the team's heavy hitter. I began to note that he was getting distinctly palsy-walsy with our curvaceous teacher.

If I hadn't known that he was hopelessly hot for my sister I'd say he was gearing up for a play at a woman a dozen years older than himself. Hey...hey.

One Saturday we were short on players. I had noticed when Miss Drake played catch at school she threw like a boy. So I suggested she cover shortstop for the practice.

She grabbed a glove and ran onto the field. "Mmm. I thought you'd never ask."

Tony at the plate hit a grounder. She speared it and whipped it to me. Surprised, I bobbled it, then fired to first base. Tony was safe.

"In this league we throw from short to first, Miss Drake." I cracked.

She laughed. "I wanted to check reflexes. You flunked, Mil-lay"

After that we treated her like one of the guys. She was a strong batter. And she could run. She would tap a bunt, then take off like an Olympic sprinter, her yellow hair flying, her calf muscles bulging below her skirt. I thought: *If the West cranks out dolls like this, California here I come.*

On a bright fall afternoon she showed up in her fancy tan bomb with Joe Tutynski sitting between her and Jack. Joe stayed in the car watching us practice. I knew there was no love lost between those two guys so I asked Jack what was up.

He shrugged. "Search me. She's got Joe on some kind of West Beach research project."

"He's sitting there scowling at us."

"He didn't want to come. But she said, 'You're coming Joe Tutynski, that's an order.' You know Miss Drake."

"The poor guy probably hates baseball."

"Poor guy? Listen, he hates everything." Jack spat into his catcher's mitt. "Okay, he's crippled. But in this life you ride with what you got."

After practice I watched the big Packard drive out. Jack and Joe were tucked in the wide leather seat beside Miss Drake. They didn't look at each other.

A Novel By George P. Morrill

Tony Tragonni

I wanted to do something so Miss Drake would notice me like she noticed Jack McGreggor. He could talk with her as if she wasn't our teacher. I overheard them at baseball practice—where she was a steady player now.

"Jack," she said, "What's the story on this broken-down barn on the Volenski property? Did Hymie's uncle have a farm?"

"Yeah—so called. One cow. He made his wife milk it out there summer and winter."

"Winter? Didn't she freeze?"

"She used to milk that Guernsey with her bare feet buried in fresh manure."

"Cut it out."

"Fact. That's how she kept warm."

"Heavens! Didn't she rebel?"

"Didn't dare. Hymie's uncle would have drop-kicked her out of the county."

"Mmm. New England. Will I ever get used to it?"

"I'm still trying, Miss Drake—and I was born here."

I decided for my writing assignment to do a short story about a girl who would defy all the taboos of West Stoddard. She'd waste her baby-sitting money on bad magazines like *Snappy Stories* and *Ballyhoo*. She wouldn't go to church. At home she'd leave her clothes lying all over the place.

"In fact," I told Miss Drake at our conference, my heart racing, "She parades around the house *naked* while the curtains are up."

I sat back, my fists clenched. She smiled, tapping her wrist lightly with the yellow pencil. I thought she didn't get it.

I went on, "She parades in front of a big kitchen window where her mother puts vegetables to ripen. She's *stark naked,* see?"

"Mmm. Sort of a peeled tomato?"

"I mean she's rebelling against all the old fuddy-dud ways that are keeping her town backward."

"Okay," said Miss Drake, looking at my notes, "She's prancing in the buff in front of the produce. Now what?"

"Well, I mean she's shocking everybody. They don't like it. That's the story."

"Let's get some action in here. Is she mad at her boyfriend and wants to lure him? Is she sore at scratchy underwear? Does she want to act out a poetic dream like the Lady of Shallot floating down the river? Make something happen—that's the essence of a short story."

We talked half an hour. She was friendly, like always. But I felt kind of foolish. I hadn't jolted her at all. I wasn't close to her the way Jack was.

Vince Bigelow

My family moved to West Stoddard in 1931, five years before Miss Drake came. We hit the New England brand of prejudice early.

That first day, my father sent me to Village Garage to buy a second-hand tire. Our Model T Ford had blown five tires coming from Mississippi. And a town cop in Irwin, Tennessee, had stolen our spare wheel. Every time we got a flat, we had to jack up the car and roll the wheel into a garage.

As I rolled the wheel into the old wooden building, a thin guy in overalls looked up from a fender he was hammering.

"Hello, Amos," he said, "Where's Andy?"

I asked did he have a used tire for a dollar?

He jabbed his thumb through the blow-out hole in the side of our tire. "Lawd Gawd, boy," he said, faking a drawl, "Yo sure nuff popped this. Was you eatin too much watermelon, boy?"

I had been through this a million times. I gave him the white-tooth grin—and was ready with the old shuffle-and-tap if he wanted it. But he just dug a rubber-cracked Goodyear from a bin and told me to pay Mr. Chapman.

We lived in a tarpaper shack behind Griffin Leather Belt, Inc.

A Novel By George P. Morrill

My father was sickly, but he took any job he could get and never regretted moving from the South.

"You go to school. You learn like ah ain't learned," he said.

My mother said, "Don't let nobody stop you, hear?"

My brother and three sisters went with me to Shoreline Grammar, then West Stoddard High. We worked and studied hard. After school my sisters helped my mother clean houses around town. Gene and I helped my father load concrete blocks at the depot.

We made fast progress. Gene and I read books all the time. So after we grew friendly with Jack McGreggor who spent a lot of time at the library, we were on an even level with his way of thinking.

Meanwhile the skinny guy at the garage—whose name was Reubin Wright—kept working us over. When we pulled in for gas he'd say, "Hey deah Snowball, how much you want?" Then, "Can this old fliver still beat a mule, Sunshine?" One day he handed me a tube of *Neverfail Suntan Lotion*, then slapped his leg and exploded in laughter.

Jack, working at Village Garage part-time, just shrugged, "Don't mind Rube the Boob. He's the end-product of Yankee in-breeding."

In 1935 Reubin blinded himself trying to set fire to an abandoned house on Old Clinton Road. And ended up in the county Home. Jack took over his job—and did more car-fixing after school than Rube had done in a day.

I suppose we were poor. But it didn't seem so. My sisters sewed pretty dresses from old drapes Mrs. Kelsey gave them. I put in a vegetable garden behind our shack. With plenty of food and hard exercise everybody except my father grew strong. Gene and I picked up muscle like a couple of horses.

One morning after Miss Drake had gotten us to link hands on Stannard Hill—with the Sound a blue glory in the distance—and made even me and Gene feel a little special, there was a traffic accident on Route 1 in front of the school. A Greyhound bus lost control, went through the 40 MPH Speed Limit sign, and ended up on its side halfway into Prue's Village Greenhouse.

In History class we heard the crash. Jack was first out the door, hollering "Come on!"

Miss Drake didn't try to hold us back. Jack, Gene and I got there just as the driver pulled himself out a window, his face dripping blood. Passengers screamed and moaned. Glass was everywhere. The sweet hot-house smell of Prue's flowers mixed with a stink of bus exhaust.

"The door," said Jack.

We climbed on top and pried it open. Propped it with a suit-case and a cane that had slammed into the windshield. We dropped inside. We pulled stunned passengers from their seats and pushed them out the door.

We moved without talking. We *synchronized*. Jack and I reached simultaneously to switch off the ignition. Gene tossed us a coat to wrap around a bleeding, half-conscious lady. In the end we made a splint out of a broken seat-metal and strapped it on a little girl with a smashed leg. We carried her sobbing to the rear and tried to open the escape door. The smell of gasoline was getting fierce.

The door was stuck.

Gene, jamming his shoulder against it, pushed. Jack and I wedged alongside him. The three of us turned on the power. The door flew open

C-clang. Gene jumped through and we handed him the girl.

We climbed out—and there was Miss Drake and the whole class. She had grabbed an armful of towels from the storage room. She and Sibyl Noyes were showing the kids how to ban-dage people. Most of the passengers sat on the playground, dazed and silent.

We looked at each other. Jack and I were splattered with blood. Gene had a lump over his left eye. We didn't know what to say. Miss Drake rose from a bandaged man and poked both thumbs-up at us.

"How to go, you guys," she called.

A minute later we heard the ambulance wail. And the State Police took over.

A Novel By George P. Morrill

Gene Bigelow

West Stoddard was a backwater town, sinking slowly—but we didn't know it. My family came from Ox Forks, Mississippi, where black kids chewed bits of cardboard to hold down hunger pains.

With me and my brother Vince growing rugged, I figured both of us were riding high. Plenty to eat. Strength enough to hold off white kids. School desks of our own. Even free books and pencils.

It wasn't until years later I realized that West Stoddard was dangerously near extinction in the 1930's. It had no industry except Griffin Leather (already down to a three-day week). It had beach rental cottages, some fishing boats, a few vegetable stands, and Prue's greenhouse. It had a couple of home industries making rope doormats, and a junkyard. That was about it.

It may have been the hardest hit township between New Haven and Providence.

The eight-room school—that Vince and I thought so wonderful—was actually a firetrap, which the state was trying to condemn. It had only four teachers, all in their 50's. Until Miss Drake arrived, August Plimpton, our oversized principal, didn't allow any athletics for fear they would damage the lawn, a half-acre of crabgrass.

Guys like Vince and Jack McGreggor (top athletes) and girls like Elaine Bordan and Sibyl Noyes (actress and physician-to-be)—how could they develop in a place like this? How could Joe Tutynski, our super brain, find a fire to light his rocket?

But in 1932 Vince and I were too excited to think about stuff like that. The first day we edged cautiously into the library, Jack looked up from a reading table and nodded. Later in the stacks he shook hands with us.

"The card catalogue's in the reading room." he said.

His friendly approach threw us off. "God, Gene," said my brother, when we were alone," You figure this white boy means to ride the river with us?"

"Don't count on it, man."

But Vince decided to trust Jack. He pulled me along with him. We started hiking with him when he visited his muskrat traps in the swamps across the New Haven tracks. Jack's folks had settled in West Stoddard before 1776. He knew every inch of the town.

"Yeah, I'm old-folks ancestry," he said, "Inherited the family slippery ass—we've been sliding downhill for generations."

Jack showed us how to ice skate, where to find greens for Christmas wreaths. He took us to Leatherman's cave, a spooky hole in a granite cliff big enough to sleep a dozen guys.

"The Leatherman was here weeks at a time in the 1890's. He wore cowhide clothes. He begged food. He had caves like this all over the county."

Jack was good news for a couple of black fugitives from the South. After awhile the three of us formed a kind of alliance—poor boys against the world.

Then Miss Drake's teaching began to come through. She said, "This Depression is hanging on. We're all in a squeeze. When this happens, everyone tends to creep into his own ball of fright or misery. Well, class, let's not. You're 19 people. Everyone here is concerned with everyone else. Each of your talents is going to reinforce others. So just forget these little two-bit defenses against each other. Get it?"

She started switching homeroom seats around. She put me between Elaine Bordan, who had a crazy family life, and Fred Millay, the richest kid in town. She didn't leave anyone close to a person he'd been with before.

"In three months we'll scramble again," she said.

Afterwards Joe Tutynski—who found himself tucked in a window-corner with Holly Millay—growled, "Am I at home here? Yeah, like a cow on the front porch."

Even I was skeptical. I told Vince, "This is nursery school baloney. You can't mix people like this."

But he said, "Shut your trap, Gene, She's moving things the way they got to go."

A Novel By George P. Morrill

Elaine Bordan

The first thing I learned about kissing was to exhale a little—so your breath goes on the boy's upper lip. It works wonders.

I grew real popular. If I liked my partner I didn't mind going out behind the Roller Skating Rink with him. But when a boy got pushy and I didn't want it, I moved him off at arm's length.

Miss Drake's ease with words had triggered a new way of talking in me. I developed a bright, snippy chatter. I used it to charm guys. I got the reputation for being a neat jazz-ball.

Boy, did this new popularity shoot me up on a cloud. After all, the Bordans had been nothing in the town as long as anyone could remember. Now I was acting in county plays. Pretty soon fellows from as far away as New Haven were giving me the rush.

One Saturday a boy from Yale named Tommy Henderson asked me to a dance after the Harvard boat race in New London. I spent the afternoon putting on lipstick and kissing grocery bag paper—to see the best print I would make on his collar.

I borrowed 25 cents from Fred Millay to take the Shoreline bus to the Connecticut Inn in Old Lyme. Three good-looking guys greeted me on the fieldstone steps. One wearing a white crew sweater said, "Hey, Tommy was right. She's a bundle."

A tall redhead took my hand. "Elaine, you look like the down-to-earth type. Have a drink?"

Glasses were tinkling on the terrace. Little spears of sunlight shimmered on the Sound. I started sipping something that made a warm streak down through my chest. By the time Tommy appeared, I could hardly see his big pearly grin through a haze.

"You feeling good, Elaine?"

I looked around fuzzily. All of us—maybe six people—had gone outside. We stood on a dark grassy place under a trellis. There weren't any girls.

I gave my glass to Tommy. "Wheresa dance?" I said, "Wheresa girls?"

97

"Oh, they're coming."

"Wheresa music?"

The redhead came up behind and put his arms around me. "I got some big music."

I felt his hard root pushing against my rear. Then all the grinning faces moved closer. Some hands unbuttoned my blouse and slipped down my bra.

"Elaine, think I can keep my mind on these two beautiful things at once?"

A hand touched my ankle and started up. "I go for low joints myself, Red."

I tried to think of something smart to say. One guy pressed his face into my neck and sniffed. "Ooo, you smell good, girly."

I said, "I slap on this junk to attract the insects."

Everybody laughed. But my voice kind of quavered. More hands slipped over me. One touched my crotch and I pushed it away.

It wasn't *friendly*. It wasn't like Fred and me getting those wonderful feelings, hugging each other.

"Take her over by the hedge, Tommy."

"Want to sit on the soft grass, Elaine? That's a good girl. Now— "

Suddenly I began to scream. I tore at the hands. A palm went over my mouth. A weight, smelling of whiskey, lowered itself on me heavily.

"Elaine, Elaine...take it easy."

"We're not going to hurt you."

At least one of them got me. I felt this giant root poking at the leg of my panties. Then sinking upward and inward—deep.

All at once a voice roared, "God DAMMIT!"

The guy on top of me flew off, his root flipping out and his open pants gaping. The other guys tumbled backward into a flowerbed. A short, rugged figure threw them like beanbags in all directions.

"Jesus, Kendall...."

"Hold it, Kendall baby..."

"You bastards!" shouted the rugged guy. His foot caught a guy trying to zip up his fly. The guy nose-dived, then got up and scrambled.

He handed me my shoe and a glove. I saw a hard, handsome face with thick brown eyebrows.

"Get out," he said.

I recognized his face. It had been in all the papers. He was Giles Kendall, the Yale crew captain. I had daydreamed over him.

"M-Mr. Kendall, I wasn't—-" I began.

"Just get out."

Walking down Route 1, I tore away the corsage dangling at my shoulder. Then the heel broke off my left shoe, and I limped, rising and falling like a cripple. I began to cry.

That's the way Miss Drake found me—a mile-and-a-half from West Stoddard in the night-sprinkle. My cheeks were covered with tears and rain. She swung her car door open. I slid across the warm, leather-smelling seats. The tiny lights of the dash reflected softly on her face.

Her eyes widened and her lips made a gentle O.

"Oh, Miss Drake...."

I sobbed in her arms. She smoothed my hair. She wiped my cheeks with a handkerchief.

"Butterfly," she said, kissing my forehead.

I stayed in her apartment at Mrs. Kelsey's all night. She cooked Campbell's tomato soup. Nothing ever tasted so good. After she had called my house and tucked in clean sheets, she sat cross-legged at the bottom of my bed.

"Now tell me—" she said.

I told her only part. If she found out I'd really been raped, she'd be down on Yale like a cyclone. Or the police. I didn't want that.

But I knew she didn't believe my story about missing the bus after my date had left me at the Saybrook terminal...about me deciding to walk to see the stars.

She patted my head. "Well, go to sleep. Sometimes just *being* a girl is a crock."

Jack McGreggor

By Monday we all knew something had happened to Elaine Bordan—and those Yalie sonsabitches had had something to do with it.

Fred said, "I haven't heard Elaine hum a note since Saturday."

Geraldine and Sibyl found her with red eyes in the girls' room. Even Hymie was upset.

"It ain't right to see old sexy Bordan turned off. Yah," he said. "You suppose one of those beach crums from New Haven tried to jump her?"

I brooded over it. At one time or another most of us guys had fooled around with Elaine (although Fred had the inside track with her). We liked her. She wasn't just a roll in the hay. She laughed and hummed—she was music in our room. And now she was our rising star.

"Elaine may be a bit of a *goof*," I said, "But she's *our* goof. I'm not going to sit here with my thumb up my ass and let a pack of Boola-Boolas work her over."

We had reached that point—we cared about each other. Miss Drake had got us farther into this unity thing than we realized. It burned us up that some college playboys thought they could cruise through shabby West Stoddard, grab what they want, and move on.

I went to Miss Drake. "Somebody hurt Elaine Bordan. The guys don't take it kindly."

Her beautiful eyes looked up from a stack of papers.

"Something happened. I'm very concerned. But she's keeping it to herself."

"Well, we're not keeping it to *ourselves*."

She followed me to the door. "Now Jack...careful thinking,

now...."

I turned back. "Miss Drake, we've been thinking and thinking."

I went on the lookout for the last college jerk Elaine had been seen with — a guy named Tommy who drove a purplish Chevy coupe. I hoped to run into him alone. But if he had buddies, I figured Fred or Tony could keep them off my back while I went to work.

One Saturday about dusk, the purple coupe drove up to the pump.

"Fill her up, high test. Radiator needs water," said a lanky, black-haired guy. He was wearing an expensive white shirt with a Y on front. Woven on the pocket, in yellow thread were the words: Tommy Henderson.

Baby!

I pumped the gas. While filling the radiator from our gooseneck water bucket, I noted there were two guys with Tommy. One, a crew-cut blond was big but fat. The other, a short bunch of muscles, could be trouble.

I looked around. Old Man Chapman was at supper. Nobody was here except Gene and Vince Bigelow out back working on a clogged Plymouth carburetor. I couldn't expect them to jump into a fight with white guys.

"Hey Fella," said Fatty, "Does a girl named Elaine Bordan live around here?"

Oh, you bastard.

I poked the water bucket in Tommy's window and tilted it up.

"HEY!"

Water gushed over all three. They jumped out. I backed off. "I thought you bastards needed cooling off."

Tommy took the first shot at me, a mistake. He swung like an old woman. I stepped inside and blasted his nose. He sat down, holding his face. Fatty charged in and I sunk my fist up to the wrist in his belly.

"Oooof-aaaaaaaaaaaaaaaa," he said, doubling over.

But then WHAM—something belted the side of my head. I woke up draped over the bumper. I struggled up and there was Bunchy Muscles, balancing on the balls of his feet, gently pawing the air with knotted fists.

"Come on, you hick," he said.

I moved in swinging. I gave one good jab—but caught six. Blood trickled into my mouth. I stalked Bunchy Muscles around the Texaco pump. I nailed him two more. But again, I took a gang of punches.

"I'm going to do a paint job on you, hick."

Not exactly. I jumped head-on into stinging fists. I grabbed him before he could pedal away. I threw him against the Chevy door. He kept up a tattoo of knuckles on my face and chest. But I got a heavy shot to his gut. He grunted.

I kept at it, digging deep. *You're outgunned, Yalie.* I was going to get him, no matter how he chopped my face. There was no way these dudes could dump on West Stoddard without paying.

But suddenly something vise-like clamped on my arm. Two arms went around my head. I ducked, throwing the body over my back—but another weight hit me. Tommy and Fatty had tumbled back in the fight. I went down, punching and cursing, and Bunchy Muscles piled on.

It happened fast. But strangely, it felt almost like a slow-motion movie. My arms moved the way a piston does in a one-lung engine: up-down, up-down. Their six fists pop-popped on my jaw, eyes, neck, belly, everywhere.

I thought quite calmly, *These bastards got me. But if Fred or Tony were only here...*

It didn't occur to me about Gene and Vince. Colored guys couldn't go brawling with whites. But suddenly Bunchy Muscles flew off me as if lifted by a derrick. A thick black hand yanked Tommy to his feet. Gene and Vince slammed the three battered guys into the Chevy and kicked the door shut.

"Git you asses out of this town, hear?" said Vince.

Gene held my forehead over the sink behind the grease pit.

Vince mopped my bloody face with a wet rag. His fingers were light, easy-touching. He chuckled—one of those deep chuckles that come out of some black people like violin chords.

"Man, you a ring-tail, knuckle-pitching gahoot, Jack. You shore enough is."

Tony Tragonni

I don't know why I got to love Geraldine Prue. She sure wasn't pretty. She had long, skinny legs and a little button-nose. Her hair was red. She was quite a switch from the curvy, big-titted Marias in my neighborhood.

I lived in the little Italy section of West Stoddard. It was woody country, six miles back from the Sound. It had ledges, bushes, and berries. Our one-story Italiano houses, made of stone and concrete, straggled along Wright's Pond road. Each back yard had an arbor piled high with purple grapes. My father made wine down cellar.

Geraldine was the daughter of the town florist. She sang solos in the Congregational Church. The American Legion always got her to do *My Buddy* at the Memorial Day observances on the Green. She had a voice like sweet bells.

She first came to Wright's Pond because of a project Miss Drake had her doing—hunting wildflower specimens. I found her standing against an oak tree, still as a statue, her hands covering her eyes.

What's Geraldine Prue crying about up here? I thought.

She took away her hands and called, "Coming, ready or not."

Then she started hunting behind trees and bushes. Some little kids—inky-headed paisanos—ran out shrieking. She was playing hide-and-seek.

That's the way she was—full of laughter and kid fun.

The next few weeks I got to know her as I'd never known her before. After school I would meet her at Wright's and help find specimens. She had a way of lifting one eyebrow and saying "O yes?" that made you laugh.

"Tony," she said, "I see you have music in your soul today."

"Music?"

"Your shoe's squeaking."

I threw an armful of hay over her. She ran—surprisingly fast—and ducked behind a tree. She looked back, her thin shoulders quaking.

"What's a pigskin used for, Tony?"

I chased her around the tree.

"To...hold...the...pig...in" she cried, fleeing toward the pond.

I caught her in a clump of gone-to-seed timothy. We sat there, breathing hard. Geraldine's flamy hair covered one eye. She laughed and her perfect teeth shone like pearls.

"I'm a dope," she said, "Really stupid."

But she wasn't. She tossed back her hair and quieted down. Her mood switched so fast that I could hardly follow her.

"What's your project?" she said.

Project? *To kiss your pink, heart-shaped lips, Miss Prue.*

"Nothing," I said.

"O yes? Didn't you sign up for anything in class?"

Well, Miss Drake had talked to me about constructing something in stone or wood. She had seen a wall I had helped my father build and said, "There's a direction for you, Tony." I hadn't thought much about it. I sure didn't want to be a mason, coming home every night with cement under my fingernails. So pooped I couldn't eat.

"She doesn't mean *become* a mason," said Geraldine, "Miss Drake is setting up targets for everyone—and they're way beyond what you think."

She said that Miss Drake had found her scrubbing flower pots in the family's greenhouse and had given her a *Golden Barrel Cactus* from Mexico—to see if she could make it grow in northern climate. Miss Drake had taken her to a farm near New Haven where a man was trying to develop a new strain of sunflower to supply seeds for birds—so the birds could winter over easily and be ready to attack bugs two weeks earlier in the spring.

"That would help farmers to grow more food."

"Might, at that," I said.

"O yes. Miss Drake says all natural things are related to each other. And I should aim for a study called *Ecology*. She said I could be a scientist. Silly me."

We talked a long time. I learned that Miss Drake had drawn up a chart with all our names on it and arrows pointing to possible careers for each of us. The arrows ended up in words like "dietician," "lawyer," "architect," "engineer," "artist."

"She's dreaming," I said, "West Stoddard isn't going to hatch brains like that."

"O yes? Who said we have to stay in this town?"

The October sun dropped. Everything turned to warm gold. We watched clouds twist slowly over Toby Hill. And the Sound start to turn purple. For the first time I glimpsed a life beyond the easy, pleasant West Stoddard way—drinking cokes at Village Garage and listening to the World Series over a scratchy radio. Me *somebody* someday?

"It's almost scary, isn't it?" said Geraldine.

She got up and shook the leaves out of her hair. Her mood changed.

"Heard the joke about the rope, Tone?"

"No."

"Skip it."

The next moment we were racing along Wright's Pond. She dodged. I went splashing for three steps before pulling out of the water and tackling her. We tumbled into tall grass and blue gentians.

She pinched my nose. "Joke...bout the ...skeleton?"

I shook my head.

"N-Nothing to it," she gasped.

I kissed her. She kissed back. We kept kissing for awhile, but that's all we did. I kept seeing her standing by that oak tree with hands over her eyes like a little girl saying, "Coming, ready or not."

Suddenly she picked a gentian and rubbed the petals into my palm. It left a weak stain beside my index and little finger.

"That print will stay there forever to make you remember this afternoon," she said, "Of course you have to believe it—or it won't."

The rest of the semester whenever I looked inside my fist I swear I saw a pale purplish tint. O yes.

Geraldine Prue

Tony showed me a water drain system he had built behind his uncle's leather shop. Water came out of a tile pipe, went down a cement trough, and dumped into a shallow pool. Then it brimmed over into a lower pool and went on to Jackson's Brook.

The pools were very pretty—shell-shaped instead of square. Tony had recessed the concrete joints and squared off the stone edges.

But the water was brown as caramel, discolored from chemicals. And it was warm enough to send up a coffee-colored mist on cold days.

Miss Drake went to look at it. She stood a long time in thought, touching a yellow curl with her finger. "That's a nifty job of Tony's—but isn't the water awful."

"It can't be helped, Miss Drake," I said. "Tone's uncle uses some kind of steam treatment in the leather shop."

"I hope nobody drinks out of Jackson's Brook."

A couple of days later, she called me to her desk. "Geraldine, isn't there some kind of plant that absorbs colors in water—a lily or something?"

I didn't know.

"It seems to me that ponds with water lilies are always clean-looking."

I asked my father. He gave me a book on aquatic plants. I

studied it for a week. I decided that lilies would die before they started in Tony's pools. But then I read:

The water-hyacinth is a hardy, vascular plant with big leaves, thick stems, and purple blossoms. Claims have been made that it removes water pollutants by absorbing them through it's roots.

I was excited. I hurried to Tony. "Why not grow hyacinths in your pools, Tone?"

Miss Drake agreed it was worth a try. My father agreed to get the plants.

"They'll probably die." he said, "Hyacinth is a southern organism, you know."

While we waited, Tony and I thumbed through encyclopedias. We wrote to the U.S. government for a brochure on water systems. Miss Drake invited us up to her room to talk. She served hot chocolate and cookies. I'd never had such a good time with schoolwork in my life.

"How are you going to solve the climatic problem?" she said.

We didn't know. But I said, "The pools are always warm from the machines. Shouldn't that keep the plants alive?"

We started them in the lower pool where the water was less stained. Every day after school we checked them. They seemed to struggle, their leaves wrinkling and developing spots. Then the weather got cold, snow fell, and Tony brought the sad news.

"They're all dead," he said.

Miss Drake went to look with us. The hyacinths were like crumpled paper, black and lifeless. But she poked a stick beneath the scum.

"The root system's still there," she said, "Maybe when spring comes they'll perk up."

We forgot about them. But Tony and I started doing more things together. He built a footbridge over a ditch behind his house. The bank started eroding under one end, so I planted myrtle to stop it. It worked.

"Nice going," said Miss Drake, inspecting the job.

One Saturday morning I walked past the leather shop and saw a wink of color in Tony's lower pool. I pushed aside the scum with a stick—and there was a tiny plant, bright green.

"Miss Drake!"

She seemed as happy as we were, walking around the pools, rubbing her hands together.

"Look at that—well, I never!" she said.

Within three weeks the pool was full of pearly blossoms. We transferred the plants to the upper pool. All summer long the hyacinths flourished. The scum vanished. Water poured from the lower pool, crystal-bright.

Tony and I got our pictures in the *New Haven Register*. The write-up praised our "natural filtration system." It was the biggest thing that had happened at West Stoddard High. In Biology Mrs. Wainwright didn't mention it, but some kids in class called us famous. O yes.

At the next planning session for projects Miss Drake said, "Well, let's not just sit here like lizards on a rock. Who's next—you, Tommy Kingsland?'

Tommy Kingsland

From the time I was five my parents concentrated on one phrase —"You'll never amount to anything if you don't—"

I was an only child. We lived in a big clapboard saltbox built by my ancestor, Amos Kingsland, in 1768 on Toby Hill. It had six fireplaces—three up, three down—and a Dutch oven big enough for me to crawl into. The roof leaked. The clapboards needed paint. The barn had fallen in.

But the Kingslands were a first family in West Stoddard, and my mother (a Meade) never let me forget it.

She said, "The Meades and the Kingslands responded to Washington's call for troops in Massachusetts. They built this country. You'll never amount to anything if you don't know your history."

My father was a stone mason—when he worked, which was less and less. Every fall he made cider in the part of the barn that wasn't collapsed. He let it ferment down cellar in some old jugs. All winter he drank the hard brown liquid and cussed the government.

"This use to be a good country, but the Jews has got it now. Franklin D. Rosenfeld. You study for a lawyer, boy. Hear? Or you'll never amount to nuthing."

The only books in the house were history volumes with cracked leather covers and the words "Meade" and "Kingsland" underlined in red ink wherever they appeared. I would pore over them when I was sick, propped up in the old brass bed in the east room. We had no inside plumbing, so I had to tinkle in the heavy amber pot under the bed. After dark, sick or not, I had to carry the pot to the outhouse—because mother was fussy about that.

It didn't take me long to realize that my parents were narrow-minded blowhards. But a kid wants to like his people. I avoided arguments. When the Old Man was muttering about the goddamn dummies in the Hartford legislature, I nodded wisely. When mother took the Meade silver from its sacred mahogany box for polishing, I helped her.

But school was a window to freedom—and I climbed through it with relief from 1st Grade on. By the time I reached 10th I was studying hard. I saw a world of glittering possibilities beyond West Stoddard. It was steamships on rolling oceans, airplanes over frozen poles, scientists in humming laboratories....

Someday I would break out.

When Miss Drake made her teacher's call at our house, I was ashamed. There was my mother, sitting stiff as a ramrod on a horsehair sofa with springs busted through on the bottom. There was Eli Kingsland, the town sot, scratching his overalls.

"You have a lovely town," said Miss Drake, "I look forward to working here."

"Good ol town," said my father, "Good ol town."

"I'll put on the tea, mother," I said, hurrying out.

"Do that, Thomas. My, Miss Drake, you look quite young for a high school position."

When I brought the tea in our China pot with the cracked lip, mother was still talking.

"There are Drakes in Wethersfield, the *old* Drakes. I presume you're of a newer branch."

"We're the Francis Drakes," said Miss Drake with a trace of a grin, "English origin, I gather."

Mother nodded, pursing her lips. "I didn't think you could be Wethersfield."

It was horrible. But Miss Drake chatted and brought sunshine to our dingy front room. Leaving, she crinkled her eyes at me.

"I just read the theme you did on dirigibles, Tommy. I was aboard the *Los Angeles* once. We'll talk about it."

Mother watched her tapering legs swing down the path. "Aren't we some punkins," she said, "No hat,"

"Aboard the *Los Angeles*, eh? I'll bet she was," said my father.

Something in me bubbled over. "S-She's just trying to be friendly, for gosh sakes.

They looked at me. "Well!" said mother.

"That what you get from all them books—rudeness?" said my father.

I didn't rebel openly for several months. But Miss Drake introduced me to her library. A whole wall of her apartment at Mrs. Kelsey's was packed with books. Fresh novels in shiny jackets...poetry in soft leather bindings...the Encyclopedia Britannica. She steered me to things that broke open my shell, Malraux's *Man's Fate* and Du Bois's *The Souls of Black Folk*.

In class she praised the book reports I wrote.

"A reading person is a free person," she said.

One week Jack McGreggor smashed his hand working on a De Soto engine. I helped him pump gas at the garage. It was my first outside job, and I made some mistakes—overcharging a customer, forgetting to replace a gas cap. But at the end of the day Jack got money from Old Man Chapman and slapped two dollars in my hand.

"You're a good worker, you bony bastard," he said, "Come back tomorrow."

We became friends. One Friday night after closing the garage, he said, "Come on down to Bigelow's shack, Tommy. Catch some good sounds."

The shack, built out of scrap lumber down by the tracks, was throbbing with music. Hymie Volenski was pounding an old upright piano with no top. Vince was slapping a broomstick-and-washtub bass. Gene was blowing a trumpet and beating a drum with one hand.

"Wing it, Gene!" Jack shouted.

Gene lowered his trumpet and began to croon:

> *"Ah wants new scenes and new faces*
> *I wants to go to the distant places."*

It was a rich, black sound. It filled the smoky room with pinewood trees, cotton fields, and the Mississippi River a-rolling. Jack tap-tapped his fist on an old sawhorse.

"Yeah...yeah..." he said, grinning at me.

> *"Mah old gal done let me down-n*
> *Cain't stand the sight of this here town-n"*

It was America opening up for me after a lifetime buried in moss. I saw the whole thing clear. Somehow our family which had started out with old Amos roaring through life, building a good house, siring a strong family—somehow the blood had petered out. We had turned in on ourselves. But these black guys from another state were alive and growing.

"I'm busting loose, by gosh," I blurted.

"What?" said Jack.

"It's late. Gotta go."

Outside I paused to watch Gene through the window still belting out the words:

> *"Some gals here still call me honey*
> *But ah'm gonna go where you git more money-y"*

In the following weeks I went back again and again. I started to drink beer. One night I came home humming, and my mother and father met me at the door.

"Get yourself in here, young man," said my mother.

My father said, "Mr. Noyes sez you been going down to that coon shack — you and that Volenski jewboy."

Both talked at once — scolding...shouting. My heart thumped. But I started making sassy answers.

"They sing church music, too, Ma," I said, "You ought to hear Gene Bigelow render, *There Ain't No Flies on the Lamb of God.*"

She gasped.

"Big as you are," said my father, "I'm gonna get me a broomstick and whale you. What you thinking of, anyhow?"

"I'm thinking I like those guys. And one of them might be a relative."

"What!"

"Gene's name is Gene Meade Bigelow. Maybe he's a cousin from the African side."

They backed away, their jaws open. Suddenly I felt sorry for them — a grim-lipped woman with worn hands and a red-eyed man in faded overalls. The world had left them behind, and I would also.

Mother began to cry. My father put his arms around her. He looked over her shoulder, his face working.

"See what you done!" he shouted.

Elvira Wainwright

Miss Drake made a habit of staying after school. Long after we senior teachers had closed shop, she'd be at her desk talking and laughing. Students who should have been off to home duties would cluster around — and you never knew what would happen.

One afternoon as I was leaving I heard music coming out of her room. It wasn't Walter Damrosch and the symphony on our educational records. It was wild jazz flowing from station WNEW in New York. A famous voice—Bing Crosby—was singing:

> "It's Make Believe Ballroom time
> The hour of sweet romance..."

I looked in. That shapely Bordan girl was doing dance steps beside Miss Drake's desk, hugging her skirt up. Her eyes were closed and she was singing along:

> "Here's your Make Believe Ballroom
> Come on, children—let's dance...."

Miss Drake had a portable radio in her lap. She was tapping her yellow pencil in time on her inkbottle. She waved me in.

"Elaine's doing research for a paper grandly titled: 'The Golden Future of Swing'. Come see the new step she calls The Saxophone Hop."

I smiled politely, But shook my head and moved on.

Tony Tragonni

If you wanted to scrounge anything at the town dump, you had to show up early. The beach people tossed out stuff that could be fixed and used—chairs with one broken leg...rusty lawn-mowers...torn blankets...things they could buy new but our folks couldn't afford.

I got a three-way floor lamp for our living room by being there at five-thirty AM—before housewives arrived looking for food cans and stuff. I re-wired it from the guts of an old toaster. My mother baked me a corn-and-berry muffin as a reward.

So when I happened to see a Columbia bicycle, lying smashed in a beach house driveway, I waited until a garbage truck picked it up. Then I ran to the dump. I lugged the thing home, busted wheels and all.

Down cellar I pounded the bright red frame into shape, by Saturday I had a bike that tilted sideways but worked okay if you leaned to the left.

It was freedom. After school I pumped myself all over town—to Wright's Pond, the Roller Skating Rink, Nathan's Swamp. I found a coke bottle at West Beach and got a two-penny refund for it at Volenski's. I bought some Blackjack chewing gum. I turned up old Clinton road chewing a sweet wad, feeling great.

I decided to check out Leatherman's cave.

I hadn't been there for a couple of years, so I was surprised to see trash paper, some empty cans, and an old shirt outside the entrance. I crawled under the crooked ledge opening. In the dim light an orange-crate desk tilted against the stone wall. A couple of books lay half-open on top of a leafy mound. Then I found a blue leather cap and recognized it as one of Joe Tutynski's.

So it was true. He had set up a wilderness base to be alone in...away from his rough old man...away from us. Geraldine had told me he went home only to sleep.

Well...it made me sad. Sure, Joe had made a fool out of me more than once. Snorting at my attempts at poetry...beating me to pulp in class debates. But here in the green stillness, with birds chirping and sun twinkling, I sensed a bitter loneliness... a suffering he couldn't detach from his wrecked self.

It would take somebody like Miss Drake to reach inside of a guy this far smashed.

On the way out of the cave I picked up a torn scrap of paper. Its ink writing was smeared from rain. It said:

Your well-written paper on the Russian system spoke of
an ideal to reach for—yes. But beware of
Totalitarians who would whip you to reach it,
Joe. Heaven save you from these perfectionists.

They'll have you on the rack for your own good.

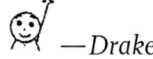 *—Drake*

Below Joe had scribbled, BULLSHIT

Tommy Kingsland

About 6:30 PM I watched Fred Millay pick up a milk bottle at Stevens Corner, walk across Route 1, and smash it against a telephone pole. Glass skidded all over the road.

"That's telling 'em Fred,"

"The whole cruddy world can kiss my ass," he said.

His Old Man had bawled him out for staying up with Elaine Bordan until 2:30 AM. And banging the Buick's fender against the garage door when he came home.

I was sore at my father for other reasons. I told Fred that a guy should have the right to stay out as late as he wants. We walked up North Road, going no place. We talked about our families...how stinky they'd become and what we were going to do about them someday.

"I know what," said Fred, "Let's get drunk."

We went down to Volenski's Store. Hymie's uncle would sell anything to anybody. Fred bought a bottle labeled Yellow Blitz. We sat under the New Haven railroad trestle sipping it. It tasted bad. I could hardly get it past my nose. But it sure made fire in the stomach.

"I'd like to do something to get my Old Man's cork," said Fred, "Something to make a big stink in the family."

"Bingo," I said tilting up the bottle.

"Something they couldn't change by just giving an order and paying some money."

For an hour we drank and talked about running away to New York. Or going to work on a Western ranch. But times were bad. We couldn't get a job. A guy had to eat.

"Les walk back to town, ol Tommie ol boy," said Fred, "and les get an idea before the church clock hits nine."

"Les do that," I said, "Idea, idea."

We climbed up from the trestle. Every few steps we took a gulp of whiskey. The road rose up and down. Fred slapped his arm around my shoulder, and we almost toppled.

"Steady, ol Tommie," he said, "or some thinkle peep we're drunk."

We hunched down on the granite steps beside the Congregational Church. It was darkening and the steps were set deep in the hill. Nobody could see us unless he looked hard.

"S'feelthy joke time, Tommie," Fred said, "Know any feelthy jokes?"

I told him the one about the rich lady in the Howard Johnson restaurant who wanted to see how the chef made those beautiful dinner rolls with the little wiggle on top. Waiter says okay. They go out to the kitchen. And there's a guy slapping dough against his belly button.

"What for, Tommie? Wha for?"

"To mak the lil wiggle on the roll, see?" I said, "Belly Button mak it."

"Hah."

"Lady say disgusting mak lil wiggle on roll, Ver disgusting."

"Hah."

"Waiter say, 'Oughta see him mak doughnuts.' Get it? Ha ha ha. Get it?"

Fred shook his head. Then suddenly he doubled over. Tears slid down his cheeks. I thought he'd choke laughing. "Mak doughnuts... hah, hah, hah."

He took a slug of the bottle. "The drunker I sit here the longer I get."

We stayed there until the clock bonged nine. We still didn't have an idea. I began to feel sick in the stomach.

Then Fred stood up and pulled me up too. "I got ver beeg idea. Ver beeg."

He whispered it in my ear. We hugged each other and

howled.

"Bes idea in whole worl," I said.

He said he'd sneak the Buick out of the garage and meet me in front of the church at ten. But when we started to cross Route 1 we wobbled against each other.

A car slowed down beside us. "What's this—the Elk's Street Parade?" said a soft voice.

It was Miss Drake, leaning on the wheel of her Packard. The roof was down. Her yellow hair was blowing around her up-turned collar.

Fred focused his eyes on her. He spoke very slowly and carefully. "We're going Noo London. Get tattoo. Beeg tattoo in Navy store."

She lifted one eyebrow. "Mmm," she said, "You too, Tommy?"

I nodded. I nodded about ten times so she'd understand I meant business. "S'all right. Tattoo...tattoo."

"Well, get in," she said, pushing open the door, "I'll make you guys a cup of java first"

Fred drew himself up. "Mus Drake, I'll bet you think we under the alfluence of inkahol."

"Heavens no, get in."

We drove to her apartment at Mrs. Kelsey's. It was lucky I was on the outside. Going around Sand Block corner I threw up—a brownish streamer of vomit. It missed the running board by a whisker. Miss Drake didn't take any notice. She was listening to Fred tell how our families had it coming to them... how they'd sure feel sorry when we came home with ten-inch eagles tattooed on our chests.

"Yes, that should get their attention." she said.

In her apartment Fred passed out on the sofa. The smell of coffee made me dizzy. I held my head where it throbbed, and Miss Drake gave me some fizzly stuff in a glass to drink.

"Feel goofy," I said.

"Why don't you lie on my bed awhile."

She tucked a blanket around my chest. Then she folded a

washcloth, dipped it in cool water and held it on my forehead. She did that for a long time.

I began to feel better. The pillowcase gave off a clean smell. *This is where she sleeps*, I thought, *This is the exact spot.*

Just before my eyes closed, I saw her hazy face bent toward me, her hands wringing the washcloth over the basin.

"I love you, Miss Drake," I said.

She grinned. "Well, I should hope so," she said.

Joe Tutynski

Since Grammar school days Leatherman's cave and I had been close. It was the only place in West Stoddard where I felt I belonged. I liked the glacial pile-up, 170 feet high. Speckled with shrubs and full of small caves. The biggest cavity was reached by crawling through a two-foot gap. You came into a stone room about six feet high and carpeted with dry leaves.

The Leatherman himself had slept there. I had found his rusty can opener. I knew his story—how he had come from France in the late 1800's, disgraced by bankrupting his bride-to-be's father in a business deal. How he dressed all in leather sewed together by himself. And wandered Connecticut backways year after year sleeping in caves. Begging food from farmhouses.

Long ago I had given him a name—Luke. And talked to him. Sitting there in the crunchy leaves I knew he was the only living thing in West Stoddard that came close to being my friend.

"Luke," I said, "We're the only two brains in this shipwreck of a town."

He and I had decided that my stupid, drunken father was to blame for my condition. My father was such a slave to liquor that his sperm had been drunk when it entered my mother. I was the bitter result.

I told Luke I'd never take one drop of that cursed liquid.

And I never had. But now it was 1937. And Kingsland and Millay getting publicly plastered had made me curious. *What's it like to be drunk?*

"Luke, I'm going to experiment..."

I had $13.50, saved from checks for correcting papers. I bought a bottle of Four Roses at Volenski's. When Hymie's uncle turned back to the cash register, I slipped a second bottle into my pocket.

Up in the cave, I opened the bottle. I sipped slowly. Hooch was fire-hot, I discovered. Pretty soon the stone walls grew hazy. All of a sudden my deformed right shoulder and snake-arm stopped aching.

"Jesus, Luke, I'm starting to float."

I felt great. Rolling in the leaves. Kicking against the walls. Great scenes flashed in my eyes—clipper ships bucking monster waves... airplanes zooming. In the midst of the fury I thought I heard birds singing.

I kept sipping. I didn't get sick at all. Finally my eyes closed. When I opened them again the sun was dropping purple stains through the granite gap. Luke was gone. I had been in another world all afternoon. Totally blacked out.

I limped out of the cave feeling wonderful. *Now I know what to do. Nobody can stop me.*

Fred Millay

Miss Drake liked music of every kind. But long before she came, we were having this love affair with Swing. We hugged the radio on Saturday night, listening to the Lucky Strike Hit Parade. Every kid in class except Joe Tutynski could dance.

There were hops down cellar at school during lunch hour. We did the Lindy and Susie-Q to recordings of the top bands—Benny Goodman, Artie Shaw, Glenn Miller.

After Miss Drake arrived, she took noon duty at the faculty table and watched. Her eyes twinkled behind her tortoise shell glasses. We really turned it on for her—throwing the girls out on breakaways...even trying air steps now and then.

Sometimes a girl flying over a shoulder would touch her feet on the low ceiling.

"Mmm. If this class could write the way it can jitterbug, we might survive the College Boards," she said.

During summer our big outlet was the Roller Skating Rink at West Beach. Local bands came there on one-nighters. They weren't much—usually amateur sidemen built around a semi-pro drummer. But they made noise. It was great. We wheeled around that polished floor, swaying and thumping. We sang the words. Outside, the Sound glittered—a romantic presence like always. Salt smells drifted up the sand.

We thought we were the best dancers this side of Harlem. Then one Saturday night we got straightened out on *that.*

The minute I walked in and dropped my quarter in the turn-stile, I sensed something different. I led Elaine past a bunch of strangers—kids with loose jackets and pointy dancing shoes. More of them were huddled around the bandstand, watching the players fit their instruments together.

And these saxes and trumpets *gleamed.* They weren't the dull, dented horns we were used to seeing. One trombone, sitting in a chrome rack, looked like it was made of sterling silver.

Hymie came up, snapping his fingers. "Boy oh boy, it's a practice gig for some of the big guys. Yah," he said, "Red Baker and Lippy McFarr from Clyde McCoy. And Skeeter Scott from Count Basie."

When the band started up, some difference! Solid blocks of sound hit the rink. A clarinet ride went up to the rafters and wriggled around like a snake. It was like a Goodman recording amplified a million times...an all-star team riddling the moon.

"Holy Moses!" cried Elaine, holding up her hands to dance.

> *I saw the harbor lights-s*
> *They only told me we were parting-g...*

We went at it. Well, that music moved into you and took over. It just grooved into the tissues. It punched through the veins and mixed with the blood. Whirling eyes, whirling hair.

Elaine flew in and out, her hips locked in the rhythms, her toes tapping. I veered her toward the bandstand. These musicians were standing straight up, their horns pointing out like guns.

Suddenly Hymie wheeled close, steering Eva Casserino. He shouted to me, "Miss Drake wants you." I looked at the entrance. There was Miss Drake waving a telegram. Before we reached her, the music stopped with a crash.

She handed me the yellow envelope. "It came in while I was in the drug store. I told Mr. Brooks I knew where you were and would deliver."

The telegram was from Chicago: MOTHER AND I STAYING ONE MORE NIGHT STOP BE HOME THURSDAY STOP YOU AND HOLLY HOLD THE FORT LOVE DAD

I waved the telegram high. Party time at our house! Elaine stretched out on our porch glider! Oh, brother!

"Thanks, Miss Drake!"

She smiled. "Not bad news, I gather."

She walked to the bandstand and paused a moment. Skeeter Scott looked up from some sheet music. He got to his feet, grinning, and took Miss Drake's hand. They started talking like old friends—with Skeeter giving her fingers a pat now and then.

"Do you see that?" said Elaine.

Hymie spoke in awe. "Miss Drake knows the Basie boys? Gees, what doesn't she know?"

The music started again—*Blue Hawaii*, a sweetie. And that's when I noticed those stranger-guys in the loose jackets cutting in. One, a drink of water in blue-check pants, tapped Tony and danced away with Geraldine Prue. Another, a chunky carrot-top, took Eva from Hymie. Then I felt a finger on my coat. "Okay, if I spin her, Mac?"

He was a pale-freckled guy, all legs and wiry neck. A celluloid button on his lapel said Shake Baby. Another, pinned to his red-leather belt, said Hot Feet Below. He swung Elaine away.

I walked over to Jack leaning against the Coke machine. "Who are these shimmy lizards?" he said.

Whoever they were, they could dance. They wheeled around,

pounding heels, leading our girls through steps we'd never seen before.

Jack's voice rose. "What's that guy doing? If he doesn't get his hand off Holly's ass I'm gonna—"

Tony laughed. "They're doing the Shake-A-Hip, Jack. These cats belong to the Glen Island Dance Club. They hire a guy from uptown Manhattan to show them the latest stuff."

The band cut into *East of the Sun*. A speed version loaded with brass. The dancing got wild—and suddenly I noticed something odd. The Glen Islanders weren't leading our girls anymore. They were doing stuff of their own. High kicks. Whirl-a-ways. When the girls couldn't follow, the guys shrugged and exchanged glances. The girls would blush and try again.

Then Pale Freckles cruised by, steering Elaine in an intricate cross-step. She stayed with him darn good until they got to floor center. Then he gave her a quick flare-out, bunny-hugged sideways—and left her stopped dead, facing backwards.

It was a bad moment. After all, Elaine was our best—and here she was totally zonked. She put her hands over her face, laughing. She tripped back to him, and that's when the sonofa-bitch showed his colors.

He danced her away in a simple Westchester. He put on this exaggerated look of boredom. When they passed us again, he had a dollar bill hanging from his fingers behind her back. Before we realized what was happening, a Glen Islander came out, took the money, and cut in on Pale Freckles.

Well! Jack and I started out on the floor at the same time. But a hand caught each of us at the elbow.

"Whoa," said Miss Drake.

She handed me her glasses. She unrolled the turban-like ribbon that was holding her hair and handed it to Jack. She walked across the floor—strong and graceful as a panther—and tapped Pale Freckles.

A moment later they were swinging all over the place. In two steps you could tell that Miss Drake was an experienced hoofer. She slipped into his designs like candy melting.

A Novel By George P. Morrill

Red sails in the sunset
Far out on the sea-e-e...

Pale Freckles pulled her in and out. He did tap steps. She followed everything, smiling in his face. I have to admit they looked good. He moved her to the center. Then he started to showboat for the crowd, putting out some fancy heel-and-toe stuff.

That was his mistake. Suddenly, as if Miss Drake had blown a whistle, the music changed to Sweet Georgia Brown. The whole band stood up and unloaded—tat-tat-tat-tat, whaw, whaw....

No gal made has got a shade
On sweet Georgia Brown-n-n

Pale Freckles started a fast Lindy, but Miss Drake was faster. She came out of the first breakaway, hair flying, two beats ahead of him. He hesitated, picked up the rhythm—but then botched it when she moved into an air step. She went over his shoulder on her own and was back two-stepping while he was looking to find her.

He blushed. I saw Miss Drake's lips form the words, "That's all right."

Then she proceeded to take him apart.

They were in the center. Everybody was standing in a circle around them clapping hands in time. Pale Freckles kept trying to lead and losing the count. He stared at Miss Drake's flying feet. His own feet got tangled. Once he tripped himself.

Georgia claims her
Georgia named her
Sweeeeet Georgia Brown-n-n-n.

I couldn't believe Miss Drake's solid, sleek-molded legs...the sweet groove of muscle that flashed and vanished on her calves. The poundage on her chest did a dance all it's own.

"Wheeeeeeee," she sang, shagging in a circle, her smooth jaw tilted and laughing.

She hit the poor guy with everything. Pecking, Trucking, and a raft of steps I never knew existed. By this time the old pros in the band were blowing just for her, pointing their horns like cannons. They drove through one chorus after another. And Skeeter Scott kept beating them on with one hand while he worked his trumpet with the other.

The last three minutes Pale Freckles just stood there, shuffling his pointy shoes. He wore a fixed smile, and his coat was sweated through. In the end, Miss Drake jitterbugged alone—like she was doing the History of Jazz Dance at Radio City, New York. And everybody clapped.

Later she danced with each of us town guys—and made us feel like Fred Astaire. She even did a classy side-shuffle with Vince that brought more clapping. But every time a Glen Islander cut in she hot-stepped him into disaster.

When the dance was over I walked up to the stand to get Skeeter Scott's autograph. The band was closing up, talking, cleaning instruments.

"Mister Scott, you know Miss Drake?"

He wrote the autograph and handed it over. "Eva Drake? Say, didn't she lay down the leather tonight?"

"What were those steps she was doing?"

He rubbed his heavy pink lips. "Bit of everything. Lindy to start. Then some Shorty-George and Hitch-Hiking. At the end she was reaching way back—Rubber Leg, Messin' Around, and Balling the Jack. Seems like I detected some Flying Charleston and Buzzard Glide in there too."

"Where did she learn all that?"

He looked at me. Did a film lower over his eyes? "How you know Eva, man?"

"She's my teacher."

He peered around. "Eva Drake lives here? Well, well. You got a damn fine teacher, man."

And that's all he would say.

A Novel By George P. Morrill

Gene Bigelow

I'd never danced with a white girl and never expected to. Where I came from they whipped black boys for a lot less than that.

But when I first went downstairs to lunch at West Stoddard High, I could hardly keep off the floor. They had Chick Webb and Lunceford blasting on the phono. Everybody rushed through lunch to get dancing. The girls were best. It was something to see Geraldine Prue and Elaine Bordan out there tapping their feet, just itching to be tossed around. But their partners, Tony Tragonni and Fred Millay, didn't do more than walk them through the standard routines.

Both guys could box-step around—even Lindy a little—but they sure didn't know how to toss a partner.

So I stood by the refrigerator slapping my hand on my hip, wiggling my toes inside my shoes—and sore at myself for not stepping out there and cutting in. I had sworn never to back off from white folks up North. But I was scared that girls would stick up their noses at me. If a guy cracked smart, I wouldn't mind telling him off. But what could I do with a girl?

Somebody put on *Isn't it a Lovely Day*, a slow Dorsey. The tempo dropped. Miss Drake pushed back her coffee and got up from the faculty table. She walked to me and lifted her hands.

"Will the gentleman ask the lady?"

I led her in classy steps—the Peabody, the Westchester. I kept my head up. Miss Drake was like mist in my arms. The melody seemed to ripple along her wide shoulders and make her whole body move in rhythm. Now and then her chest touched my shirt. Firm...heavy.

She followed everything I did. She made me feel like Bojangles Robinson-in-Slow-Time. Pretty soon the kids were making room for us, just watching. She was some stepper.

Then a funny thing happened. I looked at her and saw the young girl she must have been—willowy and carefree—before that serious little crinkle grew above her brow.

You were going on your way-y

Now you've got to remain-n-n....

Before we sat down I felt something moist on my collar. I touched it and glanced at Miss Drake. She smiled back crookedly. Her eyes were shimmering—but definitely clear.

Yet I could have sworn that the wet spot was a tear.

After the dance, the girls flocked around me. They knew I could show them plenty. In the next weeks I taught Eva Casserino to do Shake Your Duster and Fall Off a Log. I hauled out stuff that my uncles had danced on the bayous—the Jig-Walk, Black Bottom, Scronch, and Shoot the Pistols.

"Where in hell did you learn to *vibrate* like that?" said Fred.

"Way down Dixie in da land ob cotton, Massah," I said.

"I'd like to see you and Miss Drake do some of that."

So would I. But except for her famous outburst at the Roller Skating Rink, Miss Drake would never jitterbug with any of us.

Tommy Kingsland

Miss Drake got us to write a theme on a subject of our choice. And take a whole period to discuss it. Holly Millay picked Clothes Fashions. Gene Bigelow picked Fishing Down South. Jack McGreggor picked the V-8 Engine.

Then Joe Tutynski read his paper: *How To Execute a Human Being.*

He said, "Bruno Hauptman has been convicted of killing the Lindbergh baby. He's going to be executed the easy way. He'll sit in a chair. The heat will go on. He'll fry. He's not going to be hurt enough."

We all sat up. Elaine Bordan put both hands to her cheeks.

"The state ought to make him suffer. The Governor should study some of the old methods. And get the Legislature to write them into law.

"Henry VIII of England had the right idea. He got his torture master, Sir W. Skevington, to build a wide iron hoop with screws that could tighten it. Put the hoop around the body, twist the screws, and you'd squeeze the prisoner to death."

The room grew quiet. Hymie Volenski and Holly looked at each other with whitish faces.

"Sometimes blood would squirt from their nose and ears..." Eva Casserino turned in her seat and stared at Joe.

"The Medieval Germans had a better rig. Called *fass*. It was a cradle with spikes inside. You put a guy—or girl—inside and rocked it."

I saw Jack make a half-smile, kind of frozen. He turned to Miss Drake who was touching her pencil thoughtfully to her lower lip and frowning.

"Torquemada of the Spanish Inquisition came up with the best—a rack that stretched arms and legs apart until they split. America ought to have something like that. Think what a show we'd have if the execution was public. Jazz music mixing with screams. People could dance."

By this time we were all listening. Holly had her fists over her mouth. Miss Drake took out a handkerchief and blew her nose.

"What I'm talking about is getting some use out of executions. Actually a prisoner should be killed exactly the way he killed. If he choked somebody to death, the sheriff should choke him to death. On a platform in front of the citizens. If he cut some girl's throat, the girl's relatives should cut his—with a razor supplied by the state.

"Everything in public, see? That way the nation would get some entertainment out of a murderer being chopped up. While justice is served."

He finished and slid his paper onto his desk.

"Well...." said Miss Drake, "Mmm...."

I saw Jack's muscles tighten on his forearms. He swung around and— keeping his back to Miss Drake so she couldn't see—gave Joe the finger.

"The whole world's eating you, hey Joe?"

Joe wrinkled his disjointed nose. Anger flashed between

them. "I'm getting used to idiots."

I thought Jack would climb out of his chair. He turned back and mumbled something I didn't hear—but Miss Drake evidently did.

"Now, now," she said.

The bell rang, Jack and Joe moved out, not looking at each other.

Hymie Volenski

Long before Miss Drake wowed everybody with her wit, my reputation for being a joker was secure. I told hot stories and slung a fast line. Yah.

Nobody knew how hard I worked memorizing the stuff from *Manhattan Talk, Ballyhoo, Shady Times* and other magazines. Or how scared I was most of the time—about everything.

Jokes were my passport to guys like Jack McGreggor and Fred Millay. But I knew that sooner or later I was going to have to take the Saybrook Bridge test—and it terrified me.

The Saybrook Bridge was a one-arm drawbridge that carried trains across the Connecticut River. When it opened for a sailboat or tanker, the counter-weighted arm rose 200 feet in the air. Every West Stoddard guy who wanted to be one of the gang had to ride that arm up—at least once.

"It's a snap," Vince Bigelow told me, "You go at night so the railroad dick can't jump you. Wait under the embankment until a boat blows its whistle. Then climb the wire fence, run onto the steel shaft at the end. Get a good grip on the rivets—"

I felt like throwing up.

One afternoon we were drinking cokes at the garage and Tony Tragonni said, "When you riding the Iron Bitch, Hymie?"

"Tomorrow night," I said.

Instantly everybody was interested. Vince, who had gone up the week before, said "Man, you can see Long Island clear from up there."

"How would you, know, brother?" said Gene, "Your eyes were shut and your teeth were clamped on a girder."

We all laughed, me the hardest.

Vince said in a low voice, "Good thing I had a cork in my ass all right."

I was sick all next day. I knew I was going to die. I could get dizzy mounting a stepladder. Here I was about to ride 500 tons of steel to the moon.

Miss Drake found me staring at my open history book with glassy eyes. She slid the book around on my desk.

"You can read better if the writing's not upside down."

"Oh...yah, yah."

She studied me, yellow pencil in her teeth, "Something wrong, Hymie."

"Wrong? Me? No, no."

She asked me to stay after school and help her move some chairs, but I said my uncle needed me at the store.

After supper, Jack and Fred showed up in Jack's Model A.

"Ready for the old alley-oop, hoss?" Jack said.

They drove me to Saybrook. We stopped at Jamie's River End for coffee—and there sat Tony, Vince and Gene. Jesus, they weren't even going to give me two seconds alone to pray.

"Me and the boys are here to catch you on the first bounce," said Tony.

"If you start to slip, just grab a couple of seagulls," said Vince.

Everybody laughed.

By nine o'clock it was dark. We sat in the bushes under the embankment waiting for the Mobile tanker that ran down from Hartford every night. Once I heard a noise and thought I saw a shadow run down the tracks onto the bridge.

"Must be a rail dick," whispered Jack, "He'll be busy at the bridge house—don't worry."

Suddenly a whistle went *bwhaaaaaaa*.

"Hey, it's a freighter," said Tony, "You can go early."

Vince patted my shoulder. "Luck, man."

I tumbled over the fence and ran out on the ties. The rails were shiny arrows coming together at a point up ahead. As I ran they kept separating, then joining again—like something in a nightmare.

I began to weep. I reached the steel shelf under the giant truss and flopped down. There was no point feeling for the rivet-ends, trying to get a good hold on a girder. I *knew* that as soon as the whole thing began to lift, my muscles would turn to putty. As soon as I looked, down and saw the river...sinking deeper and deeper....

"Hi, Hymie." A ghost figure in dungarees stepped from behind a girder. It sat down beside me.

Good Christ! Miss Drake.

"Surprise," she said, "My girl-spies told me about this tradition. I trailed your car over."

"Gees, Miss Drake—"

She looked around, testing a bolt-end with her hand. "Mmm. Now, show me how to hang on."

There was no time for anything—not even panic. We shifted positions, tried this grip and that grip. My brain suddenly flipped into action.

I said, "if we lie on our backs with our legs up on this I-bar, the I-bar will become our seat as we go up. Now, hold this bolt...grip this edge of the girder..."

"Very good," she said.

With a rumble, the bridge started to rise. Up...up. It was like riding a giant Ferris wheel—without the safety bar in front or the carnival jukebox playing Whistle While You Work.

Miss Drake peered down. "Here comes the ship."

I opened my eyes. Far below, tiny lights moved on the bridge-gap we had made. They looked like rubies, emeralds and diamonds dragged on the water. Smoke puffed from the freighter's stack and trailed off below our feet.

"Gorgeous, Hymie."

The river was a horn of silver. It narrowed down from the northern hills, flowed below us, and fanned out into the Sound.

Long Island flowed darkly in the distance. All up and down the shoreline house lights twinkled like jewels. And the scent of the salt marsh floated up, sharp and sweet.

I felt my muscles relax. Miss Drake said, "They ought to sell tickets to this."

When the bridge-arm stopped at the top, we half-stood to get a better view. It was like being in an airplane. Way out toward New Haven we saw a tanker steaming, its porthole lights making little gold discs on the water. Up toward Middletown, stars flowed over lump-shadows.

"Hold onto me," she said, "I'm going to take pictures."

She pulled a small Kodak out of her shirt. I hugged her legs, firm and soap smelling through the dungarees. She clicked shots in every direction. Then she sat down and handed me the camera.

"You get them developed, Hymie. Keep the whole set. If the school board finds out about this, I'm a dead pigeon."

The trip down was nothing. We jounced together gently. I wasn't nervous even when the giant bridge parts came together with a grinding *c-c-clunk.*

"I hope you wasn't uneasy, Miss Drake," I said.

She tilted her head. "I was lucky you were along. Not a word to anyone, now."

She told me to get the guys out of there so she could sneak away. I ran down the track and waved them back.

"How'd it go, hoss?" said Jack.

I said, "They ought to sell tickets to this."

Driving to West Stoddard, Vince kept looking at me. "You wasn't jittery? Not once?"

I took the camera out of my pocket. "I was too busy sizing up angle shots. Yah."

The pictures came out good. The lighted coastline looked very distant. One picture showed the shadow of a girder in one corner and the shadowy outline of the freighter about a mile below.

I said, "I had to lean out a little for that one. But it was worth it."

I became a hero. Fred couldn't get over it. "Je-zus. I brought along a roll of shit paper for old Hymie. I should have brought a box lunch."

Even Joe Tutynski looked at me in a new way—interested.

Miss Drake never mentioned a thing. Not to me or anybody. But when I wrote a theme titled Great Bridges of New England, she put one of her little drawings on the last page.

The right eye was winking.

Gene Bigelow

After elections the Federal government gave the town money to fix the roads. Every guy young or old applied for a job. Three bucks a day. Me and my brother rode the back of a Ford truck, shoveling gravel onto hot tar.

A record cold snap was predicted for nightfall. We felt good—stripped to the waist, making the gravel sing off our blades. Backs were rising and falling on three trucks behind us.

"You guys gone to sleep?"

It was Hymie Volenski, two trucks back. Vince gave him the finger. Hymie's soft body was sagging over his shovel. We'd all been surprised that he showed up for dig-and-sweat work.

"What you doing?" he shouted, "The Mississippi Shuffle?"

All us guys booed him. He slid down from his load and vanished in the cab beside the driver. At lunch break he emerged, and made a speech denouncing cheap labor in the enlightened Swing Age. Then he walked away.

We were all parked on a stone wall eating sandwiches when Miss Drake drove up and stopped.

She held out her hands, palms up. "Radio says freezing tonight. Can you believe it? There go the budding peaches outside my window. Crop kill in September? Cut it out, New England."

We crowded around the snazzy Packard. Vince said, "Not to worry, Miss Drake. I'll spray your tree with water. It'll freeze and protect your fruit."

"Really?"

I butted in, "That's right. Old Vince Bigelow here knows his agriculture. He's the top field nigger of West Stoddard."

Vince twisted my arm behind my back. "Don't mind kid motor-mouth here, Miss Drake. His brain got chewed by boll weevils down south."

"My brother wants my house nigger job," I hollered, "But he's not up to it."

"Now, now..." said Miss Drake. She drove off.

That night my brother and I soaked her peach tree with water. It froze okay, twinkling in the chill dawn-light. But later on, high winds broke off the hardened limbs. Eva Casserino took a picture of our teacher standing beside the splintery, wooden wreck.

"I'm not sure they'll believe this on the Coast," she said.

Fred Millay

Elaine Bordan led me a cockeyed chase. Soon after our West Beach clinch she got interested in other guys. She broke dates, went to dances. She took gifts of cokes and bracelets from any joker who offered them.

But not one of these guys—not those New Haven hotshots in their Ford V8's or those summer jocks from Hartford—had the hold on her that I did. She always came back.

"You're the kind of boy I could love—if I could love anybody," she told me, pressing my fingers to her always-cool lips, "That's not much of a compliment. But it's something, isn't it?"

"Yeah, I guess."

"Miss Drake worries about me. I'll bet she thinks I'll get beaten to death by an alto sax."

She had grown taller, shapelier. All eyes turned to her at the Saturday hops at the Roller Skating Rink. She could jitterbug or waltz. The out-of-town acting had busted her out of the ancient

West Stoddard attitude that compelled girls to sit back and wait. In class she spoke up, surprising everybody with her wit.

Her recklessness was a big part of her charm. But sooner or later she'd be chopped down—and I dreaded it.

One afternoon when Miss Drake was lecturing on German aggression before the Great War, Elaine slipped a note on my desk: *Have you any European territorial demands to make, Herr Bismarck?*

I looked at her half-grin, full of meaning. I wrote back: *I'm asking for African concessions.*

Her lips formed the word *o-kay* soundlessly. My heart thundered the rest of the period.

We went to our newest place—the bleach room in the deserted piano key factory up in Ivoryton. The sun poured through the narrow windows where ivory had once been set out to whiten. I swept the dust off a table. We undressed. She lay down on the table and held out her arms.

"Don't believe what I say in the next five minutes, Freddy."

Afterwards we sat on the edge of the table with ribbons of sun making stripes on our bare flesh like zebras. Elaine had a way of trembling involuntarily at a time like this. I always put my arm around her as a comfort.

"I suppose I'm bad," she said.

"No...no...."

"If it just didn't feel so darn wonderful."

She pulled on her panties and smoothed them down. She pinched my arms. "These ropy muscles all over you—no wonder I get bruises."

She was quieter than usual. She walked to a dust-streaked window, the sunlight rippling on her naked breasts. Outside a couple of seagulls settled down on broken fence posts lining the factory entrance.

"Sometimes when I'm on the dance floor, Freddy, I suddenly wonder what I'm doing. I mean the ghost-me pulls apart from the rest and stares at that girl giggling and shaking. Then I get scared. How's that little dope going to make it in the world?"

I gave her a hug. "Aw, Elaine…"

She pulled away and dropped her voice to a whisper, "Sometimes if you bite your lip as hard as you can, you don't think everything's crazy. If something can hurt that much, there must be a reason for it."

Jack McGreggor

I was fitting a hose gasket to Mr. Chapman's 1933 Chevy when Holly walked by the garage.

"Hey, good-looking," I called, "No spik to proletariat?"

She hesitated, then turned back. "Hello, Jack."

I set my water-pump pliers on the fender. Her cheeks were wet. She wiped them quickly.

"What's the matter?"

"Nothing."

I mopped my hand on a rag and took her elbow. She pulled away.

"I said *nothing*, Jack."

Then she was gone, holding her head high. She didn't look around. I watched her sun-tanned legs hurry across Route 1 to the library.

I knew what was wrong. That bastard Joe Tutynski was working her over again. He was making a full-time job of blasting every project she tried at school. When Miss Drake called for general criticism up went his good arm. Then the cracks started—some bright, some humorous. But all edged with meanness.

When Holly wrote a poem about an ocean storm seen from her bedroom window, Joe said, "No storm ever sounded like that. This poet was just belching hiccups."

When she took a walk-on part in one of Elaine Bordan's skits, he said, "I gather the supporting role is supposed to be sympathetic. Well, this actress has our sympathy. She's all wood."

Ordinarily I can handle a mean guy. I let most things go. But if real bullying sets in, I seek the guy out for talk. And things cool down. But when I confronted Joe he fired back.

"What's it to you if I question the intelligence content of a weak-minded broad?" he growled.

"Watch it, man."

"Watch what? Am I supposed to sit in silence while a spoiled lawyer's kid performs stuff that her two-bit talent can't support?"

I walked away. I wanted to stand him on his head, but couldn't. A cripple can win a fight without exchanging a shot. Miss Drake sensed how the guy bitched me off.

"What's this flap between you and Joe Tutynski?" she said.

"Flap? Nothing."

She pinched my nose lightly. We were in the deserted classroom. "Let's have it, fella."

So I told her how Joe was zeroing in on Holly Millay, my girl. She couldn't say it's a nice day without him giving a snort.

"It's unnatural. I hate the bum."

She sighed and rubbed her chin slowly. "Well, unnatural may be correct. But we all know the burden he carries. We must make allowances. You don't hate him. I think you pity him. But pity isn't right either. We've got to find a way to bring a brilliant young mind into our fold. Maybe you can help me do it."

"I doubt it, Miss Drake."

She gave her soft smile—different from her laughing smile and her surprise smile. It always made us melt. "I don't. Keep in mind if you hold a grudge against somebody it doesn't hurt him at all. It simply chews your guts."

She tapped her yellow pencil on my shoulder.

"You can move beyond that, Jack."

Vince Bigelow

Miss Drake liked me from the beginning. I could sense it. She questioned me about Mississippi. I started with the usual—big moons, hound dogs, Spanish moss. After all, she was white folks. I didn't want to disturb her dreamy world.

But she waved me off. "I know all that. Tell me about life back from the railheads. I mean what's doing with a 300-dollar-a-year family out beyond ol Colonel Booby's plantations?"

So I told her about the falling-down shacks in Ox Forks, my village...the stink of coonskins drying on a board...the smell of violence when the sheriff and his deputies rode by on big black horses with rifles sticking out of their saddles.

"Down there if you have an enemy you want to hurt," I said, "Just put his name in a dead crow's mouth and let the bird dry up."

Miss Drake was fascinated. "You're kidding."

I grinned. "That trick will give the enemy a stomach ache. But if you really want to kill him get horsehair, gunpowder, and a rattlesnake skin. Wrap it in a rag. Hide it under the guy's doorstep."

She stared at me, her blue eyes wide.

I spread my hands. "He'll fall down dead."

"Do people actually believe that?"

I laughed. "Naw, not everybody. My folks never did. But they found my sister hiding a cockroach and a snip of hair in a matchbox—so a girl she didn't like would go bald. That's when they decided to move north. Hard to fight that old witch stuff down south."

Miss Drake took me and my brother Gene along with the white kids whenever we went to the Peabody Museum in New Haven. We ate in diners with her like everybody else. I still got a bit uneasy eating with white folks, but Gene gave me hell about that.

"Up North don't take anybody's shit," he said, "It's different here and we got to back it up."

One night we came home from the State Library in Hartford—me Gene, Tony Tragonni, Elaine Bordan, and Holly Millay in the Packard with the top down. Miss Drake pulled up at Bailey's Sidecar in Deep River. We were eating cheeseburgers when a fight broke out at a nearby table.

It was between two Negro guys. About 30, medium-sized. One, in a pressed tan suit, got up and backed away from a guy in a tattered red sweater. Red Sweater snapped open a straight razor.

"You bastard, Cord," he said, "Ah'm gonna cut you three ways—deep, wide, and frequent."

Everybody scrambled out of the way. Mr. Bailey, who was rubbing the beet-tinted linoleum counter, dropped his rag and backed toward the shiny coffee urn. "Now, gentlemen...gentlemen..."

Cord and Red Sweater circled each other, the table between them.

"Now wait a minute...hold it..." said Cord.

I'd been in these situations before. Red Sweater was feeling the best he ever had in his life. Everyone was backing away from him, both white and black. That had never happened before—at least in just this way. He was puffed up bigger than a sow's belly.

"You been ass-kicking me long enough, Cord." he said, louder.

I slid out of my chair and walked into the open space. "Okay, man, let's have the razor."

Red Sweater's eye fluttered. These violent boys are often stopped by an unexpected move. He lowered his razor.

"Git your ass outa here, kid."

"There are a lot of people here. We don't want anybody hurt. Now give me that."

I put out my hand, palm up. He hesitated. The ball game had suddenly changed. Now Red Sweater wanted to get out of this. But he wanted to be a big shot too. It was a confused second—the *split second* for action.

My hand shot out. Grabbed his wrist. Twisted. The razor clattered to the floor.

"Goddam!" he roared, sinking to his knees.

Then I was holding off Cord who ran around the table aiming

a kick. Keeping Red Sweater down with one hand. Bumping the razor across the floor to Mr. Bailey with my shoe.

My brother stepped up with doubled fists, about to pile into Red Sweater. I nodded him back.

"Cut it, Gene," I ordered, "Hunker down."

I stood over the two guys until the police arrived. Then I looked for Miss Drake. She had moved to a counter stool. She was watching without saying a word, her fingers locked in her lap.

Driving home, everybody chattered. Tony said, "Gosh, Vince is a hero...a living hero..."

All I could do was mutter, "Aw..."

Miss Drake let me and Gene off last. She leaned over the Packard's big wheel, her yellow hair tumbling on the fancy chrome spokes.

"Extraordinary," she said.

Gene left for the house. I started to get out.

"Vince, have you ever thought of going into police work?"

I shrugged, She should know better than that. A little ol Mississippi boy with a black skin, I said, "Po-lice? There ain't a chance— "

"*Isn't* a chance," she corrected, "But there is. Big changes are coming. You'll see. America will shuffle a lot of ideas after the war."

She mixed me up. War?

"Yes, war's inevitable I'm afraid. All the warning flags are up. How I hate it." She put her fist to her lips and rocked slightly. For a moment her eyes were closed and her lashes added something gentle to her creamy forehead and cheeks. "Afterward young men who can keep their heads in a crisis will be in demand."

I cocked my head at her. Her eyes were on me like warm honey—so interested, so friendly a crazy thought flashed in my mind: *I guess an angel must look like you, Miss Drake.*

"Think about it," she said, "I'll get you a book on Federal services tomorrow."

Sibyl Noyes

Before mother died I promised I'd take care of my little brother Shelly in second grade. I fed him and my father on five dollars a week. It was terrible when he cried for an orange or a cookie and I couldn't give him anything but a cracker sprinkled with sugar.

He'd holler for his mother and punch me. I don't know how many times I slapped him—and then hated myself for it. So when his birthday came I was determined to buy him a present. But the night before, there was only 17 cents in the cracked cup over the stove.

I had to go to Bailey's Remainders on the back road behind the dump. In a barn full of stuff—rusty lawn mowers, splintered furniture, lamps without cords,—Mr. Bailey had piled up Lucky Boxes, cartons of surprises. They sold for 10 cents.

You never knew what was in them. And you couldn't get your money back if you didn't like it. They were marked "clothes" "hardware" and so on. I gave Mr. Bailey a dime for a box marked "kids toys".

At home I found a mixture of Lincoln Logs, Erector Set pieces, roller skate keys, a cork pop gun, lumps of bubble gum, Tinker Toy bits, a collapsed rubber ball, four Fort Apache lead Indians with the paint rubbed off, two pencils without erasers, and some metal coat hangers.

I wrapped the box in colored funny-paper and tied it with white string. I wrote "Happy Birthday, Shelly" with my father's old Griffin marking pen. When he was asleep I set the box at his feet. In the morning I heard him shout and start tearing the paper.

I felt so good the rest of the day that I told Miss Drake about it. She gave me a hug. Then she rummaged in her desk and took out a little pencil sharpener in the shape of Lindbergh's *Spirit of Saint Louis* airplane.

She said, "Add this to the treasure trove."

Vince Bigelow

I've always been able to nose out trouble before it hits. As a 10-year-old kid back in Mississippi, I pulled my brother out of a fistfight with a drunken cousin who had stolen a bicycle wheel Gene was saving. I got the wheel back. (As it worked out, Gene never assembled enough parts to make a bike anyhow.)

Later up North, I stopped him from piling into Reubin Wright at the garage over some stupid racial insult.

So when Miss Drake said I might give a thought to police work, I began to wonder. Were changes on the way so that a coal-black guy could get into an outfit that fights crime? She brought me some U.S. Government pamphlets describing the FBI, the Immigration Authority, and others. They seemed to indicate that careers were open to anyone.

"You think it's worth a shot, Miss Drake?"

She beamed. "Yes, yes. Definitely, definitely. I'm going to take you to New York. We'll talk with Federal people."

But then the news intervened. On the radio, in the newspapers, stories of collapsing world peace filtered into West Stoddard. Poland refused to cede Danzig to Nazi Germany...Japanese warplanes sank the U.S. gunboat *Panay*. It looked to me that sooner or later the real need for trained personnel would be in the big theater.

"I've decided that after graduation I'm joining the Army."

"Oh!" said Miss Drake.

"Crooks have to be stopped. This guy Hitler is a crook."

She looked at me, smoothing her pencil with her wide, muscular fingers. "I know better than to try to dissuade you, Vince. You're one of those rare young people who thinks ahead. Okay, the Army. You'll put up with the military kookiness and build a topnotch career. I predict it."

Then she got up from the desk and planted a kiss on the top of my head.

Sibyl Noyes

All the church buildings in town were falling apart. Even the big Congregational had broken concrete steps and a leaking steeple. The tiny Baptist church was unpainted and missing clapboards above its eight windows.

The worst was the Methodist, an old Cape Cod that sagged against a lop-sided brick chimney. With each rain its rotten wooden shingles broke apart and skidded down the roof.

My mother had belonged to the 24-member congregation. So I still went there every Sunday. I listened to Bible-readings by Mrs. Kelsey, sermons by Mrs. Kelsey, organ playing by Mrs. Kelsey. Without Mrs. Kelsey the church couldn't have survived 15 minutes. So whenever she called for help you had to step up.

On the Sunday that Miss Drake visited, Mrs. Kelsey met me at the door with tears in her eyes. "The organ just broke down and I can't fix it," she said, "You'll have to do key duty on the piano this morning, Sibyl."

I had been dreading Miss Drake's visit to our crummy little church. What could she think after the magnificent churches she must have seen? And now *key duty.*

This duty involved standing by our out-of-tune piano when Mrs. Kelsey played, bending, and quickly flicking up the keys that stayed down as her fingers ran over them. You had to work fast. Sometimes the stuck-down keys would pull on your fingernail. Sometimes you'd miss.

"Be alert now, Sibyl, When I start *Rock of Ages* we mustn't lose any notes."

It was embarrassing standing on that platform in front of six or eight people in unvarnished pews...jabbing your hand around the keyboard...trying not to smell the mustiness of the battered piano. I was hard at it—and singing with the others—when Miss Drake walked in.

I wanted to drop through the floor. But then she opened a hymnal, pushed back her hair with two fingers, and began to sing. Old Mr. and Mrs. Huntington in the next pew nodded. John MacFarland, town handyman, lifted his rugged hand politely.

"Rock of Ages...cleft for me-e-e..."

Suddenly I recalled what she had said just Friday in English. She had quoted Marcus Aurelius: "Remember this—that there is a proper dignity and proportion to be observed in the performance of every act of life."

I was a poor girl in a poor church in a poor town. But I was going to be a doctor, wasn't I? Yes, I was. I leaned closer to Mrs. Kelsey as she hit the last chords, sticking three keys down. I snapped up all three.

Then the singing was over. I straightened my sleeves carefully and went over to say hello.

Tommy Kingsland

When Miss Drake gave us the new assignment to write something just for ourselves—a thing to show nobody—I felt good. I decided to write about her. I could say anything and not worry about anybody seeing it.

Here's how it went:

Miss Drake is a looker. She sits at her desk, tapping a pencil on anything handy—blotter, thumb, forearm—smiling a half-smile when she looks at you. If you say something funny, she laughs. Her white teeth shine, and a little dimple comes out in her cheek.

But if you say something dumb, her left eyebrow goes up. She says, "Mmm." Or "Wait a minute, fella." And she chimes in with her idea. But she never does this in a way to hurt your feelings or make you blush.

She makes *me* blush, however, when she walks up to the board. Her full hips shift slightly under her pleated skirt. Passing your desk, her legs make a kind of swish-swish. And you can't help noticing up top the sweet mounds that bulge under her open-collar shirt. When she bends over you in conference there's a faint perfumy odor from her throat and bare arms.

It's enough to make a guy want to crawl into her lap like a four-year-old kid. Nuzzle your head in the soft gap between her cheek and shoulder.

Somehow she finds time to know about everybody in class. What we're doing. What we want to do. She's even got Joe Tutynski working on a beach project, although he can't say a decent word about her.

I know I'm too shy with Miss Drake. I could never tell her how she's making things good for me. Because of her I'm trying to understand my folks.

Just yesterday my father shouted at me, "That's right — don't shut the screen door. Let the bugs in. Kid, if you can't close a screen door you won't get to Square One."

I felt like talking back, but didn't. I just latched the door and said, "Oh, I'm sorry."

I washed the dishes and hurried outside. I walked down to the state road drinking left-over coffee in an Orphan Annie mug. I stopped to smell the wild roses piled on our broken-down wire fence. Suddenly Miss Drake's big convertible hummed up the Clinton cut-off, its roof down. She saw me and stopped.

She said, "Is that Tommy Kingsland, I spy? Guzzling hot arbuckle as he saunters amidst the flora?"

Her voice loosened up something in me. I leaned against her car door. For a second I felt like Jack McGreggor who could joke with her almost like an equal.

"Arbuckle?" I said, holding the mug up to her face, "No, mam. This is Chase and Sanborn's *Stomach Buster Special.*"

She sniffed it. "Smells like Mexican arbuckle to me. At the ranch you dump in the mud. Boil it a couple of hours. Toss in a horseshoe. If the horseshoe floats, she's ready."

She gunned the car. She waved, her yellow hair flying.

I hollered, "I'll try that, Miss Drake!"

Joe Tutynski

Experimenting, I discovered that alcohol gave me about 40 minutes of normal life. I could feel the glow coming on after taking five strong swigs. My limbs stopped aching. The muscles seemed to grow in my snake-skinny right arm, deformed shoulder, and gimp leg until I had a body that matched my rugged left arm.

I'd crawl face-down on top of leaves I'd built into a mound. Hugging them I'd be a normal guy in my mind. Singing to myself. Laughing with a pretty girl. Walking. Running. Swimming at the beach. At last, dozing...

Then suddenly I'd wake up, breathing hard. It would seem as if I'd dozed only a moment.

But I'd find myself lying outside the cave. The sun was down. Hours had gone by.

That's why, on my next booze afternoon, I brought an old Big Ben clock and clamped my fist on it. When I woke up, stars were shining through the trees. And the radium dial told me I'd been blotto for four hours and 32 minutes.

Totally blacked out.

Jack McGreggor

Miss Drake treated me more and more like a grown-up. But I was careful not to get too chummy. Something told me she needed my give-and-take. But she couldn't let me too close.

She said, "Mr. and Mrs. Kingsland seemed a bit frosty when I visited."

I nodded. "Standard. But they'll warm up when they see the exhibit Tom did. You pointed him right."

She said, "I hope I didn't screw up on the poetry assignment. The nuts-and-bolts critics in town are hot for business letters and non-fiction."

I shrugged. "The class is glad we're doing something different."

By April she was probing me steadily about Joe Tutynski. What was his background? Why did he resist friendly approaches?

"We've tried a lot of stuff, Miss Drake."

"Nothing has worked?"

"Well, maybe the booze sessions up at Leatherman's will loosen him up."

"WHAT?"

I grinned. "That's news to you, Miss Drake? Joe's hitting the bottle. I see him weaving home Saturday nights."

"Good Lord, where's he getting the liquor?"

"He buys home brew up in Little Italy. Heavy stuff from Volenski's."

"Where's he getting the money?"

"Mostly he uses the dough he gets correcting school papers."

She blinked, banged her forehead with her hand. "Holy smoke!"

I couldn't help laughing.

She shook her finger at me. "There's nothing funny, Jack Mc-Greggor."

I left her sitting at her desk, tapping her yellow pencil on her blotter.

Elaine Bordan

Miss Drake got me to stay after school to rehearse my part in the *Golden Boy,* which was opening in New London week after next. It was my biggest chance. I started to read aloud, softening and hardening my voice in places—the way she showed me.

"Good...good," she said, "You're putting the bite in there. Now come down on the word *otherwise*. The emphasis needs to be—"

Suddenly she stopped. She looked out the window. She

pushed back her chair. "Golly, Elaine, I have to go."

At the door she paused. "We'll do this tomorrow. Read over the second act and try to modulate in the places I marked."

I watched her from the window. She hurried to her car, shoving her arm into her blue cashmere sweater. She fumbled with the ignition key, then pushed the starter. *Ga-rummmm.* As she pulled out the parking lot, I noticed a figure down on Route 1 weaving slowly over the cracked cement pavement toward the Clinton cut-off.

It was Joe Tutynski hitching along in his drag-foot way. He was weaving more than usual. All at once he tumbled, his cap falling off, his snake-skinny arm doubled under his waist. He was slowly pushing himself to a sitting position with his rugged left arm when Miss Drake stopped and got out.

They started talking. She tried to help him up. He yanked his arm away. I went back and sat down at her cluttered teacher's desk. *All right, Miss Drake. If you think more of Joe Tutynski—that drunken jerk—than you do of what I'm trying to do...well...*

I sat there, mad at her. I was doing what she said, making a new person out of myself. And she had just walked out on me.

Then I looked down at her blotter. It was ink-splattered and the edges turned up. I picked up a magnifying glass she'd bought to help Sibyl Noyes dissect a frog. Here was a note that said: *On the other hand, Jack, maybe there's something faster than the speed of light. Mankind conceives any distance instantly...*Here was a torn eraser, a bent paper clip, a stack of scribbled sheets marked *Hymie's humor stuff.* Books, papers, a pencil-sharpener shaped like the Woolworth building. Also a little plastic statue of Snow White lying feet-up on a pile of attendance cards.

I put my face in my hands. My awful thought about my special teacher flew away. I would never admit even to myself that I'd thought it. I saw that Miss Drake—touching all these dull school things—had blessed them with her goodness.

Jack McGreggor

Hymie Volenski's mean uncle had once been a professional fighter. In the early 20's he'd gotten as far as having his name listed in the *New York Daily News* under New Crop of Ring Hopefuls before getting finally flattened. He kept his hand in by punching Hymie.

It got so Miss Drake noticed Hymie's black eye or bruised cheek in class. She'd joke with him about the damage, thinking it was only teen roughneck stuff.

But one day she asked me: "Is somebody I don't know hanging those lamps on our budding Mark Twain?"

I said, "Hymie? His Uncle Ned belts him now and then."

"WHAT?"

"That's right. Once Doc Winters thought he had a broken rib. Hymie told him he'd done it falling off a stepladder."

Miss Drake tossed her pencil down on her desk. A little flash of red grew in her cheeks. "Mmm. Well, well..."

I saw my chance. I said that Volenski's was no good for West Stoddard. The store stocked everything from tobacco and rot-gut hooch to dirty pictures. It kept Hymie supplied with practical joke stuff like stink bombs and exploding cookies. If I was going to marry Holly and stay there I didn't want it around. But at 17, what could I do about it? Maybe Miss Drake could throw a punch?

She was frowning. "I want to show you something, Jack."

We walked out to her car in the school lot. On her seat she lifted a Scotch tartan robe and handed me an empty bottle. It was, a Four Roses fifth.

"I hiked up to Leatherman's on Sunday and found it outside the cave."

We both knew it was Joe's. I told her it had probably come from Volenski's

"I didn't know that store had a liquor license."

"It doesn't," I said, "But you could probably buy a sawed-off machine gun there if you wanted it. Volenski's is a bootleg holdover."

"Well, I never."

The following week Hymie stopped at the garage to pump up the tires on his bike.

He said, "Jesus, Jack, you should have seen Miss Drake in the store last Monday. She blew in like a cyclone. Hair flying. She pointed at Unk Ned's office. He walked in there like a kid about to get whacked. Staring down at his feet. She set an empty bottle on his desk. She paced back and forth, talking.

I was hammering a rim on a Mack wheel. "Yeah? What'd she say?"

"I couldn't hear. I was hiding in the Used Clothing aisle. But on her way out, I heard her crack, 'And I don't want to see one more bruise on your nephew—got that, Mr. Volenski?' Gees, I ought to bring her a box of grapefruit.

Eva Casserino

If my father had ever known I was sneaking down Friday nights to sing at the Bigelow jazz shack with Gene, Vince and Hymie, he'd have disowned me. Yes? A go-to-Mass Catholic girl belting out *Tiger Rag* in a smoky two-by-four room! With Jack and Tom and Fred Millay slapping their hands, chanting: "Hold that tiger!" *Wow.*

If he'd known how much I cared about Gene, he'd have *double* disowned me.

When I was soft-warbling *Stardust,* I'd look at Gene's strong, dark hands tapping the slow rhythm, his eyes closed, his powerful shoulders swaying in time. I'd think he belongs in some class outfit in New York or Chicago. Ellington, Dorsey, Calloway—an orchestra like that.

It was Miss Drake who had got us together. After she'd danced with Gene in front of everybody in the lunchroom, she talked to me.

"Eva, I hear you humming pop songs a lot. Ever try singing

with a band?"

"Gee, I'd love to. But..."

"I understand Gene Bigelow has a noisy little outfit. Let me put in a word."

Gene was naturally surprised. A bit nervous too, I guess. But that first Friday I performed in a jammed room and everybody clapped. After that he and I sometimes walked home together. We never even held hands. But we'd talk about the way Miss Drake was changing things.

He said, "Maybe the world you and I grow up in is going to be different, Eva."

I looked at his handsome, jutting jaw. "I hope so."

One summer night we finished a wild session at the shack and stopped for cokes at West Stoddard Drugs. We walked up Stannard Hill drinking from bottles. Gene turned and looked back down Route 1.

"Oh-oh, Eva, look at that."

Joe Tutynski was weaving in the center of the empty, star-lit road. Hitch-dragging along in his way—but more floppy than usual. He slipped. Sprawled.

"Wait here." said Gene.

He started for Joe. A car's lights swung down from North Road, and stopped with a squeal of tires. Joe got up and shook his heavy left fist at the car. In the white glare, his misshapen jaw bulged like a balloon. Gene halted. I came down and hooked my arm in his.

Joe was shouting at the headlights, "Ga-wannn...ga-wannn!"

A woman jumped out of the car. "Stop being ridiculous. Get in here."

It was Miss Drake. We recognized the rugged swing of her torso as she grabbed Joe's' good arm. She half-dragged him to her Packard.

"Naw...naw," he shouted.

But all at once he stopped objecting. She pushed him onto the wide seat. The big convertible took off. Garum-m-m-m. Its red taillights winked up North Road.

Gene and I looked down. We had unconsciously locked our hands together. It felt so good. We walked on—and didn't separate until we reached the big hedge outside my house.

Hymie Volenski

Eva was our best vocalist at the jazz shack. But Elaine Bordan could belt out a song, too. And she threw in torchy moves to go with it. Old Lady Wainwright was shocked at the way she danced and crooned *The Saxophone Hop* at school.

Well, she ought to have seen her at the shack doing: *It Must Be Jelly Cuz Jam Don't Shake Like That.*

Elaine Bordan

As I moved into acting under Miss Drake's guidance a funny thing happened—I grew smart.

I'd always thought of myself as harebrained. I hadn't read anything. My parents were drunks. I knew I was pretty—but that was the sum-total. I concentrated on having friendly sex with boys I liked.

When I started studying the theatre with books Miss Drake brought from Hartford Library I discovered I liked *all* books. I went from novels to biographies to histories. I became a speed-reader. And that brought me closer to Jack McGreggor.

Jack was set for Holly. We both knew that. In the past, it hadn't stopped us from having some good sessions together. But now we talked more. He gave me a paperback about Emily Dickinson's life. I swapped stories with him about the colonial founders of Old Saybrook.

One day he said, "Elaine, how about going up to Nathan Swamp with me? Maybe we can find something from the bog works."

Walking through the maple woods off the Clinton road, we

wondered what had finally happened to the Fenton brothers who had run the iron works in the Revolution. They had produced wagon wheels and cannon balls for Washington's army.

Jack said, "The legend is that Joshua and Abe Fenton had a fight over a girl."

"I read that, too."

"Abe joined the army. While he was gone Joshua stayed home with Abe's girl and ran the works."

We exchanged laughs. I said, "He ran the works all right."

We reached the coarse grass-spread where the swamp began. I poked around the stone ruins. Jack said he thought there must have been a shallow pit nearby.

"According to rumor, Abe came back and wrecked their home-made wooden pump, flooding the pit. Joshua went west with the girl."

We searched but found nothing. I picked up a small hunk of slag. The sun was hot, so we went on to Wright's Pond where the remains of some heavy wagon wheels lay 12 feet down. We stripped to our underwear and dove in. Together we swam over the shadowy wheels. I tried to tell myself that they must be originals from the Revolution. But when we both came up blowing bubbles, Jack shook his head.

"I used to think those were the real thing. But the water wouldn't protect them that long."

I said, "Are you sure? Miss Drake said marine companies purposely sink barges to preserve them to use later on."

"Well Elaine, we're talking over 150 years here...."

It was a good time. We sat in the sun, drying. Jack said that the cemetery showed 46 guys had fought in the Revolution and War of 1812.

"The women stayed and ran the farms," I said, "How the deuce did they do it?"

We talked about books. We talked about plays and movies.

Finally we put on our outer clothes. Then we looked at each other and laughed. A year ago we would have tangled in the clover before this.

Jack gave a smile—kind of sheepish. "Well, it's just like the newsreel says, Elaine. Time Marches On."

Tommy Kingsland

Miss Drake told us to write something about home...something we liked about it. So I wrote NIGHT SOUNDS. It was about my favorite hours in our old falling-down house.

Those were times after I was in bed in the unheated cubicle above my mother and father's bedroom. I'd hear a freight train starting up on the Old Saybrook sidetrack *chug-chug-chug*, then *skiiiiik* as the wheels skidded on the ice-coated rails. Finally the *chug-chug-chug* would grow constant. The train would rumble through West Stoddard heading for New York. In early morning the *pum,pum,pum* of fishing boats heading down Algonquin River to the still-dark Sound would kick in. then the *garum-garum* of a Greyhound bus would grow and quickly die on Route 1.

If it was raining I'd hear the soft *ping-ping* of a roof leak dropping on the maple-stained orange crate I used for a bureau. After awhile a couple of other leaks would make *flap-flap-flap* sounds on my ancient quilt. I'd have to pull my feet up so they wouldn't get wet.

Miss Drake read the theme aloud. "This is a perfect example of what we're after—personalized detail. Nice work Tommy."

I brought the paper home marked A+ ☺ *top job—Drake*.

Mother said, "Why didn't you erase the smudges on page two?"

My father slammed down the afternoon *Register*. "Great! Now the whole town knows the Kingsland roof leaks. All right, young man, you're going to get up there and fix it."

He bought a roll of tarpaper at Volenski's. I hauled it up on the roof. I had never realized how high our Colonial peak was. I looked down on roofs and winding driveways. The

Congregational steeple seemed about level with my eye. I inched the tarpaper toward the north end.

"Watch you don't drop the hammer. Don't break more shingles. Cover them cracks good now," my father shouted from the ground.

I tried. But the shingles were moldy. I slipped on them, broke off pieces. The nail box tipped over.

My father yelled, "Watch it...watch it. Good God, if you don't learn to handle a hammer you'll never amount to nuthing."

I hitched myself over to where I thought the leak was. At the end of the ridge, I looked down. Suddenly the ground seemed far away—way, way down. Our cat walked by down there, small as a mouse. I stared, kind of fascinated. I felt myself leaning over... over.

"Look out, look out!" roared my father.

Miss Drake...Miss Drake. You tucked me into your own bed...with your own pillow...

I felt myself falling, then everything exploded in colors of red, violet, and splintery yellow.

Vince Bigelow

By the time they got Tommy to Hartford Hospital he was dead. He was buried up in Blackthorn Cemetery. The whole class attended. Gene and I volunteered to be pallbearers. But the Kingslands didn't want that.

"Thomas Meade Kingsland will be carried by his own," Mrs. Kingsland said.

We offered because my brother and I had come to like the guy. He'd come down to our jam sessions and sit there grinning, tapping his feet. Sometimes he'd sing scat. Gene had loaned him an old sax and started to show him how to make it howl.

Miss Drake talked to us, her face showing only calm and quiet. "Grief must run its course. We're all having it right now. Let's accept it like an old acquaintance who will warm us awhile, then wave goodby. Sooner or later we'll turn back to our duties here. Keep in mind that's the way Tommy would have expected us to do."

Elaine and Holly made a wreath out of evergreens and gold colored wire. We all signed a card attached to it. Jack placed it up in the cemetery and sprinkled grass seed on the fresh mound.

A few days later he found it dumped over the Blackthorn stone wall. In its place was a tarnished silver-plate vase, monogrammed with a K and stuffed with artificial flowers.

"Well, the Kingsland's are squeaky high-tone," said Jack, "They're big vase people."

Gene said, "I'm thinking we-all was more buddies to ol Tommy than his own folks."

"You can bet your sweet ass on that. His old man and old lady never knew what they had."

A month later Miss Drake talked about grief in a way that got us wondering about her past in California. She was sitting in homeroom, tapping the eraser end of a pencil on her knee.

"Sorrow. Mmm...sorrow. Well, now we all know what it is. When it first hits, you think the sun will never shine again. But it does. You think you can never laugh and shout like you could before. But you will."

She looked out the window, her eyes squinting as if she was trying to make out something in the distance.

"You go back to what you were," she murmured, "Yes, you do."

Suddenly she sat up, poking the pencil behind her ear. She grinned and gave a little yelp. "Okay-y-y, Hymie, let's have that demented theme of yours. The title, folks, is How To Beat The Depression. Front and center, author."

Hymie Volenski

You beat the Depression by being funny. I told Jack that once I got lost in the woods. I fired three shots in the air—but nobody found me. He said I was supposed to keep doing it so rescuers could spot my position. I said I did.

"I kept firing. But ran out of arrows."

He stared. Then laughed and whacked me on the head.

Miss Drake helped me without knowing it—because she just naturally played along when we talked. One time in conference I mentioned a paperback I wanted to report on.

"What sort of book is it?" she said.

"A sort of book-like book," I said, "Very booky."

She closed one eye and squinted with the other. "Just one page after another?"

"You got it."

"What's the title?"

"Don't Kick Cow Chips on a Hot Day."

"Mmm. Will Rogers?"

"Yeah. Or I'll do his other one: *Never Slap a Man Who's Chewing Tobacco.*"

She half-smiled. "You might consider: *A Student Too Big for his Britches will be Exposed in the End.*"

We both laughed.

In my speech I said to be funny you have to see the ridiculous in the ordinary. Once I accidentally sewed the only shirt I had to a curtain while repairing it in a chair by the window. I started to put it on and ri-i-i-ip—the whole curtain came down on me.

At first I was sore. Then I told myself my brains were in dead storage. When my mind wandered I just went along. If I had more sense I'd be a half-wit. I awarded myself an M.D. degree—Mentally Deficient.

I said all this in my class presentation. And added a lot of jokes from magazines. I got everybody laughing.

Miss Drake's comment on my written notes was "This is

your best work, Hymie. Outline good. Delivery lively. Maybe you should think of a newspaper career. Humorous commentary is in demand in this glum old world.

"Correct the three misspellings I've marked. 😊 *—Drake"*

Sibyl Noyes

Wolson's Food Wagon parked every Saturday on Horse Hill road. It was an old orange school bus with a row of dented cans and dry vegetables inside. Mr. Wolson sold powdered milk in envelopes, coffee beans by the cup, soap flakes by the brown bag, sugar by the glass-full—and anything else you had to have to exist until he came again. Junk stuff at rock-bottom prices.

I owed him 87 cents because I'd been stupid enough to charge a box of Rinso last time. I said, "Mr. Wolson, I can't pay for that soap yet. My father gave me five dollars for the week."

He said, "So? You know the rules. That 87 cents doubles up. It's now $1.74. Let it go another week and it's $3.48."

I started to shake inside. But I shouted, "All right, I'll give you the 87 now. That leaves me $4.13 to spend today. Give me a bag."

"Just a minute young lady. You have $3.26 credit today—no more."

I was scared but started down the aisle. "I'm taking $4.13 worth, Mr. Wolson."

He blocked my way. "Leave the Food Wagon, young lady."

I snatched my five dollar bill from the dashboard counter. I ran home. I told my father we'd have to eat pears from our tree for awhile.

"Why? I give you five whole dollars. What you do? Spend it already?"

"Oh!" I tried to explain. If I shopped at the A&P we could get food for only one week.

"What'sa matter with the Food Wagon?" he hollered, "Since

when we trade at high-cost A&P?"

"Oh!"

I went out, slamming our broken screen door. I couldn't tell him about my Rinso purchase...how I'd *had* to wash my hair and clothes because I was starting to smell bad in school. I ran into Elaine and blurted the whole story. I couldn't stop crying.

She got mad, "That stinker Wolson! Wait till Miss Drake hears about this."

Elaine Bordan

"Why, that's usury," said Miss Drake.

"That's *what*?" I said.

"Look it up, Elaine. I'll get out of this bathing suit."

As she dressed in the bathroom I thumbed her big Webster's dictionary. I found that usury meant an *exorbitant rate or amount of interest*.

Driving to the garage she told me this Mister Wolson could be arrested for what he was doing to Sybil. But she wanted to check a few points with Jack. He always seemed to be on top of things like this.

"Yeah," said Jack as he worked on a GMC truck motor in the garage lot. "Wolson's a cheat. But he feeds a lot of people with his scrape-up food business. He has to fight for pennies."

"But for heaven's sake, Jack! He's illegally gouging Sybil," said Miss Drake.

Jack tossed a wrench in his toolbox. "He's illegal all right. Still, at the moment, the town needs him."

Miss Drake stiffened her back. "Well I never!"

Jack grinned. "However, yesterday I rebuilt his muffler. I haven't written up the bill yet."

A week later he told me how he had handed Wolson a bill for $5.87 for the repairs.

Wolson had blown up. "You told me five bucks! What the hell's this 87 cents?"

Jack had said, "That's the 87 cents I'm going to rub off your bill after you rub the 87 cents off Sybil Noyes's."

Jack McGreggor

By mid-November I realized there was a certain recklessness about Miss Drake. I found out she had climbed the Old Saybrook bridge with Hymie. I'd witnessed her wild jitterbugging at the West Beach Rink.

But I liked the way she mulled things over, then didn't back off from any tough action if she thought she was right.

So she and I grew even closer. She talked to me almost as if I was another teacher, a guy who understood the way she operated.

She said, "Jack, what are we going to do about Joe Tutynski? He's the only one in the whole class not working on a project. I started him on a study of Long Island Sound. But now he seems to scorn it."

"I say boil him in oil. Shoot him."

"Shame on you. This is no joke."

"I could add up a dozen times we've tried to get to him. He's the clam that won't open."

She turned, her swivel chair creaking. Outside the window, the town's one rickety orange school bus was moving out. A crow flashed by, cawing. She took off her glasses and stared at the Congregational steeple.

"Out West we don't leave a balky sheep beyond the fence. I'll think of something."

Elvira Wainwright

One evening I ran into Miss Drake dining alone at the Chowder Pot in Hartford. She was wearing earrings that looked like diamonds—a bit much for West Stoddard, I thought.

But then I saw she was correcting student papers. Jabbing

her yellow pencil over the pile as she ate with the other hand. I was about to go to her table and say something pleasant when I noticed her pour amber liquid from a Budweiser bottle into a pilsner.

I gave a polite wave and found a seat at the buffet.

Fred Millay

When I could get my mind off Elaine Bordan, I worked on the project Miss Drake had talked me into—A History of West Stoddard. I dug into records at the town hall. I roamed back roads. I found out that Ezekiel Stannard had set up a company in 1697 to extract salt from the Sound. Joshua Kingsland had murdered his wife and neighbor Abraham Coe with an axe in 1703—and was hanged on the village green. Jonathan Griffin had come home from the French and Indian War in 1762 and built a schooner to trade in the West Indies. He'd piled up a fortune in cod and molasses. He'd delivered West Indian slaves to South Carolina.

Miss Drake sometimes found me after school at the library with notes scattered over the Reference Room table. She'd pinch my shoulder.

"What's doing, historian?"

"Here's what," I said, sliding a pile of notes under her eyes, "The Griffin saga: Major Ethan Griffin wounded at Saratoga, 1777. George Dibble Griffin elected Governor of Connecticut, 1803. Brigadier General Ely Griffin killed outside Atlanta, 1864. Griffins all over the place."

She examined the notes. "Mmm."

I told her that the family mansion was that big pile of granite you could see beyond Toby Hill on an elevation named Saratoga Rock. It had a greenhouse on the roof. Each generation had added something to the property—horse barn...bridle paths... tennis courts.

"A generational showplace?"

"Yeah. Closed up now. They sailed high—until the money ran out. Griffin Leather Belt made it easy. Clay Griffin was the last one. He took off in 1931. Owing everybody, people said. My father was his lawyer."

She lifted an eyebrow. "Did you ever see him?"

"Once. He came into dad's office, dumped a handful of jewelry on the desk, and left carrying a tennis racket."

She walked to the window. "What did he look like?"

I shuffled my papers into rough order. Miss Drake swung around so her curvy back in a white cashmere sweater and blonde mane of hair was all I could see.

I said, "Big guy. Built lean and rugged. I remember he stooped to tie his shoe. His red hair fell over his eye. He patted me on the head and walked out."

Miss Drake turned to the stacks. "Well, I'm glad the project is coming along."

I left early. Outside I ran into Joe Tutynski, hitching up the library steps in his crab-like way. He was swinging a book to keep his balance.

"Queen Bullshit in there?" he said.

Jack McGreggor

Miss Drake had two ways of talking—King's English to town grownups, West Coast swing to us. She was mindful not to mix them together at meetings or church suppers. So the old folks of West Stoddard never got to know her like we did.

She said, "Jack, I asked Mr. Chapman to let you service my bomb from now on. The ignition's scratchy. Also I think something's whacked out in the carburetor."

I opened the hood. I tightened a loose wire hooked to her supercharger. She watched a few minutes, then hitched up her briefcase and walked off.

"Road check her, okay? I'll be back in a couple of hours."

Thirty minutes later I gunned the big Packard up North Road.

I stopped at the cemetery and worked the automatic top, up and down. I punched on the radio. Baby! This boat had *two* speakers on both sides of the dashboard. Music floated out, strong and clear.

I got out and walked around the car twice. I slid underneath and felt her oversize axle housing...her double-barrel mufflers. No heap this fancy had tooled around West Stoddard since the last Pierce-Arrow of the Griffins in 1931.

For ten minutes I sat on the heavy cowhide seats. I listened to the low growl of the engine, smooth from the new spark-plugs I'd put in. I stared through the curved windshield's thick glass at tiny sailboats on the Sound.

Then I started back and saw Holly walking from Doane's Woods, her arms full of flowers.

"I don't usually stop for good-looking skirts stealing gold-enrod."

She got in. "I don't usually ride with strange men swiping high-powered convertibles."

I turned up the Stevenstown road where the state had put in a wide asphalt highway. I punched the accelerator. The car leaped.

"Jack, where are you going?"

"Canada. We can get five thousand for this clunker. Hold tight, Holly."

"*Jack!*"

We reached the straightaway. I pushed the car to 80. Then 85. It seemed we were flowing. Smooth...smooth. Then I slowed down, listening to the purr of the quietest power-machine I'd ever heard.

"Come up for air, Holly. I'm just road-testing for Miss Drake."

She made a pretty O with her lips. "Well...thank heavens."

We cruised all over town, then headed for the garage. We both clicked on and off the radio...tried the recessed door lights...pushed the pearl-topped button that started a soft hum of air conditioning.

I said, "This is the kind of boat I'll drive you to our wedding in, Holly. You'll wear diamonds and high silk heels."

"I'll have to pawn my school ring."

"It'll probably be a Deusenburg. Straight twelve. With twin superchargers."

"Vases for flowers in back?"

"White wall tires...double fog lights..."

We turned onto Route 1. A 1928 Studebaker was parked beyond the curbing, one rear wheel lying flat beside a rusty jack. Two kids about our age sat on the grass. I pulled up.

"Need a hand, guys?" I said.

They looked at the Packard. The taller guy in overalls said, "Yeah, tell your old man to buy us a new convertible."

It wasn't friendly. The guys stared at Holly holding her goldenrod. The smaller guy laughed.

"You got a spare wheel in that ocean liner, rich boy?"

My impulse was to get out. And ask just what did that mean? But I felt Holly's hand on my arm.

"Let's go, Jack."

I gunned the engine. A voice followed us, "We'll make out okay, rich kids."

I drove Holly home to Stannard Hill. I dropped the Packard off at the garage. Then I slid into the seat of my Model A, and hit the starter. She kicked off, rattle-bang. At my house, I rubbed an oil cloth on my scratched dashboard. It was going to be a long time before that Deusenburg.

And now I didn't know if I wanted a jewel box like that anyhow.

Fred Millay

By June some of us were worried that Miss Drake might not come back next year.

Hymie said, "She's heading out. She's had it with West Stoddard."

Eva Casserino said. "If she leaves, I'm gone. I'll hitch to New

York and sing in a band."

She had got us going in directions we'd never thought of before. Hymie was editing a mimeographed school paper...Eva singing on weekends with the Hartford Sax Boys...Elaine acting in County Players. I was in my father's office sneaking up on a law career. Miss Drake had pushed all of us except Joe Tutynski into some kind of action.

One day my father got me to drive our Buick Roadmaster up to the old Griffin mansion to pick up some papers. I took Elaine along for company (hoping for more, also). We turned in the pot-holed drive, past broken trees, up to the granite big house with its jutting porte co-chere.

"Hello, ruin," I said. As a kid I'd romped on the velvet (now shaggy) lawns here. Picked flowers in the formal greenhouse. I'd jounced on a pogo-stick under the red awning (now in tatters) that had stretched from the doorway to the crushed-stone drive. Sometimes I'd played in Colonel Griffin's Pierce Arrow parked nearby.

Elaine was wide-eyed. "This is me, Elaine Bordan, folks. I'm twinkling my ring-finger at the maids. I'm nodding to the gardener."

I turned the bronze key in the heavy lock. Elaine patted her smooth hip. She dipped her shoulder gracefully. She eased into the oak-paneled vestibule, her arm extended.

"How do you do, Mrs. Griffin," she said "May I see your pile of money please?"

The living room was huge. Its chairs and sofas were covered with white, protective cloths, fitted precisely. This morning at breakfast my father had shaken his head. "That boy should have done something. The roof needs attention."

"What could Clay have done?" said my mother, "He's in the military. He was a good lad—no matter what they say."

"Good at sprinkling money around. Unfortunately All-American doesn't pay a salary."

I went into the downstairs office and opened a file cabinet. I lifted out a locked strongbox marked Deeds in red crayon.

"First lesson of law," I said, "Never keep documents where they can be stolen. Mama Griffin should have turned this box over to Millay and Paton long ago."

Elaine was lifting some large photographs out of a cabinet. "O pooh to Millay and Paton."

The pictures were backed with expensive poster board. They went back to the 1900's. Here was H. Sherwood Griffin, President, holding a shovel of dirt at a ground-breaking for a factory extension in 1906...Matilda Griffin, grandmother, bouncing a fat baby in a two horse carriage with a uniformed driver....

"Fred, look."

Elaine was staring at a 12" by 14" photo. A rugged handsome boy in a football uniform was holding a girl up high with one arm. Her hands were pressed into his palm, her arms straight. Her hair was blown, her plain skirt curling over her knees.

It was Miss Drake.

The same squarish, laughing grin...the same image of energy untamed. Her body looked more limber...more young-girl-ish. But her tapered calves, hanging in mid-air, hinted at the strength we were used to when she strode into the classroom.

"Who's the guy?" whispered Elaine.

"It's Clay Griffin."

"Where is he now."

"Who knows? He joined the Foreign Legion in 1931. I guess Miss Drake was his girl. One of 'em."

She looked at the picture a long time. Then she tucked it back gently in the cabinet. "Does he ever come home?"

I shrugged. "Somebody said he got hit in Spain. Maybe he's dead."

"Oh, how awful."

She got up. I put my arms around her. I felt her full thighs against my leg. I slipped my hand up under her blouse. That sweetness I could never resist started to build in my body. Elaine, baby....

She pushed me away. "I want to do something for Miss Drake," she said.

Jack McGreggor

Elaine told me she wanted to do something good for Miss Drake. I said I got just the ticket—a ride on an old West Stoddard rum-runner's boat.

My Uncle Terry's battered fishing boat belonged to me. I'd given him $25 for it after he got out of prison and turned to truck farming. I kept it at the abandoned wharf up Baylor Creek. I tinkered with the super-charged engine—just to see how it worked.

Miss Drake was delighted. "Mmm. Should I bring my sawed-off shotgun?"

She and Elaine climbed aboard. I had draped clean canvas over the half-rotted fantail. She was wearing her pale blue bathing suit, Elaine her red one. I tried to keep my eyes off them, but it was tough. Sitting there with their tan legs crossed, they were about the best-looking twosome this side of the Ziegfield Follies.

I said, "Hang on to the rail."

Ka-bank...Ka-bang...Ka-bang! We chugged into the Sound. Bright sunlight winked on low waves. The shore shrank away, tan and yellowish.

Miss Drake stretched in the warm, salt breeze. "Eeeeeeee—this is paradise."

Elaine came down to the engine pit where I was kneeling with an adjustable wrench. "Wow," she shouted above the thundering, "I didn't know fishing boats needed such big motors."

I shouted back, "This baby is a double-acting, four-stroke powerball, made by Harland & Wolff in Belfast, Ireland. Uncle Terry needed it all right. If he couldn't outrun the Coast Guard cutter he was a dead duck. A government sea plane finally nailed him."

She put her hands over her ears. "Noisy."

I shouted, "Noisy? Listen to this."

I pushed the throttle to full. KA-BANK...KA-BANG! The bow pointed up. Miss Drake steadied herself on the fantail,

166

her honey-glow hair flying. She laughed. We roared along the Sound.

"Whe-e-e-e!"

Right then I discovered my big mistake. First a chunk of the fantail broke off. Cra-a-ak-k-k-k. It bobbed in the wake. Then water began spouting up through my knees. Quickly I throttled down. The old boat lurched, digging in at the nose. Elaine and Miss Drake lost their balance. Miss Drake skidded and dove overboard.

She came up laughing. I idled the engine. With a strong crawl, she caught up and climbed aboard. She looked at water squirting in the pit.

"How's the life preserver situation?" she said.

I looked around the splintery deck. My throat went dry. I didn't have an ounce of cork—or anything else floatable. I looked at the shoreline. It seemed miles away. *If the Coast Guard saw this, they'd hang me up by the balls.*

Elaine grinned at me, wrinkling her nose. "Ahoy, Captain, What's your next bold move?"

"Mmm," said Miss Drake, "The Ocean seems to be coming in. You got a bailer, Jack?"

One rusty coffee can—that's what I had. I started bailing, cussing myself under my breath. The engine idled on. And we headed slowly for the beach.

Miss Drake was moving around the pit, splashing. She said, "Jack, the biggest intake seems to be a half inch above the exhaust. If we get our weight off right away, I'll bet the leak will rise above water level."

We all dropped overside, hanging onto the gunnels. Yard by crippled yard, the idling engine towed us toward Baylor Creek.

After 30 tense minutes, we made it. Climbing out at the dock, Miss Drake stretched.

"Let's see—did we deliver the rum?" she said.

Elaine said, "Some bailing, Jack. You looked like King Kong throwing coconuts."

Hymie Volenski

A month before Miss Drake went West for summer vacation, I had a scare on the town Green. I was tossing a baseball with Vince Bigelow in bright sunlight. All at once a dark shadow passed over us. High up, engines whined. The dirigible *Hindenburg*—huge, powerful looking—slid by, so low it seemed to brush the elms. The big swastika on its tail gleamed blood red above the Congregational steeple.

My stomach turned over. Our history class had zeroed in on horror stories from Nazi Germany.

Vince smacked the ball in his glove. "Maybe the bastard will blow up, Hymie."

And that night—May 6, 1937—it did.

The next day Miss Drake brought the *New York Times* to class with a picture of the *Hindenberg* falling in flames at Lakehurst, New Jersey.

"The world moves on," she said. "Sometimes justice is brutal."

Afterwards, Jack warned us not to spread that remark around. At the moment the U.S. was neutral, anti-war. "Some nosy sonofabitch who doesn't like her style will moan to the school board.

In spite of our caution, her bold opposition to dictatorships—German, Spanish, or any other—got out. And by the time she drove away, Jack suspected that someone was working to cancel her contract.

Through June, July and August Jack and I added up the good changes that had come since Miss Drake had been our teacher. They were our ammunition. If No Balls made any move against her, Jack said he was going to sound off all over town. I had started a school weekly. I was simmering down my joke-craziness. I was studying newspapers, and building a vocabulary—yah.

Jack was digging deeper into history. At the garage when he pumped gas people got used to seeing him reading a paperback.

Fred was buried in his old man's office, picking up points of law. He was always giving us constitutional razzmatazz—such as how the Supreme Court had just okayed the minimum 'wage for women. And it was going to revolutionize the workplace.

Eva Casserino was singing weekends with semi-name bands—The Providence Dixie Cats...Mel Bancroft's Shore Orchestra. She was putting her money in the bank for voice training. She was also sticking close to Elaine Bordan who was acting in summer productions.

Elaine was our star. In the past she'd been over-friendly to most of us guys (particularly Fred). But that only made us the more proud of her. Besides, everyone knew that Jack had set himself up as her protector. And he didn't take kindly to any wiseguy cracks. She hummed songs. Kidded around. Swished her sexy legs past our desks.

But when she was learning her lines or listening to Miss Drake's advice her doll's brow would be laced with little creases, her heart-shaped lips set tight.

By summer her laugh had become a soft, happy sound. It almost made you forget that grown men without jobs were hitchhiking through West Stoddard. And housewives were wearing dresses made from window drapes.

Geraldine Prue was cleaning beach houses, saving for college. Tony Tragonni was working on Hartford Bridge construction with a state engineer who Miss Drake had contacted. The Bigelow brothers had joined a debating club in New Haven. They practiced public speaking in the jazz shack. In August Vince stood up in the town meeting and asked the selectmen to give the school an athletic field.

Practically everyone in the class of 1938—except Joe—was into something. We haunted the library. Scribbled in notebooks. Prowled beaches and woods in search of new thoughts.

And summer raced by.

ᴏᴑᴑᴑᴑ

PART THREE
1937 – 1938

Eva Casserino

Miss Drake came back from California on Labor Day about two in the afternoon. It was raining hard. Mr. Chapman let us stand in the open garage with a big bouquet of yellow roses Holly and I had picked. Her snazzy Packard pulled up at the Texaco pump. She ran for shelter, tugging her trench coat collar up...skidding through the big door on one foot.

She shook water from her hair and said, "Quack, quack."

Then she glanced at each of us in that warm, golden way that made you think you were special. And kissed every guy and girl.

"Well, new Senior Class, what's been doing?"

Everybody chattered. Each time a kid laid out what he'd done, she shook her hands over her head like a winning prizefighter and said, "How to go."

Then she looked around and said, "Where's Joe Tutynski?"

Joe Tutynski

I was standing in the old Congregational carriage shed when Teach drove up to the garage. Rain was drumming through the splintered roof, wetting my face. Now and then I'd guzzle from the bottle I'd lifted from Volenski's. Good, 190-proof stuff.

Across Route 1, Teach ran from car to garage. The sheep fawned over her. Elaine Bordan scurried from the library through the downpour to hug her. Jack McGreggor pulled off

173

his work glove and grabbed her hand. Eva Casserino, Holly Millay and the others got into the act, yaking and laughing and grinning like assholes.

Teach played her part, talking to each. Now and then she'd lift her arms in the old boxer's high sign.

Get out of here, Tutynski, before you throw up.

I yanked down my blue leather cap and hitched myself out onto the Clinton road. The rain was easing to a heavy sprinkle. I headed for Leatherman's. I hugged the bottle under my belt. At the cave I crawled into dry leaves—drinking, sucking, licking the bottle. In the following two hours I drank myself into a sweet half-dream. No pain, no crooked limbs, no moose-jaw. Only me, a body of steel to match my mighty left arm.

Then—as was his custom—Luke appeared.

Luke the Leatherman was now my brother. He emerged along the back of the stone wall, sliding over cracks and moss. His lumpy shoulders were encased in a leather shirt. His thick legs wore leather trousers.

"How you doing, Luke?" I said.

His boots, sewed from stiff cowhide scuffed the rock floor. "Tolerable handsome, Joe."

"You got the life, Luke."

"Yeah. That likker good, Joe?"

"The best."

"Gimme a snort."

I hugged my bottle. "Nahh."

"Come on."

He made me sore. I waved the bottle at him. "You did *nada* to get this likker, Luke."

He began sliding along the wall. Everywhere I looked his thick face with holes for eyes stared back at me.

"Common, Joe. We're rummies,"

I tried to stand up. "I'm no rummy."

"The hell you're not."

I fumbled in the leaves for a stone. I hurled it at Luke. It bounced off his face. His leather shirt shook with laughter. "I'm still here, Joe. You're my rummy-buddy. You ain't gonna put me down.

I stumbled and fell. I got up. I flung stones at Luke. "I read books, hear? I got—"

Luke laughed. "You got me. And a cave in the woods."

I staggered around, scooping up stones, dirt, leaves. Heaving it at Luke. I crawled to the wall and beat his image with my fists. My fingers began to bleed. Luke didn't fade. He kept laughing and sliding along the stone.

"A cave in the woods...a cave in the woods..."

I slammed myself at him, head down. The stone wall exploded in colors of red, purple and blazing orange.

I woke up on my back in a pile of rotted branches 50 feet from the cave. Soaking wet. Night had fallen. Above the trees a white moon looked down—and grinned.

Tony Tragonni

Some guys would call Miss Drake sweet meat—with her nifty jugs and all—but we guys didn't think that way. Sometimes when she walked in, Fred Millay's eyes followed her swishy skirt all the way to her desk. But he never cracked wise.

Jack set her role: "She's this class's big sister."

I showed her my rickety, patched-up bike. She took a ride on it, leaning to left the way you had to—even peddling across the playground with no hands.

"And you built this down cellar—hurrah!" she said.

She took in a stray dog at Kelsey's Beach and named him Nebuchadnezzer. She taught Neb—a brown half-terrier with a pink nose to lie quietly under the blackboard in homeroom.

It was natural that when I had a scary experience up at Leatherman's I'd turn to her in a hurry.

I had gone up there on my bike to try out a slingshot I'd just made from pig bone. And to catch butterflies in a Shredded Wheat box for Geraldine. I pumped into the rough trail from the Clinton road, hauling my bike over the two brooks this side of the cave.

Joe Tutynski was lying face up at the entrance. He was drunk. Out cold. But his eyes were wide open, glazed over.

Jesus, he's dead!

I stuck my hand in his grimy shirt. No—the heart was beating. I tried to roll him onto his side. He was stiff as oak.

"Joe!" I said, "Joe...Joe!"

He made no sound. The eyes kept staring.

He's dying.

I pulled and lifted. I tried to get his good shoulder up. I kept talking and panting. He stayed rigid.

I don't know exactly when I decided to go for Miss Drake. I guess it was when I figured Joe was hardening to a corpse right in my hands. I peddled at high speed back to Mrs. Kelsey's. She wasn't there. I raced to school. Old Jake the janitor said she'd gone to the library. At the library she'd left for Middletown Players with Elaine Bordan 15 minutes ago.

Night fell. At home I tried to phone her. No luck. I went to bed chewing on the idea that I should call the police. But Joe hated cops. And if this was only another crazy binge for which he was growing famous, I'd be judged a rat.

In the morning I found Miss Drake, fresh as a flower in a pink dress, talking to Joe at her desk. He looked tough and mean as ever.

Geraldine Prue

Tony helped me nail in a wooden seat at the top of the giant oak in our wood lot that I liked to climb. Sitting up there I could see across the tree-tops his house in Little Italy, and Wright's Pond beyond. Looking the other way, I could watch freight trains stop on the New Haven Railroad siding to let passenger trains pass.

One afternoon I saw a train slow down and ragged figures jump out of boxcars. They stumbled and fell but got up. They vanished in the woods where the hobo camp was.

One small figure wore a skirt. O yes.

I sneaked over our hill. I saw about a dozen people around a fire. They were cooking something in a big tin can. The little girl was barefoot. Her dress was made out of brown cloth with letters on it—a fertilizer bag.

I gulped hard, then stepped out in the open.

"Hello," I said.

Bearded faces turned. The little girl ran to a bald, stooped man wearing faded overalls.

"Whatchoo want?" somebody said.

They were skinny—all of them. There was one grown woman wearing dirty dungarees. She walked to me.

"Yo-awl got any food, miss?"

They were hungry. I'd never seen hungry people before. I said, "I-I can get you some."

Somebody laughed in a rough, gurgling way. "Yo-awl do that, honey chile."

I ran home. It was the first time I'd heard a down-South drawl. These folks were out of a strange world. My parents weren't home, so I ransacked our refrigerator—hamburg, beets, carrots, everything. On the way out I grabbed a milk bottle and a loaf of bread.

When I reached the camp my arms gave out. I dropped the big paper bag. Everybody stared.

"Land a Goshen!"

The woman snatched the milk. The men peeled the vegetables with jackknives and dumped them in the can. A tall, smelly guy with a grease-streaked cap bowed to me. His voice was deep and slow.

"Gawd sent you, miss. We thank Him and you."

I had to tell my parents. Dad listened gravely, but said nothing. Mother simply crinkled her eyes, "You be careful, daughter."

The next day I saw three State Police cars drive by with those people inside. And Fat Augie gave us a speech:

"It's been reported that questionable elements stopping in town have been visited by somebody in your age group. One of these uninvited callers mentioned a girl."

He hooked his thumbs in his vest pockets—like he was speaking in town meeting. "I don't need to tell you that this sort of behavior is unladylike at the least. And dangerous at the most. If one of you is involved, I'd like that person to come to my office."

I was nervous. I told Jack what had happened and how I dreaded talking to Fat Augie about it.

He shrugged. "Don't go near the old goat. He'll give you that rape-murder-danger stuff." Then, tapping me on the shoulder, "Hey, you walked right in there with food?"

I said maybe I'd talk to Miss Drake. Because she'd understand.

"Don't do it, Geraldine. She'd have to give you the same stuff—the line about steering clear of tramps. You and I know she'd rather praise what you did."

Later in the week Miss Drake put her arm around me when I came to her desk. I think Jack told her the whole thing.

Jack McGreggor

One Saturday I picked up a blue Arabian rug at Sears Roebuck in Middletown for Miss Drake. Geraldine and I unrolled it in her living room and knocked over a maple coffee table by mistake.

I picked up a sprawling book. It had wide pages and a rawhide cover.

"That's her journal," said Geraldine, "She writes in it every day."

Joe Tutynski

After my discovery that liquor blocked out painful thoughts—then total blackout for hours—I did anything needed to get a bottle. I cleaned cars in the town parking lot. I corrected papers for Teach. Stealing was easy. I picked up coins at a grocery counter. I stole extra brew out of a Little Italy cellar when the old Wop owner was selling me a bottle.

I kept a supply up at Leatherman's hidden in the leaves. After school I'd go up there and drink.

I'd guzzle until everything got wild, misty, and whirling. The stone walls would pulsate. I'd roll in the leaves. I'd talk with Luke and float out of consciousness.

Usually I woke up around suppertime, my dungarees sticky around the crotch. Then I'd limp home to my old man who cooked oatmeal every night.

One afternoon I was heading up Clinton road to the cave when Teach stopped. Her dog Neb was sitting beside her.

"Get in," she said, swinging the Packard door open.

"Naw," I said.

"Come on, Joe. I'll take you home."

"Naw, naw, naw," I shouted, "I said naw."

I yanked myself away from the car. My short leg whipped out from under me. *Wham-m.* I hit hard, tasting the asphalt on my lips. I felt a sharp pain on my skinny snake-arm.

Then warm arms were lifting me. They were strong and soft at the same time. They smelled like Ivory soap. As I straightened up—my powerful left arm groping for balance—the full weight of her thigh pressed into my oversize hand. I tore myself loose and hop-limped to the trail entrance.

I turned and hollered, "I said naw, didn't I?"

Gene Bigelow

One cold day I went with Jack checking his traps. The first trap on the salt meadows behind West Beach had a chewed-off muskrat leg in it. The next two had nothing. The next, set in the marsh below Orsini's Hill, was missing. Its short chain hung down, still attached to a tree.

"A trap-jumper," growled Jack, "Some wiseguy is looking for a fat lip."

Four more traps were empty. We trudged on. Up a snow trail toward Essex...down the old Spencer Plain road. Both of us were tired and disgusted. Jack was mad.

"Now who'd steal a trap? Joe Tutynski maybe—if he could haul himself as far as Orsini's."

He said it in a tone I'd never heard—irritated. I was feeling a little sour myself.

I said, "You're nuts, Jack. Joe wouldn't do that."

He stopped. He looked at me, unsmiling "No? You don't know the bastard. You see how he lands on Holly in class?"

"That's just noise."

"He gets away with that stuff. He's riding his cripple-horse all the time."

"Well, he's got plenty of hurt all right."

We walked on. Then we got to the last trap and it was empty. Jack yanked it loose. He hung it over his shoulder.

"Everybody's got some hurt, Gene. A real guy rides with it. But that sonofabitch Tutynski, he—"

This didn't sound like Jack. He was a fair guy, always in control. But this time he was blowing off. He finally added he might pop Joe, no matter what.

I stopped, looking at him. "That's smart, you think?"

"Whadda *you* think?"

"I think Joe's dragging a tough red wagon. And you won't look good if you pop him."

We hiked on to Route 1, not talking. A kind of wall was rising between us. What did Jack know about the red wagon that

Vince and me had had to drag down South? If he'd had our experience maybe he'd understand Joe's red wagon.

We'd reached West Stoddard Center when Miss Drake's Packard pulled alongside, it's roof up. She beeped her horn and made motions in the window. Jack opened the passenger-side door.

"Thank heaven! Get in here, guys. Hold these kittens."

Four tiny black and white cats were crawling and mewing on the seat, the dashboard, in her lap. Jack and I slid in. We caught the squirmy little buggers. I put two inside my shirt. Jack tucked one in his coat pocket, held the other.

We drove to Mrs. Kelsey's. In her apartment she put down a saucer of milk. We sat there watching the little fur-balls drink, their spike tails sticking up. Neb sniffed at them but kept his distance.

I said, "What are you going to do with them, Miss Drake?"

She bit her lip prettily, then folded her hands under her chin. "Well, here's an idea...."

As it worked out, she talked each of us into taking two kittens. We had homes, didn't we? And every home needed mouse protection, didn't it?

"Besides," she added, "Look how cute they are."

In the end Jack and I were climbing into her car, holding sleeping little cats in two pink blankets. Miss Drake was giving us strategies to win over our families. "Why, we have six cats on our ranch at the Coast...."

Jack grinned at me. "Maybe Joe will take one up at the Leatherman's."

Jack was okay again.

Sibyl Noyes

Miss Drake could be tough. She once told me to stop griping about the other teachers and study harder. She gave Jack an F on a theme with six misspellings he dashed off sitting in his

Model A with Holly Millay. (Jack showed it to us with a laugh and said, "You guys still figure I'm teacher's pet?")

One afternoon when I was sorting books in the stock room down cellar, I heard her get tough with Joe Tutynski. Leaning near the hot air conduit to homeroom upstairs I caught every word:

"...disappointed at your attitude, Joe," she was saying, "You are letting obstructionism and pettiness interfere with what should be a time of glorious development. Why, your brain is capable of brilliance—I'm sure of it. But you insisted on hostile reactions to everything attempted in this class."

"Teach, you getting paid to stick your nose in my private methodology?"

"That's impudence. But yes, I am concerned with your life pattern, Joe. Particularly how you scorn *everyone* and *everything*. It's a negative approach that can deliver only misery in the end. Yes, *misery*. Now, come on. Take a positive slant. You've shown an interest in the human brain...its normal development...its distortions. Okay, I'm setting up an interview for you with...."

I heard a chair scrape back. Then the thump-thump as Joe slammed out of the room.

"Teach, what do you know about misery?" he shouted.

Later I passed homeroom door. Miss Drake was sitting silently at her desk, hands resting beside her yellow pencil on the blotter. She turned and smiled.

"Hello Sibyl," she said in a weary voice.

Hymie Volenski

The County Relief Carnival rumbled in one late afternoon in October. Three Mack trucks streaked with mud unloaded a Ferris wheel and merry-go-round behind the town hall. It took six heavy-muscled roustabouts only four hours to get the machinery up and working. By suppertime we had a brand new little village of lights, music, and game booths.

"No assignments for 24 hours!" said Miss Drake, "It's Carnival time!"

Her face was like the sun. For a few seconds we saw the girlish glow behind the schoolteacher. After supper, six of us piled into her car at Mrs. Kelsey's. We drove off singing and laughing. Neb was aboard, whining and wagging his tail.

Everybody was happy. Yah. But we were nervous, too. I had 15 cents. Sibyl had a dime. Even Jack had only two quarters. We weren't going to do much riding on the big wheel.

At the hall Miss Drake parked in a group of about 30 cars. She was backing into an open space when a carnival truck veered off the roadway and hit us. It slammed along the Packard's side from rear to headlight. *Sk-r-r-r-r-ik*, metal tore against metal.

"OH!"

Miss Drake thudded into me, her full chest flattening on my face. The girls shrieked.

"Anybody hurt?" shouted Jack.

We untangled our pile of arms and legs. Miss Drake got out. A man came running back from the truck.

"My God...my God," he was saying.

There were no injuries. It developed that the man owned the carnival. It was in bad shape financially. His steering wheel had been slipping and he hadn't fixed it yet.

"Now, I'm in a mess," he said, looking at the long scratch on the Packard, "My insurance payment is overdue."

Silence.

"Well, let's think about this a minute..." said Miss Drake, edging away from us.

For about five minutes she and the man conferred. Then she called Jack over to examine the damage. After awhile, she shook hands with the man.

She and Jack came back grinning.

"We didn't swap a nickel," she announced, "Jack can fix this for peanuts."

Jack said, "Less than peanuts, Miss Drake—five rides on the

Ferris wheel."

She gave a thumbs-up. "It's a deal. Here we go, folks."

The owner had been glad to give Miss Drake free tickets to everything for her crowd tonight. We rode the Ferris wheel and the merry-go-round till midnight.

On the way home Miss Drake sang Flat Foot Floogie with the rest of us. She said, "Wait till Fred Millay hears how we handled the legalities of the big wreck. Hymie, here's a scoop for your paper."

Elvira Wainwright

Heaven knows we wanted to welcome Miss Drake back. I told Virginia and Susan that perhaps a year of absorbing West Stoddard's ways was all she needed. We invited her to tea and maple cake at the faculty table.

She was charming. Telling us about horseback riding on her family's ranch last summer...visiting an art gallery in San Francisco. But then she got up, stretched with a kind of boyish arch of her arms and said, "I hear a carnival is coming to town. Hooray."

So when I learned later she'd had a wreck—with her fancy car full of students—I shook my head. I told Mr. Plimpton we veteran teachers were troubled about a junior colleague escorting the town's youngsters into harm's way.

He said he was thinking about the incident very carefully.

Jack McGreggor

On a warm October night the Griffin mansion caught fire. I was bobbing off Salt Island in my rum runner's boat—testing the Harland-Wolff engine I'd cut down to two cylinders in hopes of saving gas.

The flames billowed high over Saratoga Rock. They colored the clouds red and yellow. Around me small waves danced with reflections. Within 30 minutes the whole of West Stoddard looked like a flickering background for some Technicolor movie about the end of the world.

I raced for shore. The wails of fire engines drifted up and down the coast. The stink of smoke grew strong.

Just as I was turning into Baylor Creek my boat rammed a sandbar. For two hours I struggled to get loose—while the biggest estate in Middlesex County blazed down to a smoldering ruin.

Fred Millay

The night the mansion burned I was sleeping on our wide back porch. I woke up just as the church clock bonged once. Two miles away I saw strange lights dancing.

"Dad! The Griffin place is on fire."

We got there within minutes. The flames towered up, engulfing the Doric columns that lined the long verandah. They lapped at the upper French casements. The firemen wouldn't let us try to save anything. It seemed, like the whole town was pulling in, getting out of cars and staring. Some wore pajamas and bathrobes.

"There goes old Ethan's office room—Jesus."

"Plenty pay checks written in there, hey Bob?"

"Ooooo. Miz Griffin's greenhouse room is going...."

My father and I hung around long after the fire engines were gone. By morning the deserted property still smoked. But we hoped to find something of sentimental value to save for Mrs. Griffin.

"I owe that family a lot," said my father, "Old Ethan paid my first year in law school."

I poked around the ruins. Picked up a couple of athletic loving cups, still warm, smudged beyond recognition. I walked around back. The limestone terrace—where gleaming Cadillacs and Rolls Royces had once parked—was littered with glass.

"Fire is the silent language of a star, Fred," said a familiar voice.

Miss Drake was perched on a stone pedestal in what was once the formal Griffin garden, now choked with weeds. She wore dungarees and a rawhide Western shirt. I walked over to her.

"You said something there, Miss Drake. Looks like the mansion got bombed by an asteroid."

She got down and examined the loving cups I'd found. "I didn't say it —Conrad Aiken did. Hey, do you suppose young Clay won these trophies?"

"Probably. He was some athlete."

We talked awhile. And walked around the devastated place. It wasn't until after my father called me and we drove home that I realized she still had the cups.

Eva Casserino

Like everybody else, I poked around the Griffin mansion ruins hoping to find something worth keeping. I picked up a charred iron kitchen ladle and a water-soaked book: *Tom Sawyer's Electric Rifle*. I was walking out the big stone gate when Miss Drake drove in.

"Mr. Millay said it's all right to take from the trash pile," I said.

She nodded. "I'm here to look too."

She examined the book. Suddenly her eyes widened. She sat down on the stone wall, staring at the title page.

"See this, Eva."

A boy's crinkly signature was written there—*Clayton Griffin*—*from Mama, Xmas 1921*. She stared at it. A kind of blush reddened her pretty cheek. All at once I got the strange feeling that she wanted that crummy book.

"W-Would you like to have it, Miss Drake?"

"Oh, no."

"Please, take—"

"No," she said, "No, no, no—but thanks very much."

Jack McGreggor

I was swimming with Holly Millay at Chapman Beach when she stepped on a clamshell and cut her foot. It wasn't much. But it gave me a chance to carry her up onto the big Millay lawn overlooking Salt Island. We flopped down on warm, trimmed grass. I wrapped her foot in her Girl Scout towel.

I'd been in love with Holly since 6th grade. But I wasn't sure she knew it.

I said, "Well, it sure is nice to recline on my ancient family property."

She opened one pretty eye. "How's that again, Jack?"

I told her that my great, great, great, great grandfather Silas McGreggor had owned the 900 acres from West Beach to Chalker Inlet. The spread included the present Millay estate. And four others on either side.

"Why, Jack McGreggor!"

I knew she was wondering what could have happened to push my ancestors out? We McGreggor's were now reduced to a rented Cape Cod three miles beyond Leatherman's.

"Couple of forebears in love with the bottle," I explained, "That's all you need."

"Gosh."

I told her that in the 17th century only farmers had owned this stretch, for fishing and seaweed fertilizer. Then tiny cottages had appeared. Then huge ugly Victorian mansions with winding porches. The rich newcomers hired Italian immigrants to build breakwaters and bulkheads.

Then the Italian masons had started buying in at both edges of the 900-acre stretch. They built ugly frame houses. Packed close together. Summer nights grew noisy with relatives swimming and singing. The old Victorians looked on in horror.

"Back in 1886 an old Army Colonel, Jonathan Crownin-shield, tried to get an ordinance forbidding more sale of the original acreage. It didn't work. But he kept a vacant lot between his property and the interlopers. The old townsfolk approved. They said Crowninshield was holding the line...holding the line...."

Holly frowned. "What was so horrible about the Italians?"

"Well, for one thing they built better masonry walls for themselves than they did for the Victorians. And they put broken bottles along the top of the barriers—to keep the rich and everybody else out. How sassy can you get?"

She opened the towel and examined her foot. "And now—Lord help us—the sassy Millays are here. Grabbing and holding the line."

I tossed a clover head into her lap. "But you won't win. Here come the sassy New Yorkers. This morning I saw a rooms-for-rent sign on the house two doors down from you.

We grinned at each other. She shrugged.

A moment later I pointed over her shoulder. "And now, for crying out loud—look who's horning in.

Down on the sand, Miss Drake had appeared in her curvy blue bathing suit. Hitching along beside her, dragging with every step, came Joe Tutynski. He wore his usual dirty dungarees and oversize shirt. His monstrous misshapen jaw was set in a scowl. And his snake-thin right arm dangled like a rope.

Holly started to get up. I pulled her behind a rhododendron bush. "Wait."

As we looked, Miss Drake swam out and began to dive repeatedly. Joe sat in the sand staring at Salt Island.

"What's she looking for?" Holly said.

Miss Drake came up, waving a large conical shell. She brought it to Joe, then went back. For the next 20 minutes we watched her bring objects from the water. Clam shells...a clump of seaweed...a rusty oarlock. Finally she hauled in a small brass lantern, corroded green, its glass broken. She handed it to Joe. Her excited voice floated up to us.

188

"How about that, Joe—straight from Neptune's Used Furniture!"

He dropped the lantern in the row of items. He spat into the sand. His voice reached up to us—like gravel on a shovel.

"What am I supposed to do with this crap?"

Tony Tragonni

Miss Drake got me to help her dig out an old metal frame she and Joe had found in the marsh behind West Beach. It was rusty and crumbling.

"This looks like a binnacle from a sailing ship," she said, "An old West Indies trader, I bet."

Joe watched, his deformed jaw bulging. His mouth had a sour downturn, as usual. But his eyes glittered. You never knew when he was going to let go some crack that told he was wise to everything in the world. And you were stupid not to understand everything too.

I was scared of him—in spite of his weak shuffling walk. He threw an insult like a punch. And you always wondered what he could do with that out-size, powerful left arm if he found a way to throw it without falling down.

"Not West Indies," he said, "That's nothing but an iron rack to hold crab scoops."

I kept digging. Miss Drake scraped mud from the frame. Her blue bathing suit was dirt-streaked.

"It looks like a frame to hold an ocean-going compass, wouldn't you say, Tone?" she said, running her finger along the exposed top.

Joe spat on the ground. "You got junk. It's a scoop rack built in somebody's back yard. It never got beyond the mud flats."

Miss Drake straightened. She paused a minute, then grinned.

"Okay, record it in our Function Unknown file, Joe."

She motioned me to stop digging. I got thinking why am I

doing this for that crazy cripple anyhow? He's stealing wine from my relatives up in Little Italy. He doesn't like anybody. He'll soon be a champion boozer.

Then I saw her smiling at Joe the same friendly way she gave to all of us. I scraped off my shovel, watching her move around the sunny, sweet-scented marsh. Her hair was gold and swaying. She started drinking in the salt air, her arms stretched toward the clouds—like one of those razzle-dazzle actresses in Hollywood.

"Wow, what weather," she said.

I said to myself: *I'm doing it because Miss Drake asked me to, that's why.*

"Tony, Joe. Look at this!"

She was on her knees beside a little hollow. Near its center a small mass of flowers with velvety purple leaves shone in the dull marsh grass. She lifted one leaf gently.

"Dwarf morning glories, I think," she whispered, "Rare—and far from where they should be."

I saw Joe turn away, dragging his short leg.

Holly Millay

Mom, Dad and Fred were gone, visiting Harvard, so I ate supper alone. Afterwards I waded out to Salt Island to look for marine mussels. But about sundown a monster storm rolled in from Long Island.

The wind screamed. The waves turned white. When the first spatter hit my cheek I hurried back to the beach. Halfway there, I turned around. On the island's highest level a humped figure was standing, one arm clamped to a small, twisted tree.

It was Joe Tutynski.

What was he doing here? How had he dragged himself up the steep slope without me seeing him? Then I saw him quiver and shake his deformed arm at the sky. He began to shout. His moose jaw strained like a crazy animal. All I could hear was a faint yahhhhhhh.

Well, he looked mad. He was yelling at the lightning flashes getting closer...at the spray starting to rise from the sea boulders. It was like he was daring the storm to hit him.

When I reached our porch I got Mom's binoculars and examined him again. He was still clinging to the tree, waving an arm. I thought: In five minutes he'll be in real danger. *What do I care?*

I turned the pages of an American Girl magazine. Rain drummed down. Lightning streaked over the Sound. I went back on the porch and lifted the binocs again. Joe was still there. Waving his arms. Sagging a bit.

What do I care?

At that moment the electricity blinked off. The house went pitch dark. The wind wailed higher. Something in my head said: call somebody. I fumbled to the phone in the kitchen.

"Miss Drake..."

In less than ten minutes the Packard's headlights bounced up the driveway.

"Where is he, Holly?"

I rode with her down to the beach. She parked the car so the lights pointed at Salt Island. Joe was in the water. Splashing, falling, getting up, hitch-limping toward shore. Miss Drake strode into waves growing higher and wilder. She grabbed his shoulder.

"Good heavens, Joe!"

He shook off her arm. He dragged himself out on the beach. In the headlights he gave both me and Miss Drake a bitter, scornful look.

"You afraid of a goddam storm? "he yelled.

Jack McGreggor

I stopped at Mrs. Kelsey's to show Miss Drake my new, secondhand tires on the Model A. I found her down cellar doing her wash. She asked me to pick up Joe Tutynski's term paper at the library.

"The librarian spotted pages lying all over the place. Joe scribbled and left them. She wants them out."

It was Saturday afternoon. I picked up a big manila envelope marked: English Dept. West Stoddard High. Joe had been absent from school three days. Instead of going straight to Miss Drake I decided to sneak a glance at his work. I drove to West Beach and started reading.

The paper was titled, West Stoddard's World of Water:

The Long Island Sound, green and slimey, is nevertheless a liquid poem that sings to our homeland...

I read the whole thing. It practically knocked me cold. Joe had made the Sound an object of high interest and beauty—in fact, the crowning symbol of West Stoddard. For nine pages he described the ships, ancient and modern, that had plied with cargoes and passengers. He described bald eagles that soared where the Connecticut River poured in. He used language unknown at West Stoddard High: "the crystal glitter of bestilled water: ... "the ramming hurricane waves that tore holes in the sea wall."

He went into fascinating detail about our historic fishing industry. He mentioned offbeat facts like the transparent larval eels found off New London...the floating kelp from the Sargasso Sea.

I reached the last page, my head ringing. Expressions like "the molten red-radiance of salt marshes at dawn" and "the broken crockery of gray clouds marking Long Island's shoreline" weren't the kind of stuff we were used to in English IV.

He finished with: "If you hold a pink shell to your ear, you'll catch the tiny thunder of West Stoddard surf. It calls you home, no matter where you are."

Joe had written something beyond all of us.

I sat for several minutes, trying to readjust. Trying to get a new slant on this weird guy. He had put into words the love song that went naturally with our gorgeous waterway. This inksplotched term paper was going to change how we dealt with him. And was going to lift Miss Drake up on a cloud.

Then I read page 10:

All this, dear reader, is a monster lie. Long Island Sound is a stinking sewer...

He went on to sneer at everything he had written, the seascape of beauty he had described was actually a nightmare of splintered reflections that would pierce your eyes...the busy shipping activity had been a whirlpool of fraud and bankruptcy. The beaches were carriers of sea garbage and poisonous jellyfish.

The Sound—which everybody blathered so sweetly about—was actually a curse.

I got out and sat on my fender. I stared at the water. When Miss Drake started reading, her face would light up. She'd give little cries of delight. "Oh, listen to this, Jack!"

I got back behind the wheel. I tore page 10 into little pieces and tossed them down on the sand. I slid the nine good pages back in the manila envelope and delivered them to Miss Drake.

Joe Tutynski

After I'd scribbled off that pointless beach report—full of allusions to flashy sunsets, ancient shipping industry, temperature variations, historic uses of the West Beach littoral, *etcetera ad nauseam*—Teach tried to trap me into scientific study.

"Joe, you simply must not let native abilities you have in abundance go undeveloped. I'm signing you up for a new Yale program. It's a secondary school search for tomorrow's white-coat leaders."

"I don't like white coats."

"Oh, *please*—that's an expression. You simply must jump at the chance to work with high-rank professional science teachers."

"I don't like high-rank professional windbags either."

But she went ahead. Even got me a stipend of ten dollars a week for transportation expenses to and from New Haven. I didn't go to the sessions. I spent the money on liquor.

I was scrounging everywhere to support my bouts up at the cave. Twice a week I was gurgling into semi-consciousness...talking to Leatherman Luke as he came sliding in along the stone walls...finally blacking out for three hours.

The day the old Griffin mansion burned I was down to 78 cents.

I watched flames licking out of the big upper windows. The volunteer firemen went to work with hoses and axes. By the time they finished, the mansion was a giant stone skeleton. Heaps of charred stuff lay around. Broken furniture. Blackened books. After everybody was gone I found two sterling spoons in a pile of kitchen refuse.

Then in a collapsed bookcase I picked up a water-soaked, leather-bound book—Volume 18 of the Encyclopedia Britannica. It covered topics from "Plastics" to "Razin."

The next week, after trading the spoons for a bottle of Yellow Blitz at Volenski's, I read every item from "Plato" to "Primates." My mind raced on like a whirring motor—memorizing each page without effort.

Bored at last, I was beginning to fade out (muttering to Luke who sat in the wall staring at me) when my eye hit *Psychiatry: Treatment of Mental Disorder.* I blinked myself awake and read: *Included in this group are persons who exhibit extreme emotional instability, characterized by explosive outbursts of rage upon minor provocation...*

That night I didn't go home. I read until light was gone, then finished the whiskey. I did my hugging thing on the leafy mound and passed out.

The next two days I stayed at the cave. I read backward and forward in the half-burnt book—Psychiatry, Psychical Research, Psychoanalysis, Psychogalvanic Reflex, Psychology Abnormal, Psychotic Reactions. I zeroed in on Psychoneuroses: Schizophrenic Delusions.

For the first time I completely lost connection with the physical ogre I was. The mystery of the human brain—its lethal power to destroy or liberate—gripped my imagination.

I was eating cold beans from a can with my fingers, reading an anthology of D.H. Lawrence, C.G. Jung, Franz Kafka, and Sigmund Freud, when my old man, a State Trooper, and a woman in a trench coat came through the woods.

"There he is!" shouted my old man, "Jesus, I'm gonna bust your nose."

"Hold it now," said the Trooper.

The woman said, "Joe, are you okay?" It was Teach. She climbed over the big stones to where I sat.

"He's okay," hollered my old man, "But he ain't gonna be. Git down here, you goddam freak."

"That's enough, Mr. Tutynski," said the Trooper.

Teach bent and put out her hands to me. I pushed her away, my fingers all gooey with bean-ketchup.

"Leave me alone," I said.

Fred Millay

I was driving my father's big Buick up Leatherman's Cave Road. Rounding the bend at Breakneck Hill, I came on Joe Tutynski dragging himself along the gravel side-path.

I wasn't going to stop. Like Jack, I was pissed off at this deformed, arrogant jerk who wouldn't say a decent word to anybody. But my foot hit the brake.

"Going my way, Joe?"

His head snapped around. His arm—the skinny one—dropped the book it was cradling. He stooped for it. He spoke, his ugly bloated jaw opening like a hippo.

"What's it look like?"

We drove on under elms that loomed like giant cauliflowers.

The silence grew awkward.

I said, "What's the book, Joe?"

"Some shit Teach gave me."

"Oh?"

"*Voices of the Brain*. Latest psychiatric crap from the head-monkeys at Harvard."

"Oh?"

"Yeah. Those guys figure they know where auditory hallucinations come from in schizophrenic brains. Some from Broca's Area in the frontal lobe. Some from the Auditory Cortex high up in the temporal lobe. One asshole says *all of it* comes from Wenicke's Area in the occipital love. Oh yeah? That can't be true because...."

I lighted a cigarette (forbidden at home). Joe growled on, talking stuff I didn't begin to understand.

"If the cause is local—a cancerous tumor in the head, maybe—how come the Jesus nuts claim a religious mainspring over-all? That's horseshit because..."

I tuned out, tapping a finger on the steering wheel. Then, glancing at Joe, I saw a curious thing.

He was sitting back. He was holding his left arm – the oversize, muscular one—across his lower face. Like he was stretching. Or maybe pointing out the window. His bulging biceps covered the hideous moose jaw. *The upper half of his face was handsome.* Wide-set gray eyes...broad forehead...crisp pitch-black hair. I shook ash off my cigarette and nearly dropped it. Why, here was a guy who was meant to be good-looking. Something had gone wrong at the start, that's all.

"...and that leads to the logical goal—*suicide*."

I let him off at the path to the cave. In the rear view mirror I saw him pull a bottle from his hip pocket and take a swig. Then he dragged himself into the woods, hugging the book.

I thought: *Miss Drake, you're dumping far-out brain texts on crazy Joe. I hope you know what you're doing.*

A Novel By George P. Morrill

Eva Casserino

It's sneaky to listen in on other people's conversations. No? Usually, I don't. But when I accidentally overheard Miss Drake and Jack talking in homeroom, I was all ears. It was after history class. They didn't see me stacking paper in the supply closet.

Miss Drake was saying, "...but Jack, If that's what's happening we all have an obligation to do something."

"Why?"

Her voice went up. "Why? Because we're human beings. There's brilliance in Joe. It came out marvelously in his beach project."

"Yeah. But that doesn't mean the class got to stick its nose in his private business. If he's decided to go rummy, he'll do it."

"You're disappointing me, Jack."

"We've all tried to get to Joe...."

"And you mustn't stop. We have a terribly wounded psyche here. Now, who's selling him liquor?"

"He gets some of his stuff up in Little Italy."

"What's the name?"

"I don't know. Every family up there makes wine. Sometimes harder stuff."

"I need a name. Can you get it for me?"

Silence.

"Miss Drake, you know what will happen? The Mirandis, the Pastros, the Tragonnis—they all live there. You'll open a real tub of eels."

"You're still disappointing me. We can't worry about damaged feelings."

Silence.

"Okay, I'll find the name. But I'm not turning somersaults about helping the guy. He's crippled. But he doesn't take step one to get along with any of us. He won't love you for this either."

Silence.

"I know that—I'll abide it."

Elaine Bordan

Jack let me drive his Ford coupe. He'd built it from two wrecked Model A's that Mr. Chapman had given him. It was the first car that anybody in our class owned. It made him more our top guy than ever—and my new link with him as a friend instead of a sleep-girl somehow gave me dibs on it.

He said, "Take Old Faithful to rehearsal tonight, Elaine. Stick on the Clinton back road. Next week we'll go for your license."

"Gee, thanks Jack."

"Just get me and Holly free tickets for your Swingtime Girl, Okay?"

I drove up Leatherman's cave road, feeling good. Warm, evening scents rose from the fields. Purple shadows of the elms winked on the tarmac. I was rehearsing my clinch line: *"What Malcolm! You're actually going to marry that...that..."* when I saw Joe Tutynski sprawled on the path leading to the cave. His short leg was doubled up and his crippled arm lay across his face like a thin rope. A cardboard crate of books had spilled onto the road. He was trying to scrape them out of the way with his good arm.

I stopped. "Joe! What happened?"

His monster jaw flapped. "What happened, what happened? I decided to sleep here. I like throwing my books around. I'm waiting for stupid people to show up with stupid questions."

There was a strong odor of whiskey from his sweaty shirt. Very familiar to me from home. I got out. I started picking up books.

"Goddamit, leave 'em be!"

I ignored him. I stacked the books in the crate and slid it up beside him. He hauled out a lumpy book and waved it. "Hey Ethel Barrymore, see this: *Somatic Treatments in Psychiatry.* And this: *Common Neuroses.* And this...and this..."

He flung the books around drunkenly. I picked them up again. Straightened pages. I was used to this.

"Well, Joe you've got plenty to dig into. Good luck."

I got back in the car.

He shouted, "Goddamit, I got it all, see? I scoop it all out, see?"

He banged his meaty left fist on his temple. "It's all up here, see?"

At rehearsal in New Haven I flowed into my part, a teen-age vixen trying to break up an affair of her older brother with a divorced woman. I remembered the time—it seemed long ago—when I had faced Joe's hostility head-on in my first part at school. Now I moved around the stage as if it were home. Thank you, Joe.

"That's exactly what we're after, Miss Bordan," said the director, "Very high marks."

Driving home after dark I felt the Ford's right rear tire go flat. I was fumbling around in the trunk, feeling for a tool, when headlights came up and stopped. A door slammed. A woman in dungarees walked around a big front fender, she was eating an ice-cream cone.

"What's this I see? An unlicensed driver on the King's Highway? Tut, Tut."

"Miss Drake!"

"That Jack McGreggor's heap? Yes, it is. Ever changed a tire, Elaine?"

"No."

"Watch close."

She handed me her cone (chocolate) and told me to take licks as it melted. She yanked the spare wheel out of the trunk.

"This is the bumper jack, see? Always stand clear when it lifts. This is the lug wrench..."

She worked at high speed, like those mechanics you see in news reels of car races. Her forearm muscles made unexpected ripples when she tightened the lugs.

"There. Now, got that, Elaine?" she stood up, panting slightly. She took back her cone, now half gone.

I said, "Golly, Miss Drake, if you hadn't come I'd have been in a mess."

She chewed the last of the cone. "I've been up to Leatherman's. Joe Tutynski burrows in up there like Rip van Winkle. I built him a fire and got him to eat a couple of hot dogs."

I told her about running into him earlier, sprawled with a bunch of books.

"He's devouring tomes on psychiatry and every kind of related subject," she said, "He retains it all. It's quite amazing."

I started the Model A. "He's smart. And not smart. I know what that's like."

She got back in the Packard and called over the windshield. "We've got to try harder with Joe."

Joe Tutynski

Out of curiosity I finally went to one session at Yale that Teach had set up. She knew the professor, a thin-faced guy with a gray mustache who looked like a timber wolf. His name was Morgenstein. I called him Wolf-Ass.

When I crawled into a seat at the rear of the room, the students nodded and went back to their notebooks. Nobody seemed interested in how I looked. Professor Wolf-Ass lectured about psychiatrists' conflicting views on the Oedipus Complex. And how infantile fixations of the libido could raise hell in later developments of neurosis.

I rode back to West Stoddard on a bumpy Shoreline bus, my mind tumbling with ideas I'd heard. For 50 minutes I was completely out of my wreck of a body.

But the next night I went back to the cave. Got dizzy-drunk. Hollered and laughed with Luke after he slid in on the stone wall. I did my thing on the leaf pile. I was back in my body with a vengeance.

School went on. I didn't let Teach know I'd started digging into psychiatry, taking in everything Wolf-Ass had to offer—and hunting for more at the library. But she suspected.

She said, "Joe, you're coming across as something of a scholar. Your short study. *How the Head Works*, was remarkable. Can't we start thinking about college for next year?"

I stared at her. This hot-looking doll with the strong, curvy body and the nice clothes. This West Coast demoiselle that rode around in a fancy car, joked with the whole class, and kept poking everybody into doing things. *Jesus!*

I said, "To hell with college."

"Now, Joe. I have scholarship material. This brochure says...."

"Lemme out of here."

She didn't try to stop me. I hitched out, slamming the door. I went up to the cave and smashed three empty hooch bottles against a dead oak.

Gene Bigelow

My brother and I had a kind of sympathy for Joe Tutynski. He was a rotten guy on the surface. Unfriendly to everyone. Arrogant — even to Miss Drake

But both Vince and I understood how the red wagon that he was dragging twisted him. Practically all the kids in West Stoddard were Depression-poor. But they didn't know any pain on the level of everyday Black living down South. So they couldn't key in with Joe's feelings as close as we could.

That's not to say we were free from his attacks. Once he referred to us as "a pair of block-headed Mississippi tar babies."

One afternoon Miss Drake sent me down cellar to search for the school's rolled-up map of the United States before the Mexican War. I found it behind the big cracked mirror that Joe sometimes sat in front of, writing homework on an old desk. I picked up a wrinkled paper from the floor.

It was one of Joe's scribblings:

I didn't ask my mind to function at the speed it has lately. It automatically locks onto one subject — the human brain. I read, read. And look for more. I forget my body completely.

The obsession dominates. Where am I going?

I showed it to Vince. He said it looks like Joe is on the edge of some kind of change.

"Let's watch and say nothing," he said, "Not even to Jack."

Hymie Volenski

Miss Drake never let up on assignments, tests, and recitations in class. But she eased the studying with jokes and foolishness. You could horse around with her, if you kept your work up. One night I came back to school with a flashlight and painted the words *Please Flip Me* on a small flat rock by the steps. In the morning we watched her pause, read it, then set down her briefcase.

She stooped and turned the rock over. I had painted *Thank You* on the underside. She came into class smiling. "You tear me up, Hymie Volenski."

Now all of us were grinding out projects. That is, all except Joe Tutynski. He had stunned us with his West Stoddard beach report, researched and written practically overnight. Now he hunched in his seat scowling. Sometimes he scribbled on paper, then tore it up. Sometimes he just stared out the window. Quite often he never showed up at all.

Miss Drake would put a mark in her attendance book. She'd inquire, "Is Joe sick? Anybody seen him?"

We all knew that crazy Joe spent his time up at Leatherman's cave. Stumbling around. Drinking. Reading the psychiatry books Elaine had seen.

Jack said, "The guy is taking a nose dive. What can anybody do about it?"

One day at the end of an English session, Miss Drake got us playing a game with words—anagrams. You wrote a word on the board and, using all its letters, tried to make another word (or words) underneath. Joe, in his seat for the first time in three days, snorted out loud. But he seemed interested. Elaine (who kept surprising us by her changes) wrote PRESBYTERIAN. Underneath it she wrote: BEST IN PRAYER.

Vince Bigelow wrote THE EARTHQUAKES and underneath: THAT QUEER SHAKE.

Then Joe heaved himself up and dragged to the board. He snatched chalk from the eraser holder. He wrote ANIMOSITY and underneath IS NO AMITY. Then instead of limping back to his seat he wrote DESPERATION. And stood staring at it.

"Mmm," said Miss Drake, studying the word, "A tough one."

Joe gave a grunt. In double-size letters he printed underneath: A ROPE ENDS IT.

I saw Miss Drake blink. Her two fingers brushed back a strand of blond hair. I think her wrist was shaking a little.

Joe Tutynski

What with stealing money, selling any article I could grab, correcting papers for Teach, and sneaking bottles from my dumb old man I promoted enough liquor to lubricate my sessions up at Leatherman's.

My stupors had no effect on my brainpower. I could out-argue anybody in class on any subject. All I needed was some scan-time of the material. My beach project was researched at lighting speed. It left everybody with their mouths open.

No imbecilic hours of study for me, see?

Teach's leaning to poetry gave me a pain. But I used the open sessions to showcase my memory—which was hypernormal. When we studied *Macbeth*, I leafed through the pages, then dumped back every soliloquy in the play. Verbatim.

Teach dropped her pencil on her blotter. "Well, I never!"

When the girls came up with sentimental verse, and everybody talked about it as if it was important, I felt like vomiting. But I limited myself to sarcasm. This always burned up the listeners, particularly Jack McGreggor. (He's dying to stick it to

Holly Millay—who might be a good chunk at that.)

"Must we eulogize this kind of doggerel?" I'd say.

Jack's jaw muscles would tighten.

One afternoon I was trying to sleep through a session of verse regurgitated by the class sheep when Geraldine Prue read her latest discovery. It was a quatrain she'd found in the discard pile at our joke of a library. The words floated across the scarred seats and nodding heads into my ear. For some reason they rang like chimes.

Later, up at the cave, I wrote them in a notebook before I started drinking. Somehow I linked them to Teach...to her tormenting way in my thoughts sometimes:

Oh, promise me that some day you and I
Will take our love together to some sky
Where we can be alone and faith renew
And find those hollows where those flowers grew.

— *Clement Scott*

Geraldine Prue

Long before Thanksgiving we'd learned from Elaine that Miss Drake had been a girl friend of Clay Griffin, that rich boy who'd gone to Exeter prep when we were grammar school kids.

Every Saturday I cleaned rooms at Mrs. Kelsey's. After Elaine's eye-opener, I looked for something to back up her story. I found Miss Drake's snapshot album in the lower drawer of her night table. I thumbed through it.

Here was Miss Drake standing on Clay's shoulders on the deck of a yacht. He looked about 20. She about 17—strong and willowy in a short-skirted bathing suit. Here was Miss Drake pointing a tennis racket—like a gun—at him as he pretended to hide from it. Then, Clay standing alone, holding two kittens on his shoulders, grinning. He was handsome in a dark way—a muscular ridge on his jaw, a chunk of unruly hair over one eyebrow, big lumps of muscle on each arm. A scrawl underneath said: *See you Saturday, Eva?*

I remembered him as a guy who drove a shiny black Model T Ford around town in the Twenties and waved to us kids. But kept his distance.

There were other shots of Miss Drake posing as a gypsy in dangling earrings...jumping over a lawn chair...winding herself up in a massive raccoon coat. There was one of her standing under the goal posts of the Rose Bowl, her mouth shouting, her hair blowing. Below her swirling skirt were the words in the neat squarish penmanship I recognized: *1930 Our big victory—oh how I cried.*

Something hurtful must have happened to lift Miss Drake out of this happy picture-album life on the West Coast and dump her on depressed New England...something linked to her Yankee boyfriend. In class I'd watch her from behind a book. We were supposed to be in study hall. She'd look along the blackboard, touching her chin lightly with her yellow pencil. She'd squint across our battered old globe in its brass frame...across our unpainted windowsill...and stare at the sunny outside.

I'd say to myself: *She's back in California, 1930. O yes.*

Sibyl Noyes

Bad things kept happening. Wolson's food bus went out of business in a scandal. Police found he was digging up piglets recently killed by the government's agricultural program and selling the meat. The A&P left town. On Horse Hill we had to get emergency food from a Salvation Army truck that came out from New Haven once a week.

I wrote a theme titled There's Darkness on the Land. Miss Drake praised its detail. But after Fred wrote Will Depression Level New England? and Hymie wrote Italy Enacts Anti-Jewish Legislation, she gave us a talk.

"All three of these papers are documented and well-expressed.

These tough subjects have to be addressed. However, —just so we don't get lop-sided in our thinking—let's balance black topics with hopeful topics."

She suggested that somebody do a review of a new book: Van Wyck Brooks's *The Flowering of New England* or Majorie Rawlins's *The Yearling.* That brought a snort from Joe Tutynski.

"Life is black," he said, "Why paint it white?"

"No," said Miss Drake, "Life is *both* black and white."

The whole class got into the argument. Jack said, "If I thought life was all black, I wouldn't bother to fill another gas tank." Eva Casserino said, "If life was all white, I'd be in New York right now, singing with Charlie Barnet's band." I said, "I think life is a mixture—but mostly black at the moment."

Miss Drake looked at us, touching her pencil eraser to her chin pensively. "Mmm. Let's try something."

She wrote the words POSITIVE and NEGATIVE on the board. Then stood aside and looked at them.

"Try this, class. For one day keep a record. After supper think back and decide where each of your thoughts should be listed."

We grew silent. "I don't get it," said Tony.

"Well, let's say you got out of bed and thought: another lousy day of rain. You got to school: you decided a classmate was snubbing you. Two unpleasant thoughts. They go in the negative column."

She wrote them on the board.

"Now, you remembered that it was a baseball day and you were pitching. In History you think you've scored a straight A on a test. Two pleasant thoughts. They go in your positive column."

She wrote them on the board. She dropped the chalk in the eraser tray. "Keep your tally-sheet to yourself—and brood over it. If the negative column keeps getting longer than the positive, it's time to re-think where you're heading."

Joe Tutynski

I decided Teach's thought-classifying idea was idiotic. But the new tempo of my mind—energized daily by reading books like Furski's *The Abnormal Brain* and Eric Tayler's *Madness Under Leash*—pushed me to try things I'd never considered before.

Before sundown at Leatherman's I wrote my Positive-Negative list for the day. Like Teach said, I tried to remember every thought I'd had over the last twelve hours:

1. Pain in my elbow. Why?
2. Teach says class college prospects better. Baloney.
3. Jack and Fred whispering. They hate me.
4. Too damned hot in this building
5. Where's my blue leather cap? Hymie's grabbed it, yeah.
6. This desk is the worst in class, jackknifed all over.
7. Paper says Fed money coming. None to West Stoddard, you can bet.
8. Who's after my sauce up at the cave?
9. Holly Millay's wearing a ring that looks real gold. Rich bitch.
10. I won't ride in Teach's damned car with Jack McGreggor.
11. Someday I'll smash every window in this bastardly school.

The list went on to 36 items. Things that had flashed in and out of my head...longer thoughts that hung there awhile. Then I classified them. I got a jolt. Only one qualified for the Positive column:

29. Goldenrod coming in along Clinton road. Yellow as topaz.

I won't say I was upset. But my brain, motoring along at its new speed, wouldn't let go of Teach's whole idiotic process. I decided to give it a full week's test.

Hymie Volenski

Everybody experimented with Miss Drake's thought-classifying monkey business—for about 24 hours. Elaine stopped me in History and said "Hey, I saw you gawk at her ankles. You were having an un-wonderful thought."

I said, "Elaine, right now I'm looking at a thought-cloud floating out your ears, bright as popcorn. Stop brooding over my good looks."

Fred said, "I sit here thinking sweet thoughts hour after hour. My brain's turning to candy."

Miss Drake said, "All right now. Let's move on."

Joe Tutynski

My one-week, thought-classifying experiment didn't come up with any surprises. The world's an ugly place. Why shouldn't my brain output be 98 per cent negative?

Yesterday, however, Nebuchadnezzar came to my desk in homeroom and licked my hand. Today the sun feels warm on my snake-arm hanging from my shirt. And I got a bottle of Old Grandad waiting at the cave.

Three positive thoughts, Teach. Shouldn't they get me into Valhalla?

Jack McGreggor

At our homeroom seat switching in November, I found myself in Joe Tutynski's old place. I didn't get around to cleaning out the apple cores and trash paper in his desk until on Friday after school. Everybody was gone. I dug into the junk, cussing Joe under my breath. Why couldn't he house-clean like everybody else?

Suddenly I pulled out a crumpled paper marked PRIVATE. It was the assignment he was supposed to have destroyed months ago. I wasn't supposed to read it.

But I did.

Then I jumped in my Ford and drove to Mrs. Kelsey's. Miss Drake was in her blue bathing suit cooking something on her new four-burner electric.

"Want a tortilla, Jack?"

I thrust Joe's paper at her. "Read it."

She put down a spatula. I told her it was something left over from a writing assignment and it was important.

"Joe Tutynski's memoir? Mmm. Why, this is private. I can't—"

"Read it."

"Why, we should burn this, Jack."

"Just read it," I said, and walked out.

Later when I was fixing the windshield wiper on Old Man Chapman's Graham-Page at the garage I saw her car speed down Route 1 and turn up the Leatherman's cave road.

Joe Tutynski

I was sitting in the leaves up at Leatherman's examining Hendrick Van Jurgin's *Abnormalities of the Ephebic Mind* (borrowed from Prof. Wolf-Ass at Yale) when Teach came running up the trail. She climbed to the cave. She looked down on me, panting.

"Joe, don't you *dare* consider anything like this!"

She threw a crunched-up blue book on my lap. I recognized it as that thing I had written last year about suicide plans. I'd forgotten all about it. But instead of telling her I was now obsessed by my probe into the brain's mysteries—and would no more kill myself than stop guzzling good booze—I replied:

"Hey Teach, wasn't that the essay that nobody but the author was supposed to read?"

She walked away. On the trail she turned and called, "I cheated. Be proud that somebody cheated for you, Joe."

Sibyl Noyes

By May my project was even-up with everybody else's. Miss Drake was driving me to nurse's basics on Saturday at Middletown. On Sundays I worked part-time at the hospital. I wrote a theme titled *Repairing Hurt Bodies* that everyone said was good. (Except Joe Tutynski, of course, who said, "It should be titled: *Band-Aids for Boobocracy.*")

I was proud...maybe even cocky. So when Joe surprised me by deigning to speak, I was in a mood for fire back.

He was coming out of the library, limping lop-sidedly. "Hey, Half-Brain," he said, "What was the history chapter Teach wanted us to cover?"

He said it in a surprising way—mild, part-friendly perhaps. But I didn't catch it that way.

I shot back, "Hey, sick-Brain, Chapter 11—if you're sober."

He looked at me with that bright, tough stare which always went with some cruel crack that could knock everybody (except Jack McGreggor) for a loop. His monster lips moved. I got ready for some sarcastic blast that would make me feel like a fool.

He said, "Okay—thanks."

I was stunned. No one had ever heard him say thanks before. I watched his lumpy shadow limp away. Suddenly I remembered Miss Drake writing the word *compassion* on her car's hood last year...and saying it was what a doctor had to have...and her kissing me...

At home I wrote in my notebook: *I will never again talk like that to another human being. Never.*

Jack McGreggor

"I guess I'm in a state of shock," said Miss Drake.

She was sitting in her car, arms out stiff, hands gripping the steering wheel. I finished wiping her windshield and peered through the glass.

"Shock?"

"I've been up to Leatherman's again. Joe was out cold and couldn't be roused. I shook him. Shouted at him."

I took her ten-dollar bill and counted out change. "Don't worry about it, Miss Drake. A four-hour knockout is routine for him."

"So Tony told me. But it's unnatural. It shouldn't be happening. I ought to report it right this minute."

"To whom, Miss Drake? School superintendent? Police? State Hospital? Joe always comes up for air—eventually."

She pressed the back of one hand across her eyes. "That poor, wretched, helpless boy...groveling in those leaves..."

Holly Millay

Winter came and went without much snow. In mid-April Sibyl's father set fire to their house. He'd just taken an eviction notice out of the mailbox.

He ran from their sagging old porch shouting, if he couldn't live here nobody else was going to. The fire department put out the blaze. But the inside was charred, furniture destroyed.

Then the State Police took Mr. Noyes away. Miss Drake found Sibyl in the library stacks, trembling but turning pages of a nursing book. She took her to Mrs. Kelsey's.

"You can sleep on the sofa, Sib. We'll work out something."

We all felt terrible. Geraldine and I wanted to help. But Sibyl had a tough way, and you had to be careful how you offered anything. She could be hurt and snappish.

Geraldine said, "Her clothes are all burned up. I got skirts, blouses, and socks extra."

"So have I," I said.

We wanted to get stuff to her. But our stuff was elegant in comparison to the hand-me-downs she'd always worn. When the others recognized it, she might feel uneasy, even resentful. Miss Drake had taught us to be cautious dealing with people's sensibilities.

So we *camouflaged*. Geraldine brought two beautiful flaring skirts, some white blouses, and tan socks to our laundry room. I brought a snowflake skirt, a frothy pair of slacks, two mist-colored scarfs, and white socks. We dyed all of it various colors—turquoise, crimson, clam-shell gray.

We took our big, neatly-packed box to the grubby little Methodist church where Mrs. Kelsey had set up a collection for Sibyl, her father and her little brother. One week later Sibyl wore Geraldine's coral skirt—now deep ultramarine—to class. Miss Drake admired it out loud. And Sibyl blushed the only time I could remember.

Sibyl Noyes

I didn't let on that I knew Holly and Geraldine had given me their clothes. For the first time I tried to think the way Miss Drake wanted me to think—not sore at being poor but grateful for a friendly act.

Then I got thinking, maybe it would make me feel good to do something for somebody. That very day I saw an ancient Sterno camp stove at Bailey's Remainders. It was old and rusty, but had six openings for heat cans and a cute little oven.

It was marked 15 cents, but Mr. Bailey took a dime. And he threw in two cans of cooking fuel.

That night I scraped and sand-papered the stove in Mrs. Kelsey's cellar. I bent the skinny legs into shape. Miss Drake found a half can of Chinese vermilion in the Packard trunk. She helped me spread on three coats. The stove gleamed like new.

"Well, I've never seen such a transformation," she said.

I felt wonderful. "I'm taking this up to Joe Tutynski at Leatherman's."

She clapped her hands. "What a great idea, Sibyl!"

After school she drove me up Clinton road. We walked in the leafy trail. We crossed both brooks on stepping stones, handing the stove to each other. She stayed in the trail while I climbed up to the cave entrance.

"Whatcha want?"

Joe was half drunk, reading a book. I said I had a little stove for him. I put it down. It looked good—bright red, sturdy. I set the two cans of fuel down beside it.

I started back to the trail. I looked back just in time to see Joe fling the stove into the woods.

"I cook over fires, dammit!"

My pretty Sterno restoration smashed against a thick maple and snapped in half. He sent the two heat-cans after it.

I looked at the broken stove. For a second my temper threatened to bubble up. But I made my voice come out in an even, natural-sounding way. "Perhaps it will be useful to you later, Joe—when you feel better."

Miss Drake's voice rose clearly. "That was uncalled for, Joe. Someday I think you'll discover the value of heartfelt things. Then you'll know what this gift meant—and you'll turn a different face to the world."

We walked out the trail. Miss Drake hooked her arm in mine and hugged it close.

"You're going to make a doctor—a good one." she said.

Joe Tutynski

As soon as I finished reading Signud La Gordon's *Warped Frontiers of the Mind* I arm-hauled and hip-struggled myself down to the trail. I picked up the wreckage of the Sterno stove and brought it back to the cave.

It had occurred to me, I could use the two tins of heat to cook a steak—if I could heist one at Jacob's Meat Market.

Geraldine Prue

I was cleaning Miss Drake's bathroom the Saturday morning a professor from Yale arrived. He sat on her sofa with the rainbow-colored Navajo afghan and talked about Joe Tutynski.

He said, "We have a very unusual person on our hands, Miss Drake."

"I can certainly corroborate that, Dr. Morganstein."

They exchanged incidents of Joe's astonishing mental powers...his instant memory of research material... his grasp of complicated diagnoses made by famed doctors like Freud and Jung. Miss Drake said Joe was really far beyond the high school level. But he was so scatter-shot in his approach to learning that there was a danger he'd never assemble a workable mind.

"I never know when he's going to explode in class and scorn everything we're trying to do."

"I'm sure he's a terrible problem," said the professor, "He's somewhat better in my class. Pugnacious, but passionately intent on a study of the human brain. He insists on probing abnormalities. These should be far beyond his ken at this stage—but they aren't. We're beginning to wonder if there's not an awesome psychiatrist lurking in that tortured body."

It came out that a number of faculty members were highly interested in Joe's potential. They were ready to devote time and money to his development. O yes.

"It could be an epic-making venture, Miss Drake. The Rockefeller Foundation has offered backing."

I peeked out the door. Miss Drake was standing, her hands pressed together. "Really? That's so exciting, Dr. Morganstein!" Then she added, "Joe's cruelly distorted body...if only...."

"That's part of the plan also, Miss Drake. Several of our surgeons at the university hospital are focused on body repair and reconstruction. They'll take him on."

"Oh!"

At the door, the professor shook Miss Drake's hand. He got in his car. "Perhaps—a few years down the road—the Tutynski rebuilding case will become a medical textbook entry."

"Oh, how I hope so...."

Jack McGreggor

I was pretty much in touch with the easy-going way 1930's morals were changing. The garage kept life flowing by. And the Old Saybrook movie house featured sexy heroines like Mae West and Lana Turner.

But, in spite of my brief entanglement with Elaine Bordan, I had old-fashioned ideas about the boy-girl link. I believed in the steady way—love and marriage. And, after you earned it, a house.

That's why I was so surprised at myself and Holly when we got caught in a rainstorm after a movie titled *Gold Diggers of 1937*. My Model A wouldn't start. We began to neck.

I put my hand on her knee. It slid up. Then further.

"Jack—" she said. Her voice trailed off. Her hand dropped onto my knee.

The next ten minutes we were shifting positions...moving this way, that way. Our hands kept exploring beneath clothes. And each time we touched it was a new thrill we couldn't stop.

Holly said, "I-I don't know why I'm—"

"Me neither," I said.

Then we were locked together. And then it was over. Holly closed her legs and smoothed down her skirt. She gave a sob, barely hearable.

"Don't cry...for gosh sakes..." I said.

"I-I'm not."

"It's all right...you'll be all right."

She adjusted a brassiere strap. She tried to smile in the semi-dark. "Let's hope so,"

The rain stopped. I got out and dried the wet plugs with a handkerchief. Finally the engine kicked to life. I kissed her goodnight in the fancy Millay crushed-stone drive. I watched her slip through the big mahogany door, her pretty calves flashing.

Well, the next week I kept telling myself that it was okay, that's the way life goes in the modern world. I was okay. Holly was okay. But a voice kept saying: *You damaged the sweet girl you plan to marry.*

It was asinine. A New England conscience, banging me in the head in this day and age? I laughed at myself. But...

I had to talk to somebody. I was doggoned if I'd unload to anyone in the gang. So I talked to Miss Drake. However, I steered all around the subject, figuring to keep it secret. She wrinkled her suntanned brow, figuring it out.

"Mmm, are you saying this couple you're acquainted with jumped the gun a bit?"

"Yeah—yeah, that's about it."

"Well, the first thing is to face the possible consequences."

"Consequences?"

With a trace of a smile, she tapped her pencil on her blotter. "I imagine your friends passed Biology in West Stoddard High."

"Yeah...I guess."

"All right, they can quietly wait. Chances are there'll be no consequences. Then they can...well, be careful from now on."

I stood there shifting my eyes to the ink well, to the blackboard, to my feet. I felt like a fool. Here I was Miss Drake's closest class friend—practically an adult. And I was mumbling like a nervous kid.

I started out.

"Jack?"

I turned. She took off her glasses. Her green-gold eyes were shimmering with a kind of warmness that went into my stomach,

"Anyhow, if your friends really love each other, consequences can be faced. The realistic world is tolerant of things like that."

Joe Tutynski

I sat in the afternoon sun outside the cave drinking. Ideas burned and burned behind my eyes. *Transference—neurotic emotions of hate and love toward somebody? Teach yaks about love and respect. What does she know?*

I stood up, kicking leaves. I drained my bottle and smashed it against the stone ceiling. I staggered around, shaking glass out of my hair. Prof. Wolf-Ass wants me to come back for his lecture: *Psycho-Analytic Profile of Freud's Oedipus Theories.* Why should I? What good will it do me to know that crap?

I crawled into the cave and opened a can of Budweiser with my powerful left hand. The metal bent easy, like paper. Wait, goddamit, look at that arm. That's a steel-muscled wing ruggeder than any kid's in West Stoddard. That's the arm of a *man*, a bone-and-sinew *man*. Railroad men in New York are talking about it.

I got every right to go where I want and listen to what I want. I'll be there, you Yalie fag.

I drank until my eyes dimmed out. I crawled toward my leaf mound. Leatherman Luke slid in along the west stone wall. He grinned.

He said, "You a man? Bullshit. You're nothing."

I sat up. Luke had a mean shadow in his jaw that I'd never noticed before. I said, "You're crazy, Luke. Lookit this arm."

"You're a freak."

"Listen, you bastard..."

"A balled-up freak. You never been near a real woman. You wrestle a leaf pile—hah!"

I staggered up. I slammed my good fist at Luke. Pain burst in my knuckles. Luke laughed and slid along the wall. Ugly lines wriggled in his face—like gashes. I staggered after him, pounding the wall.

"Freak...freak...hah!"

I swung and landed. Blood splashed on my wrist. Even my snake arm bled into its dwarfed, three-fingered hand.

"Get out!" I screamed, "Beat it!"

He shook his head. He twisted his lips in protest. But his face began to fade. A moment later the stone wall was empty. I finished my bottle and flung it at a tree. It missed and skidded along the leafy floor, unbroken.

I sank down in the leaves and blacked out.

Then a strange thing happened. A faint, hazy dream floated through the solid nothingness that made up my blackout. A shadow seemed to drift in from the outer dark. It slipped against my sprawled body. I was vaguely conscious of a softness and a firmness I'd never felt before. I buried my monstrous jaw in soft strands of perfumed hair...

When I woke up stars were winking through the trees. In the distance the Congregational clock bonged twelve times. I'd been zonko since eight o'clock.

I rolled over and went to sleep again. When morning came, Prof. Wolf-Ass and two other Yale guys—grown men with beards—were sitting on a big oak log outside the cave.

"We're here with an idea that will change your life, young man," said Wolf-Ass.

They talked about me studying in New Haven...having operations...starting a new existence...for once I listened without saying a word.

But when we started down the trail one of the tall, gray-haired guys smashed my last unopened bottle of whiskey against the ledge and I yelled.

"HEY! What the hell you doing?"

He pointed both forefingers at me. "We're going to work on *everything*, son."

Holly Millay

I told Geraldine this year was going faster than any in my life. It was May already. Graduation loomed. Exciting letters were coming in from colleges. She'd been accepted at Mount Holyoke. And I was going to the University of Connecticut.

"Miss Drake's got everybody headed for something," she said, "Only Jack is holding back."

That made me defensive. I said that Jack was ahead of college freshmen anyhow. He was reading all the time...learning about motors at the garage...

She laughed. "I knew you'd say that. When you getting married?"

I threw a pillow at her.

Miss Drake now had us drawing and painting. On sunshiny afternoons she'd get the whole class outside sketching the school building.

"Yes, this is History class, Mr. Plimpton," she said, when he objected, "Our building is pre-Revolutionary. I want students to see its Colonial pedigree and Christopher Wren simplicity. And they'll have a picture to remember."

It was surprising how good some of the sketches were. Miss Drake showed us elements of perspective, artistic shading and all. Her own drawing showed a stately, smooth-clapboard farmhouse, framed in imaginary elms. It made us stare. Could this old wreck of a school have had a stylish history like that?

"Keep this art with your memory things," she said quietly, "It will grow on you."

Life was looking good. Our tattered baseball team was cleaning up in shoreline games. Sibyl Noyes had won a scholarship to Connecticut College. The Red Cross had brought in two truckloads of groceries for Middlesex County. West Stoddard selectmen had distributed our share to hungry families in the back woods.

We were working on a plan to find a classy present for Miss Drake—to have a swing dance and try to get her performing—to cook a great graduation dinner of roast beef at the West Beach Rink—to go out in a blaze of glory.

Then—to our shock—the whole thing fell apart.

Tony Tragonni

Miss Drake got sick. Six days before graduation I saw her sink down on the school step, letting go of her briefcase. I had ridden my bike in early.

"Miss Drake!"

She sat up and reached for some papers that had slid out. She smiled weakly. "Tony, what are you doing here at 7:30?"

I carried her briefcase into homeroom. She eased down at her desk and said thanks. She started correcting papers, her face very white. After leaving, I looked through an outside window and saw her lower her head on the blotter.

At 12:45 No Balls came in and said, "Miss Drake has been excused. Miss Wainwright will be in charge the last two periods."

Well, we all knew Miss Drake would expect us to be polite. But when you glanced up at the familiar desk and saw mean-looking wrinkles instead of a pretty mouth and twinkly eyes you felt gyped.

Hymie slipped a note on my desk: *What's Al Capone's grandmother doing at West Stoddard High?*

I wrote back: *The bone bag is for sale. Make an offer?"*

Elaine ducked behind a book and took a compact out of her gold-bead pocketbook. She started jabbing bright red lipstick on her lips.

Jack drummed soundlessly on his desk with his strong fingers.

The two periods dragged. All the while Miss Wainwright wrote with a scratchy pen, not even looking up. Once she walked out of the room. Hymie jumped up, tip-toed to her desk, and started reading what she'd written. His mouth dropped open. He stared...stared...and barely got back to his seat as Miss Wainwright came in.

The bell rang. Outside, Hymie told what he had seen, "She's done a hatchet job on Miss Drake. No Balls told her to write it."

Jack McGreggor

I told Fred we had to get a copy of No Balls' charges. Within 24 hours he and Hymie had faked Miss Wainwright out of the Biology room and rifled her desk. Geraldine made copies. The original went back without the teacher knowing a thing.

I wasn't surprised at the report. But it made me boil:

At your request, Mr. Plimpton, I am listing the activities and qualities of Miss Eva Drake that you might want to consider in presenting this case before the board.

—Elvira Wainwright, Biology 1 —

1. Her classes are noisy, interfering with other classes.
2. Her language is slangy, especially unacceptable for a teacher of English.
3. She takes students off school grounds during class hours, sometimes into the evening hours.
4. She leads students into subjects far removed from her properly stipulated English and History.
5. She practices unhealthy social informality with young people, endangering local custom.
6. She once left her class unsupervised to go swimming.
7. She joins students in competitive sports (baseball) wearing inappropriate, unladylike garments.
8. In class she reportedly suggested approval of the Communist creed.
9. On another occasion she had a student deposit a money gamble for her on a golfing contest.
10. In sum, she seems unable to practice the down-to-earth methodology of educating young people that has served West Stoddard successfully so many years.

Fred Millay

Next morning we were alone the first period. In homeroom Jack read No Balls' charges aloud. My sister exploded in a completely uncharacteristic way—she threw an ink bottle at the blackboard. Eva Casserino pounded both fists on her desk.

Vince Bigelow, calm like always, said, "Hold it down. They'll send somebody in."

Tony said, "We got to do something."

"Yah," said Hymie, "...like murder."

When Jack got to the sentence saying Miss Drake was unable to practice down-to-earth methodology, Elaine jumped up from her desk. She stalked out, her nose in the air. Through the window I saw her jogging down Sand Block Road toward Mrs. Kelsey's.

Sibyl Noyes

Jack planned our defense of Miss Drake. We wrote up our personal experiences, her one-on-one help to each of us. We noted the slow, steady rise in our grades. We listed the colleges interested in us. Vince added the places she had introduced us to: Hartford Public Library, Peabody Museum, historic Newgate Prison, Mystic seaport, Yale art exhibits, Coast Guard Academy displays, natural scenes like state beaches and old village sites.

Jack wrote, *She opened up our eyes to stuff all over New England. She linked History, English, Science, Current Politics and everything else in the kind of mix that life really is.*

He got quite eloquent. He tore into the complaint about Miss Drake approving the communist creed. He slammed the criticism that she was too informal with young people.

He wrote, *It's 1938. Miss Drake knows it's time to touch shoulders with students, not turn away.*

We decided to mimeograph our two pages secretly in Fat Augie's office after hours. Distribute them all over town.

"I'll unload a bunch at the garage," said Jack, "Hymie, punch them into bags at your store. Fred, dump some at Millay and Paton's."

Geraldine said, "Maybe we can get a town meeting!"

It was Friday. Over the weekend we didn't see Miss Drake because she'd been sick. But we were excited about the coming fight. We figured Miss Drake would let go some devastating California punches when Fat Augie tried to attack. Every one of us wanted to be at her hearing with the school board—which Jack said, would have to be open.

"Come early," he said. "It will finish quicker than Joe Louis—Max Baer. Miss Drake—by knockout."

Hymie Volenski

Saturday night I walked up to Tommy Kingsland's grave and talked to him. I said, "Tom, don't worry, Miss Drake's going to make mincemeat of No Balls. I know what she meant to you. She has been my great protector, too. We can both celebrate.

"I'll give you a blow-by-blow tomorrow."

Tony Tragonni

Sunday afternoon Miss Drake drove out of town, taking Nebuchadnezzar with her. She left a note for Mrs. Kelsey saying a couple of students would pack her things and send them to California.

Jack McGreggor

I couldn't believe it. But Mrs. Kelsey said yes, Miss Drake had left, taking only a suitcase and Neb. She had designated me and Geraldine Prue to ship her things to California. She'd contact us by mail.

Well, the whole class was stunned. This was not our gutsy teacher...this shrinking away from a challenge. She must have known darn well that we and most everybody in town would have supported her.

I ran into Elaine walking across the Green. She didn't seem to droop the way the rest of us were. It griped me.

"Well Jack, that's life, right?"

I stopped and stared at her. "Can you hack it that she simply bugged out because of Old Lady Wainwright's squawks? Did you expect her to scram like this?"

She looked down her pretty pug nose. Then grinned. "Want to know something, Jack? She didn't leave because of those stupid charges."

"What?"

"She had a different reason."

"Different reason?"

"While you were reading those charges to everybody, I ran down to Mrs. Kelsey's. I helped Miss Drake pack her suitcase. She was all smiles and bright talk. Said she loved us. But she had to get out."

"Why?"

"Because."

"Because what?"

"Just because."

I grabbed her wrist. "Hey, come on..."

"I promised myself not to tell."

"For the love of Mike, Elaine...!"

"Wild horses can't drag it from me."

I tightened my grip on her wrist. Her beautiful chin went up. One eyebrow rose—Joan Crawford defying Clark Gable on the silver screen.

"Boil me in steaming oil. Crush my limbs with medieval torture. Never will I..."

I felt like standing her on her head. She walked away humming. *Nice Work If You Can Get It.*

Elvira Wainwright

I don't know how my judgements of Miss Drake—assembled on Mr. Plimpton's order—found their way into students' hands. They were intended for board members' eyes only. I fear he was careless with them.

Well, we all approved the judgments. Student anger wouldn't last. In later years these young people would understand that we were motivated by their best interests.

Meanwhile to show our respect for our beleaguered—and not too confident—principal, Virginia, Susan, and I decided to give him a token of respect. We couldn't think of anything better than a box of his favorite cigars. Virginia found he bought them at Volenski's, a rather disreputable store we always avoided.

She said, "Don't worry. I'll get young Hymie Volenski to bring them to Chem class."

We gave the boy four dollars apiece. The next day he brought a box of Optimo Kings and said, "I hope Mr. Plimpton likes them."

Sibyl Noyes

Our fury at Fat Augie reached bounds I'm sure Miss Drake would have called absurd.

Tony said, "The least we can do is knife all his tires at night."

Eva said, "Dump molasses in his gas tank."

Jack sat in homeroom, opening and closing his fists. I was afraid he might turn violent. Since Miss Drake's disappearance the whole class was stumbling from Biology to Chem to Industrial Arts like zombies. We'd stopped talking about graduation only two days away.

Fat Augie came in and told us to review back assignments in History, he met stone silence. He turned pale.

Later after the final bell, he hurried out to his car. He pulled a cigar from his shirt pocket and lighted it with a quivering hand. He took a long puff.

The cigar exploded.

Jack McGreggor

When Miss Drake's letter arrived it didn't explain much. Something urgent had called her back to California. She was sorry she couldn't stick around for graduation. Would I please give her congratulations to the wonderful students who had enriched her life? They were truly on their way to the stars. She'd be cheering from her family ranch outside El Centro.

Enclosed were two checks. One for freight costs. The other for me and Geraldine to divide.

She added, with a kind of mystery that corked me off: *And you, Jack the Seeker, keep growing. I'll watch. When we stand shoulder-to-shoulder, we'll talk again.*

Geraldine Prue

Jack and I packed Miss Drake's things. Under her bed we found a box of papers, letters, clippings, college reports—private stuff. We read it all.

Miss Drake had graduated from Southern California with Phi Beta Kappa honors in 1929. She had won a state tennis championship in 1931. She had gone on an archaeological expedition to Egypt, explored Colonial sites in Virginia, edited an historical magazine in Chicago. Hollywood studios had offered her contracts.

She and Clay Griffin had been in love for years. Dancing, traveling, dining together. Talking about marriage, but never getting there. Then suddenly he had awakened to feelings of indebtedness. The world was catching fire. The only thing that privileged young folk like them could do was respond.

"Eva, you and I have lived in a fairyland of delight. Football

roughneck and brainy coed sipping at America's flowing fountain. Now we have to pay the ticket."

Over her protest he had joined the Foreign Legion—hopefully to fight dictatorships. Simultaneously Griffin Leather Belt had gone broke. It was too late for him to save the company that had kept little West Stoddard perking for generations. But after much thought, he had decided to return there as a teacher when Franco was defeated. It would be an attempt to pay back for everything the town had given him since childhood.

Jack and I read in silence. Once with a grin, he handed me a faded clip from the Los Angeles Times:

> FOREIGN LEGION RECRUIT &
> HOLLYWOOD STARLET WIN
> GRUELING DANCE CONTEST
>
> Legionnaire-to-be and Paramount
> Actress Wow Spectators. Fellow
> Hoofers Fade in Exhausting Event
>
> Clay Griffin & Eva Drake pounded
> timber at the Palace Dance Floor
> for 37 hours yesterday to cop the
> Annual Gold Toe Championship. As
> an estimated 900 dance devotees
> clapped and shouted.....

"No wonder she could jitterbug," he said.

I picked up a couple of letters in Clay's jagged handwriting. One said that his love for her surpassed that of Dante for Beatrice—whoever they were. The other said that when his enlistment was over he'd bring her to West Stoddard. And after awhile she'd see why he treasured this place.

We found a letter Miss Drake wrote but never sent. It showed a flash of irritation at her lover:

> So you're hell bent to go into the
> Legion? Who are you? Beau Geste?

When our kid revelry was over, we were
going to get married, remember?
Okay, I'll wait. But I'm not going on
the New York stage as you suggest. I'm going
East to work in that little town in Connecticut
you say you're so obligated to.
Watch my smoke, savior of humanity.

Jack nodded "So that's why she came."
We packed the next-to-last suitcase and were about to lock
the apartment when I spotted a card scotch-taped to the underside of Miss Drake's bed. It was placed so she could read it as
she lay on her side:

*Clay, darling. I'm through crying. The
Official report of your death in the retreat
from Valencia came last July. Ever since,
I too have been dead.
Now, no more tears. I'm here doing the
thing you planned to do. I'm teaching in your
little New England town. I'm reaching into
every corner, trying to lift things the way you
wanted.
I'm touching every student with love—just
as we talked about it before you left. It was the night
we slept on that mountain in the Rockies, remember?
Goodnight, sweet Legionnaire,*

Eva

Jack turned his back and blew his nose. I stared out at Mrs.
Kelsey's beach, fists pressed on my cheeks.

oOOOo

PART FOUR
1955

1.

Jack finished supper in silence. Holly, lost in thought, had forgotten the red-checkered dishcloth draped over her shoulder.

"I'm sure Miss Drake would want you to use a very light hand in this, Jack..."

"I know, I know."

In the living room he sank into his easy chair. The *Register* headline said: EDEN TAKES OVER. Beneath it was a picture of Winston Churchill shaking hands with Anthony Eden. He started to read...then laid down the paper.

So Miss Drake wanted to spill it all? He picked up the phone.

"Elaine Van Taunton residence," said a clipped voice.

"Is Elaine there?"

"Mrs. Van Taunton is in seclusion."

"Tell her it's Jack."

Her voice cut in. "I got it, Clive. Hello Jack. My car finished?"

"Elaine, Michael Drake is coming next week. Here. West Stoddard."

Silence.

"Holy cow, who says?"

"I got a note from Miss Drake."

"Gosh, Jack. Last month I bunked at the ranch during Paramount shots. She didn't say a word about this."

"She wants me to unload the whole story on him."

"*What?*"

He went on, asking her to be in on the meeting. He couldn't think of anybody better suited.

She laughed. "You mean I've quarterbacked life-in-the-bizarre? My three ex-husbands might agree. Okay. Let me know when the historic parley takes place. I'm between scripts. I need an oddball interruption. Now, put Holly on..."

While the women talked, Jack stepped out on the porch. A ragged cloud was basking in moonlight. Up on Stannard Hill he could see the lights from Elaine's glass-sheathed country house whitening her broad lawn. He smiled as he often did, musing how attorney Fred Millay must feel each morning in the family Colonial as he shaved. Looking out at his old sweetheart's fancy vacation residence while his English war-bride cooked breakfast downstairs.

Miss Drake, will I even recognize your son?

He hadn't seen the boy since he was five. Way back in...let's see...1943. He returned to the living room and took Holly's old photograph album from the mantel. He thumbed through yellowing pictures to a faded snapshot of himself dressed in a U.S. Marine uniform. That's how he had looked back in San Diego on the day their beloved, runaway teacher had reappeared...

"Hey, Lieutenant McGreggor — over here!"

He turned. Behind Dock 4's wire fence a woman in red skirt and white blouse waved vigorously. It was definitely, *incredibly* Miss Drake. Tall and shapely. Wisp of gray in her hair. Clinging to her hand, jumping in excitement, was a little boy in a blue sailor suit.

"Jack ...Jack!" she called.

He jogged to the fence. Behind him the line of armed Marines continued trooping up the *USS Fort Taylor's* gangplank. A bell clanged... Army trucks rumbled down the dock. She pressed her face against the fence.

"Kiss..."

His lips brushed hers through one of the steel-wire orifices. His eyes slipped over her trim shoulders and shiny yellow curls.

"I'm trying to believe this," he said.

She dabbed her eyes with both forefingers. "I've trailed your career from West Stoddard High, through Paris Island, to here, Jack. Five years. You've grown so...*military*. Oh, this is my son. Poke your hand through the wire, Michael."

Jack shook the sturdy little fingers. "Hello, Mike."

"I know you're headed out. Japanese waters, I fear. Can you have a peacetime lunch with your old schoolmarm?"

He held up a clipboard. "After check-in I have one free hour."

They ate at Howard Johnson's. Following dessert, little Michael fell asleep in the booth. Over coffee she gave Jack her warm green-eyed gaze. She didn't mention her 1938 abandonment of New England so he avoided it.

"Okay, Lieutenant sir, what's happened to everybody?"

He said that Fred Millay had left Harvard for the Army. Tony Tragonni had won a grant to the Colorado School of Mines. Eva Casserino was lead singer in a Chicago swing band. Hymie Volenski was 4f in the draft because of a broken eardrum. He was writing for the Hartford Times. Sibyl and Geraldine were in college somewhere. Elaine Bordan had grabbed a bit part in Broadway's *Watch on the Rhine*.

She pushed back a yellow lock with two fingers, wiggling slightly with pleasure. "The Bigelow boys?"

"Athletic scholarships to Ohio State—but in the Army now. Training as fighter pilots at Tuskegee."

"Holly?"

"Botany at University of Connecticut."

He lighted a cigarette and peered through smoke as Miss Drake touched her little boy's sleeping cheek gently.

"None of us knew you were married," he said.

"I'm not."

She ignored his startled blink, his sudden silence. Spreading both hands prettily, she explained that Drake Ranch, inherited from her family, was her total occupation now. She had to fight rival cattle outfits, and it wasn't easy.

"I'm happy you never saw my ruthless side, Jack. You West Stoddard kids brought out the decency in me. In my present business I'm a meanie."

He fiddled with his coffee. He was trying to adjust his thinking. Miss Drake with a child and no husband? Well...

"All right, New Englander," she said, nodding her head at him gently, "A new day has dawned—and you need an explanation. Take a look at my little boy."

Tenderly she pushed aside the child's collar. The small, handsome face puckered, then settled back to sleep. Jack peered across the dishes.

"Do you see a resemblance?"

He stared. He felt a sudden skip in his breath.

"Well?" said Miss Drake.

He fumbled his cigarette. He wiped his lips with his napkin. All at once his stomach seemed to shrink away—as if he had stepped into an icy shower.

"Miss Drake, do you expect me to believe that—"

She opened the boy's collar wider. The trace of elegance in brow and upper cheekbone...it was distinctive. He'd seen it. Yes, he'd seen it many, many times.

He said, "I can't accept that you...."

"Look again."

He looked. And it was the child-face of Joe Tutynski all right. Joe's upper Grecian half molded to a small perfect jaw. He exhaled, searching for the dropped cigarette.

"Now Jack, you listen to me."

She told him to muffle his Yankee conscience. Think 1943. Think Western. Yes, Joe Tutynski was the father of little Michael. She had stopped at the cave to drop off some books.

"He was lying there semi-conscious. Stupefied with whiskey. Hugging a hump of leaves...."

Jack turned away. "I'm having a tough time with this, Miss Drake."

"Jack! That poor, wrecked half-human. I saw the one person I'd failed to reach crying for some kind of comfort...some kind of link to the species..."

He was conscious of his hands tightening to fists beside his cup. She was looking straight into his face, her green-honey eyes calm.

"He stayed blacked-out the whole time. But when it was over, his broken body seemed to sleep like a normal person's. I walked back to my car with no regrets."

So...so. His mouth felt dry. He heard himself give a long sigh.

"I still have no regrets."

He heard only faintly as she went on. She'd found herself pregnant. Her initial alarm had quickly changed to acceptance, then to happiness. If a child was building in her body, she *wanted* it. She'd intended to stay in West Stoddard for 1938's graduation. But severe morning sickness had changed her mind.

"I started throwing up all the time."

They talked on, trying to reach across a new awkwardness. She said that after Michael's birth at the El Centro ranch, she had decided to raise him alone.

"I mustn't allow Joe's murderous philosophies to warp my son's formative years."

He nodded and looked away. "Well, here's the big surprise, Miss Drake—Joe has stopped drinking. Right after you left he went after that Yale stuff you started him on. Began corrective surgery. Picked up some kind of a scholarship at Columbia. I tried—like you said—to get to him. He told me to mind my own goddam business."

She stirred her coffee. "Mmm. I'm afraid there won't be much change in him. The unreachable wounded inflict their own kind of dictatorship on the rest of us."

"That's sure the truth, Miss Drake."

They left the restaurant. Michael walked between them, holding his mother's hand. Jack, fumbling with the facts, managed to say that this explosive story should not be spread to West Stoddard, didn't she agree?"

"Why broadcast it? Time will tone it down."

Her eyes twinkled. "Ah, the Yankee treatment—repression."

He couldn't look at her, "I'll tell Holly. That's enough. We're getting married my next leave. Does Elaine know?"

"I guess so. She helped me pack. I didn't confide anything—but she had lively intuitions."

When they said goodby he felt a stiffness, a withdrawing of intimacy. It made him set his lips and nod formally. But Miss Drake pressed her head against his shoulder, then looked up with swimming eyes. For a second he felt her perfumed cheek slide coolly against his chin.

"Try to savvy the Western approach to life, Jack. California swings to a different rhythm from Connecticut." She patted his tan Marine necktie softly, "Here's my philosophy: if the hurt is great and the need overwhelming, a body is such an easy thing to give."

2.

The next 24 months were all explosion. For Jack the war became an eruption of mud and flame at New Georgia...a slog through bloody waters at Tarawa...and finally a blasting off his feet on Iwo Jima.

In June 1945, back in San Diego, wrapped in surgical gauze, he was looking out a hospital window when a nurse tapped his shoulder.

"You have a visitor, Lieutenant."

"Am I too soon, Jack?"

Miss Drake bent over the bed and kissed him. Her warm cheeks smelled faintly of roses. Her eyes drifted down to his leg bandages with a mild purse of her lips.

"Sit down," he said, "Just don't split an infinitive or use a double negative."

She took off her glasses. "I'll try to stay in one tense."

They talked of time and their long-gone West Stoddard days.

Yes, all the kids were surviving the war—so far. Fred Millay was on Eisenhower's staff in England. Both Bigelow brothers had been shot down in Italy, but escaped unwounded. She said a movie scout had spotted Elaine Bordan in *Watch on the Rhine* and she was coming to Hollywood.

"I'm bunking her at the ranch," she said, "I'll send her down to you."

He asked about little Mike. How much had he grown in the two years since their meeting? She said his teachers had skipped him into Fourth Grade, saying he needed the challenge. She had bought him a sorrel colt.

"He has some of Joe's brilliance. And he's amazingly athletic."

"I told Holly about him. She sends love."

"You'll see him someday—all of you."

"Meanwhile," he said, rising on a elbow, "You, me, Holly, and Elaine will keep this thing secret—okay? You know how West Stoddard is, Miss Drake."

She smiled gently "Any way you want it, John Cotton Mather."

Three weeks later he awoke with Elaine Bordan's strong lips pressed against his mouth. He inhaled a wave of Channel No. 5.

"The Phantom of Footlights?"

She explored his bedclothes up and down. "You're in one piece—glory be." She wiped her eyes, then laid her cheek on his chest. "I couldn't have stood it if you'd been chopped up, Jack."

They exchanged surprise at the way life was racing on—war winding down—careers building. She mentioned how Miss Drake's little boy was melting into Western ranch life. Riding. Roping. Even competing in runt rodeos.

"He's only going-on-seven, Jack. Wouldn't you be scared to have a kid doing that wild stuff?"

"Miss Drake told me he was pretty bright, too."

"Bright! He speaks Spanish, German and Chinese. Slang

picked up at the bunkhouse. Now Miss Drake says he's into deciphering codes. He unravels messages that are scrambled on the ranch's short wave. That kid's an electric light, going day and night."

"Got any of Joe's bastardly vibes?"

"None. Swaps cracks with his mother like a grownup. Miss Drake adores him."

Before she left, Elaine pirouetted and struck an erotic pose, her fine thighs pushing out. "I'm building a routine like this to seduce directors. How's it look?"

"I'm panting. Tell me Elaine, did you really know Miss Drake was pregnant when she took off that day?"

"I spotted a book on her coffee table, *Childbirth at Home*. And I knew she'd been morning-sick. Neat guess, huh?"

"So you pretended you'd promised to keep a secret you didn't know existed. I should have stood you on your head."

She paused at the door. "You're addressing the new, stream-lined Mae West. Respect her station, please."

"Well, keep one thing in mind, Mae. Miss Drake's off-the-wall move—and its result—is known only to her, you, me, and Holly. I want it to stay that way."

She stepped back in and hugged him." Get well, Marine."

3.

Joe Tutynski relit his cigar. The voice on the phone had said "... please be there, Mister Celebrated Attorney." It sounded young and tough. Crackpot, maybe? Should he alert the police?

Miss Fox walked in carrying papers to sign—and he let it go. He had just finished when she spoke through the intercom: "A Mr. Drake to see you, sir."

The tooled mahogany door swung open. A young man en-tered wearing a red plaid shirt with rolled-up sleeves. Two muscular hands were hooked in his belt. Above a handsome, jutting jaw, shiny black eyes stared at him without blinking.

"How do you do," said Joe rising.

The young man didn't move. His eyes moved slowly from Joe's face, up and down his body. Then he took a step closer, squinting.

"Can I help you, young man?"

For almost a half-minute neither spoke. Then the young man's voice, low and imprecise, came softly from lips barely moving:

"Yeah...maybe. I guess...yeah, yeah..."

He turned. Giving a backward wave with a rugged arm, he walked out. From the front room, he called, "I'm leaving some papers for you to read, sir. My address is there. We'll meet again, soon I think.

Joe sauntered out to Miss Fox. "Where'd that guy come from?

"I have no idea. He just barged in."

She handed him a folder of typewritten sheets. He walked back to his office pleasantly aware—as always—of the painless *click-click* in his rebuilt legs. In his easy chair he munched on a chocolate mint, conscious—as always—of the pleasant tightness that went with movement of his artificial jaw.

He opened the folder and started to read.

4.

The Saturday Michael arrived, Jack left Ted Millay in charge at the garage. He and Elaine drove to Chester Airport in her fuchsia Cadillac.

"I didn't expect the kid to come in his own plane," he said.

Elaine chuckled softly. "Wait till you see this 20-year-old dynamo, Jack. He's not only the brainiest football player Southern Cal ever produced. His talents run in all directions—science, engineering, English lit. He rebuilt his old WWII plane on the ranch airstrip."

They turned off Route 154, through cleared fields to the

terminal. Elaine parked beside the small hanger.

Jack said, "I still haven't figured out how to tell him. Have you?"

"Nope. I just pray he's as tough as I think he is?"

Michael's P51 monoplane glided in, engine coughing. A lank, square-shouldered youth jumped off the wing. Elaine walked across the tarmac and kissed him.

"Welcome to Yankee land." Jack said.

He shook the hand of a powerfully structured young man with an uncanny resemblance to his old enemy. The Tutynski wide-set eyes and broad forehead were startling. Almost unnerving.

Michael tossed a purple musette bag in the car. "My mother warned me not to try squeezing the McGreggor hand. He'll crush you, she said."

Elaine drove slowly under leafy maples to West Stoddard. She cleared her throat several times, then began. "Michael, there's something your mother wanted us—"

"Yeah, I know."

"Facts from the past," put in Jack, "Facts that demand understanding..."

"Yeah, I know."

They were stumbling. *Michael knew what?* The Cadillac pulled into Elaine's swank carport. She and Jack turned in their seats facing the rugged figure sprawling in back.

"What we're trying to say, Michael—" began Elaine.

They groped awkwardly. Michael listened, his lips in a half smile. Jack started to describe Joe Tutynski and Joe's connection with Leatherman's cave. He brought in Miss Drake's involvement...her concern for a troubled student...

"How's that again?" said Michael, "This guy lived in a cave?"

"No...not exactly," said Jack, "The fellow I'm talking about was a student of your mother's and..."

Suddenly Michael laughed. He gripped his knees with sinewy hands. "Hold it. I have a confessional to deliver. I'll unload it in Mrs. Van Taunton's beautiful crystal house—where I gotta go to the bathroom."

Inside they reclined on Elaine's 20-foot mulberry-silk divan. Clive the houseman brought corduroy pillows. Michael rummaged in his musette bag. He tossed a small rawhide-backed book on the coffee table.

"Here's the confessional—my mother's old diary. It's in her self-invented shorthand. She used to kid with me that no one but her royal self could read it. I disputed that."

Jack opened the pages. It was the book Geraldine had shown him long ago. It was crowded with tiny images that reminded him of the little figures Miss Drake used to draw at the end of themes—*great, good, so-so, terrible.* Between them, alphabet letters were sprinkled in crazy unreadable paragraphs.

Elaine was fascinated. "You mean this gobbledygook says something?"

"Yes mam," said Michael. "I took advanced cryptography my freshman year just to crack this baby. Navy Intelligence in San Diego gave me some help."

Elaine gave the distinctive pixy grimace that had charmed fifty million moviegoers. "Spy business?"

"Yeah. Well, two weeks ago I read all about this Tutynski guy you mention. He was a case, I gather."

Jack's heart began to thump. Michael tapped a forefinger to his chest.

"Then I discovered the truth—the guy is my father."

Silence. The tinkle of Clive moving glasses on a tray sounded like bells ringing.

"Well, son," said Jack, "This situation was…"

"M-Mike, you mustn't judge harshly…" stammered Elaine, "Your mother was the most loved… You invaded a private diary and you…"

Michael spread his hands. "Shameful me - exploring my mother's private stuff. I admit it. But I cracked the mystery. And I'm glad I did. After all, she's getting me to take over the ranch in June lock, stock and barrel, so I should know everything. I found out my old man is a distinguished lawyer in Washington. And just before I came here I looked him up in his office."

More silence.

Jack said, "Elaine, if you have any Scotch, I'll take a shot."

Clive passed drinks around. Michael, pacing in short athletic steps, talked on quietly, "Am I stressed over this? No I'm not. I've traced my mother's day-by-day life as a teacher here in New England. She did okay, it seems to me."

"Better than okay," Jack managed to say, "She brought hope here—and reason."

"She brought love," said Elaine.

Michael stood up and stretched. "I was surprised, of course. But marriages, divorces, and strange hook-ups aren't all that unusual out our way."

"Or here either these days," said Elaine.

"There's no reason why my parents should be married - ever. But I think they should have a passing acquaintance with each other. I left an account of all this with my father yesterday in Washington."

In the morning Elaine stopped for gas at the garage. Jack, stacking tires in the used rack, waved her into his office. She sat with her matchless legs propped on some Exide batteries.

"Whew, that's over, Jack. Now I'm hauling my good-looking houseguest to Doane's Woods, Little Italy, and what's left of the Griffin mansion on Saratoga Hill. He wants to see every place Miss Drake put in her diary."

"Where's he now?"

"West Beach. Looking for an English brick in the Rink ruins."

He handed her a cup of coffee. "Miss Drake must have described the famous jitterbug stomp at the Rink. Remember those Glen Island hoofers?"

She laughed. "Boy—was that a night."

They agreed that Michael's stunning revelation had been a break for them. He had seemed calm about his unique parentage.

Sooner or later, of course, he'd want to visit Leatherman's.

"You taking him to the cave, Elaine?"

"I doubt if I could find it today."

Jack lighted a cigarette. He hadn't been up there in years.

"Maybe the trail's grown over. Let's take a look."

Through flickering sunlight, the yellow jeep bounced up Clinton road.

"Hello," said Elaine, "Company."

A gray Lincoln limousine was parked at the trail entrance, its front wheels blocking the way. A blue-uniformed chauffeur was draped over the wheel, asleep.

They stared at it. "Do you see what I see, Elaine? D.C. license plates?"

They walked around the limousine quietly. In a low voice she kept saying she couldn't believe it...she couldn't accept that Joe would come back here.

"He hates West Stoddard."

Jack helped her on stepping stones over a brook. "But Michael left him a written history of all that's happened. If he's overwhelmed he might do anything."

Rounding a cluster of low spruces, they saw him. Joe was climbing high on the stone rubble at the cave entrance. They stared, their mouths open. Joe was metamorphosed. His body was pared down, un-lumpy. His movements were natural—if slightly hesitant. He looked like a middle-age vacationer sightseeing the outback.

"Is that our monster?" said Elaine, backing off the trail. "This knocks me out."

Jack crouched beside her. They watched Joe drop to his knees and easily enter the cave. Minutes passed.

"Keep hidden," said Jack.

Joe emerged. He was carrying something in both arms.

"What's he lugging?" whispered Elaine.

"Shhh."

Joe climbed down the trail. He passed within six feet of them, his jutting jaw at an elegant angle.

Elaine stepped into the trail. "Did you see that?" He was *striding*. His shoulders were straight. His arms nearly even. His hump is gone. Jack, can you believe it?"

"I wonder if they rebuilt his brain."

"Did you see what he was carrying?"

"No—something in pieces."

She looked down the trail. "Gosh, it's a miracle. It makes you think Miss Drake was right when she said life was worth the fight. Jack, I'm going to bring her here to meet him. Yes, I am."

"This is Elaine at her craziest," Jack said, as he put on his pajamas, "Five of us at dinner, pretending all is well in a lunatic situation."

Holly was brushing her hair. "Oh, maybe not. It will be wonderful to see Miss Drake anyhow."

"If she's smart she won't come."

All afternoon he had argued against the dinner party. Elaine had been adamant. She would fly west and bring Miss Drake to meet the father of her son. She'd cornered the new Joe Tutynski at the drug store, had coffee with him, found him transformed in mind and body. She'd talked him into staying at Kelsey Motel and accepting her invitation for a Sunday banquet. No, she hadn't told him Miss Drake would be there. That was the surprise part.

"Surprise? *Explosion* is the word. What's Joe supposed to say to his old teacher: 'Sorry I impregnated you.'? What does Miss Drake say: 'I apologize for luring you when you were comatose.'?

Holly sighed. "Oh, don't be silly."

"Then the surprise baby says, 'I exist. Which one of you two is to blame?'

"Jack, be sensible."

"I was sensible years ago when I said that Miss Drake had made one hell of a mistake. I still don't want West Stoddard to know."

"Maybe she and Joe will get together. They're only ten years apart."

He winced. "Happy landings, Miss Lonely Hearts."

"Stranger things have happened."

Jack paced the living room. He couldn't think of any way Joe and Miss Drake could navigate the gulf yawning between them. Why would they want to anyhow?

Holly sat up on the sofa. "A gesture might be a start."

"Gesture?"

"Yes, some little, gentle thing. Just a smile. Or a dumb little present."

Far out in the Sound, a freighter *bah-h-h-h-ed*.

"Jack, sometimes the tiniest of offerings moves people to do things. Miss Drake and Joe Tutynski—imagine!"

Before they went to bed, Elaine called from San Francisco. Miss Drake had agreed to come East. Could Jack pick them up at Brainard Airport, Hartford, Thursday afternoon, two-thirty?

Thursday was going slowly—the way Jack liked. He washed the Texaco pump. He helped Ted Millay attach a new side-mirror to his father's 1953 Buick. He wasn't due at Brainard for six hours.

"Big wheels coming in," said Ted.

A gray Lincoln limousine stopped by the stone fence. Its bulky rear door clicked open. Joe Tutynski stepped out.

"Hello, Jack McGreggor."

The voice was the same. Low, grainy. Everything else was different—balanced shoulders in a trim coat, two straight-looking arms, legs that held his heavy torso erect. Most striking was the lower jaw, lined with tiny surgical scars. It jutted normally, even handsomely, over a mango-colored collar.

The two men examined each other, their ancient hostility floating faintly in the morning sun.

At last Joe smiled, a slow alteration for his new face—the lips curving stiffly. "Jack, it's been over 17 years. I'm supposed to be an articulate lawyer. Does it do any good to say at this moment I'm a confused and humbled man?"

"Welcome back, Joe."

They shook hands. Jack felt a slight tremor in the strong grip. Their bitterness seemed to fade.

"I'm here for a very strange reason..."

Joe said that a young man in Washington was claiming a close relationship to him. Day before yesterday the guy had left him a detailed fact sheet that had almost bowled him over. It had prompted him to rush up here. Last night at Kelsey Motel he had re-read it, probing for truth.

"It's not possible, of course. But the pictures he enclosed look exactly as I would have looked at his age without my old deformities. He's coming to West Stoddard, his supposed ancestral home, for the first time."

Joe rubbed his jaw with a heavy fist, which quivered slightly. Then glanced at his watch.

"I'm to meet him at four o'clock at West Beach."

"Come on in, Joe."

The office smelled of oil and old rags. Joe sat on a new crate of General Motors exhaust pipes. He said that their classmate movie star, Elaine Van Taunton, had met him at the drug store and invited him to dinner. The young man would be there also.

"She invited me and Holly too," said Jack.

Joe looked at his hands. "I don't know how to say this...aaa... the fact sheet mentioned some kind of connection with our old teacher Eva Drake...aaa... I don't understand exactly...in fact..."

Jack edged the talk to local topics. Old West Stoddard High School had burned 12 years ago...Sibyl Noyes had gotten her M.D. at Yale and moved to Detroit. The Bigelow brothers were operating a profitable Chevrolet agency in Boston.

"The beaches are jammed with small craft, Joe. We need another marina."

Half-an-hour passed. The easy atmosphere, fueled by nostalgia, misted over stark memories. Jack showed him around the small, neat garage. Joe patted the new hydraulic lift...picked up Snap-On tools that gleamed on each bench. He walked into the tiny carpenter shop Jack had built on the back side of the office and beamed at the expensive Milwaukee lathe.

"I've got a layout like this in my apartment. I use it a lot. It's a relief to take hold of a chisel after yaking all day in a court room." He grinned. "Matter of fact, last night at Kelsey's I got into the motel hobby room and did a bit of repair carpentry myself."

Leaving, Joe looked at the Sound, gleaming blue-and-white around Salt Island. "Still a jewel, isn't it," he said, "Long ago up at Leatherman's I used to climb above the cave to gaze at it."

Jack smiled. "We remember your famous essay."

Joe lifted his finger. "Say! Wait a minute."

He got a briefcase from the limousine. He pulled out some scribbled sheets and handed them to Jack.

"Joe, don't tell me..."

It was his article on the Long Island Sound—nine dog-eared pages. Miss Drake's handwriting slanted across the title page:

Super excellent, Joe. This love song to our beautiful waterway stands alone. 😊 😊 😊 *—Eva Drake.*

"A triple," said Jack. "Nobody else ever scored like this."

Joe shrugged. "Why do I keep it? Because of those three little figures, I guess. I was an impossible snob, as you know. I wasn't nice to our teacher, or anybody else. Those three little guys put me out in front—in a normal way. Now I carry them in my briefcase for luck."

Climbing into the limo, Joe added, "Funny thing, I wrote another page—page 10—condemning every word I said. Called the Sound a sewer and a menace. It was the standard hate bucket I dumped on everything in those days. She missed it—thank God."

"That was a break. See you at supper."

5.

Elaine and Miss Drake came down the ramp, talking brightly, their high heels clicking. Miss Drake, her hair sandy gray, wore a peacock-blue jacket and white skirt. Her tan legs flashed past an airport poster saying *Caution—Wet Tile*. Elaine, in pink sweater and mocha slacks, hugged her arm.

"Jack McGreggor!"

Miss Drake's firm curves pressed against him. A familiar rose-scent drifted from her open collar.

He said, "West Stoddard humbles itself before the Queen of the Pacific."

She looked around smiling and waved her hand. "Arise, all ye humble."

Driving home, he mentioned that Clive had organized the dinner for eight o'clock. There was a French chef from New Haven... imported wine from Naples.

"Good Heavens, Elaine," said Miss Drake, "I fear this rendezvous is doomed to shipwreck anyhow. Now it will go down in history as a conspicuous-consumption bust."

Elaine squeezed her hand. "This is an epic moment, Miss Drake. There'll be no shipwreck. Nothing but gilded excess will do. We have quail from Spain, morels from Paris..."

Miss Drake walked through Elaine's shining house, touching the paneled walls. She exclaimed over each bright implement in the chrome-and-porcelain kitchen.

"And you live with sunshine on every rug! Well, I never saw such an open, jewel-like living room."

They drove around town. Miss Drake stared at the wide fishing boat docks...the new town hall, a remodeled Colonial home. They stopped at the yellow brick high school that had replaced their old battered classrooms. She got out.

"I'd like to stand here a minute," she said, "Hello, Tommy Kingsland. Hello, Vince. Hello, Gene. Here's Tony on his goofy bicycle. And there's Hymie and Fred tossing a baseball. Eva Casserino, no humming in study hall, please."

Jack stiffened to attention. "And the whole menagerie is saluting, Miss Drake."

She laughed, holding her cupped hands to her eyes like binoculars, "Ah, is that Dr. Sibyl Noyes I spy—attaching a splint to a broken neck on the baseball field?"

They stopped at Mrs. Kelsey's beach. The Sound was glowing, a gentian expanse checkered with sailboats. Briny scents blew along the sand. Beyond Salt Island a crazy-quilt of white clouds drifted over the water.

"My swimming niche," cried Miss Drake, "How lovely."

She slipped off her shoes and waded a few minutes. Then they were back at Elaine's, drinking sweet cider in her elegant living room. Clive reported that Michael had gone up to West Beach with a gentleman named Joe Tutynski. They would be back at dinnertime.

Miss Drake said, "Mmm. You can never count on Michael being where you expect him to be."

Elaine frowned. "Those two guys better get here."

Slowly the talk moved to the issue of the moment. Miss Drake sat up in her rustic cedar chair.

"Well, all of you know my story. There's nothing to hold back. I'm here because Elaine invited me to meet the father of my son. She thinks something good might come of it."

Elaine lighted a cigarette, her hand quivering. Miss Drake smiled at her fondly.

"I have an opposite view. I told Michael to come to West Stoddard because he had decoded my diary, after I foolishly said he wouldn't be able to. Now that he's wise, he should see the place where this irregular plot unfolded. Also it's time he met his Old Man, regardless of what his mother thinks of the guy. But me? Meet with Joe Tutynski, *now?*"

In the silence, Elaine's antique grandfather's clock chimed five times.

"I'm afraid Joe is locked in a psychological pattern that has stayed with him too long. I hear he has become a criminal lawyer in Washington—a very successful one. I guess the courtroom is the place for his kind of toughness.

"Well, I've dealt with tough, unrelenting men for years. I've learned to steer around them whenever possible—for my own sanity. That's one reason I'm getting out of the cattle business. Michael can battle those hard-boiled guys from now on."

Nobody moved. In the chartreuse dining room Clive was silently laying gold-edged plates on a lace tablecloth.

Holly said, "What will you do, Miss Drake?"

"Oh, I don't know. Go someplace...any place I want. Try something new. I'll maneuver around tough guys like Joe, that's for sure. I've been growing too much like them. My nickname at the bunkhouse is Mama Hatchet."

Jack lifted a finger. "Wait a minute, Miss Drake. Joe was at the garage this morning. He seems different—not tough at all. I had quite a long talk with him. He does ordinary things. Carpentry in the motel hobby shop, for instance."

"That's right," said Elaine, "Two days ago we saw him take some broken junk from the cave. He looked so...so normal."

Miss Drake shrugged. "Mmm."

Saffron twilight was tinting the room. Everybody stood by the glass wall. They looked down on the glittery, blue-gold Sound. Miss Drake wondered out loud what it would be like to own a private sleep-aboard boat in the new marina world of West Stoddard.

"Murmuring water...tiny waves slapping. How nice," she said.

At seven-thirty, Elaine put on an unrehearsed display of her Hollywood talent—anxiety, irritation, hopefulness, resignation, anger.

"Where *are* those guys?"

Miss Drake stretched out on the divan. "Michael may be having a seminar with his new paterfamilias, Elaine."

A half-hour passed.

"Clive, bring on the lobster bisque," ordered Elaine.

They had reached the main course—tenderloin lamb—when

the gray limousine pulled in. The chauffeur opened the rear door. Michael stepped out. He was carrying a package wrapped in white tissue tied by a wide blue ribbon.

"Hello, Mother and everybody. Sorry I'm late." He dropped into a chair. "What an afternoon. We sat in the sand and talked. My father told about his crazy youth...his physical distortions...the mental battles. He said he was shocked at what had come out...particularly his actions reported in your diary. But he sort of liked the overall result—me! How about that? And he'd thought he hated West Stoddard. But now he's glad he's back. So—"

Elaine rose. "Clive, bring this mad youth some cold bisque." She walked to the polished glass wall. She looked up and down the driveway. "Where's Joe?"

"He didn't come."

Paralyzed silence.

"*Didn't come!*"

"No, I tried to talk him into it. But he said no." Michael tapped his fingers lightly at the table edge. "It wasn't right just now, he said."

Elaine tossed her napkin on her plate. "Not right? What's he talking about? Damn that bum!"

"Whoa, Elaine," said Jack.

"He said, 'I have my reasons. Just give this to your mother. And tender my apologies to Mrs. Van Taunton.'"

Michael planted the beribboned package in front of Miss Drake. Elaine paced, clenching and unclenching her fists.

"I might have known, West Stoddard's never-say-die rebel would toss a monkey wrench into this!"

"Now, Elaine..." said Holly.

The room grew quiet. Michael ate the cold roast lamb and gravy. Elaine sank into her chair, her lips grim. Miss Drake reached across and pressed her hand.

"It's a beautiful dinner, dear."

"I planned it hoping something could be pulled together for you, Miss Drake. Now that guy—that...that..."

Michael pointed his fork at her and grinned. "Easy. He's my old man."

Elaine made a faint wail. "Joe's wrecking everything—as usual."

"Hold it, honey, said Miss Drake, "Perhaps your old teacher's unorthodox action of 20 years ago isn't meant to be pulled into the light today. It was an unscheduled happening that—providentially—created a beloved life. I'm content with that."

Elaine covered her eyes. "Don't mind me—I bawl at times like this."

Silence. Michael bit into a caviar-topped biscuit. "This fancy chow almost makes me forget I'm a curio."

Miss Drake gave him a hug. "A *treasured* curio, cowboy."

In the living room they all sank into Elaine's enormous, pillow-studded divan. Miss Drake asked Holly to open the gift package.

"I'm a little wary of this, Long ago I had so many disappointments with your father, Michael. I couldn't get on the same track with that brilliant, savage, uncooperative mind."

Holly snapped the blue ribbon and tore off white tissue.

"Holy cats!" cried Elaine, throwing up her hands.

Holly lifted out a six-burner Sterno stove, painted red. Its tiny oven was nestled beside the canned-heat nooks. Four metal legs had been reinforced with short steel pieces, linked together.

"Well, look at that." said Jack.

Elaine shook her fist. "A crummy piece of junk—patched with more junk!"

"But it's cute, Elaine," protested Holly.

Elaine slammed a corduroy pillow on the floor. "We get your message, Joe! Did you have to insult the best teacher in the world?"

She was crying. She rushed into the kitchen.

Holly rose to follow. "She'll be all right, Miss Drake."

Miss Drake walked to the window overlooking Salt Island. The stove was light and tinny in her hands. She ran a finger

252

along the enameled sides. They had been carefully joined at a break at the center. Sanded and painted with a craftsman's hand. She touched the small oven door. It popped open.

There was something inside.

Quickly she stepped through the tall French door. She crossed the dew-wet lawn to Elaine's four-car garage. Under a carriage lamp she examined some paper sheets. They were: *West Stoddard's World of Water* by Joe Tutynski. The title sheet carried the three daffy little figures of excellence she had drawn.

She sank down on a driveway bench. Mmm. She visualized the new-minted Joe bending over a workbench...repairing the cheap little stove he had wrecked at the cave...painting it with quick-dry vermilion.

And tucking the famous term paper inside.

And holding himself back...staying away from her.

A gush of sea breeze tumbled up from the Sound. It tugged at her collar, and hurried on to Doane's woods. At the French door she paused, hand on the latch.

This little town with its tilting gravestones...its Revolutionary cannon wheels sunk in an old pond...its battered houses leaning away from the water...it was really a solid homestead of the Republic. Suddenly the whole place seemed warm and familiar. And beckoning.

She clasped her fingers beneath her chin. "Well, I never," whispered Miss Eva Drake.

**Thus do Coastal gods—hidden in sea-mist —
Lay down their lures before the vulnerable.**

∞OOOo

— Worthington, Krantz Fiction —

Printed in the United States
200312BV00001B/2/A